Harry Castlemon

Marcy the Blockade-Runner

Harry Castlemon

Marcy the Blockade-Runner

ISBN/EAN: 9783337384340

Printed in Europe, USA, Canada, Australia, Japan

Cover: Foto ©Andreas Hilbeck / pixelio.de

More available books at **www.hansebooks.com**

CASTLEMON'S WAR SERIES.

MARCY

THE

BLOCKADE-RUNNER

BY

HARRY CASTLEMON,

AUTHOR OF "GUNBOAT SERIES," "ROCKY MOUNTAIN SERIES,"
"SPORTSMAN'S CLUB SERIES," ETC., ETC.

Four Illustrations by Geo. G. White.

PHILADELPHIA :
HENRY T. COATES & CO.

FAMOUS CASTLEMON BOOKS.

GUNBOAT SERIES. By Harry Castlemon. 6 vols. 12mo.

FRANK THE YOUNG NATURALIST.   FRANK ON A GUNBOAT.
FRANK IN THE WOODS.   FRANK BEFORE VICKSBURG.
FRANK ON THE LOWER MISSISSIPPI.   FRANK ON THE PRAIRIE.

ROCKY MOUNTAIN SERIES. By Harry Castlemon. 3 vols. 12mo. Cloth.

FRANK AMONG THE RANCHEROS.   FRANK AT DON CARLOS' RANCH.
FRANK IN THE MOUNTAINS.

SPORTSMAN'S CLUB SERIES. By Harry Castlemon. 3 vols. 12mo. Cloth.

THE SPORTSMAN'S CLUB IN THE SADDLE.
THE SPORTSMAN'S CLUB AFLOAT.
THE SPORTSMAN'S CLUB AMONG THE TRAPPERS.

FRANK NELSON SERIES. By Harry Castlemon. 3 vols. 12mo. Cloth.

SNOWED UP.   FRANK IN THE FORECASTLE.   THE BOY TRADERS.

BOY TRAPPER SERIES. By Harry Castlemon. 3 vols. 12mo. Cloth.

THE BURIED TREASURE.   THE BOY TRAPPER.   THE MAIL-CARRIER.

ROUGHING IT SERIES. By Harry Castlemon. 3 vols. 12mo. Cloth.

GEORGE IN CAMP.   GEORGE AT THE WHEEL.   GEORGE AT THE FORT.

ROD AND GUN SERIES. By Harry Castlemon. 3 vols. 12mo. Cloth.

DON GORDON'S SHOOTING BOX.   ROD AND GUN CLUB.
THE YOUNG WILD FOWLERS.

GO-AHEAD SERIES. By Harry Castlemon. 3 vols. 12mo. Cloth.

TOM NEWCOMBE.   GO-AHEAD.   NO MOSS.

FOREST AND STREAM SERIES. By Harry Castlemon. 3 vols. 12mo. Cloth.

JOE WAYRING.   SNAGGED AND SUNK.   STEEL HORSE.

WAR SERIES. By Harry Castlemon. 5 vols. 12mo. Cloth.

TRUE TO HIS COLORS.   RODNEY THE PARTISAN.
RODNEY THE OVERSEER.   MARCY THE BLOCKADE-RUNNER.
MARCY THE REFUGEE.

Other Volumes in Preparation.

CONTENTS.

MARCY, THE BLOCKADE-RUNNER.

CHAPTER I.

MARCY HAS A VISITOR.

THE boys who have read the first volume
of this series of books, in which we followed the fortunes of our Union hero, Marcy
Gray, and described the persevering but
unsuccessful efforts he made to be true
to his colors in deed as well as in spirit, will
remember that we left him at his home
near Nashville, North Carolina, enjoying a
brief respite from the work he so heartily
detested, that of privateering. He had made
one voyage in the *Osprey* under Captain
Beardsley, during which he assisted in capturing the schooner *Mary Hollins*, bound from
Havana to Boston with an assorted cargo.
When the prize was brought into the port of
Newbern the whole town went wild with ex-

citement, Captain Beardsley's agent being so highly elated that he urged the master of the *Osprey* to run out at once and try his luck again, before the capture of the *Hollins* became known at the North. But Beardsley, who was afraid to trust landsharks any farther than he could see them, declared with a good deal of earnestness that he would not budge an inch until the legality of the capture had been settled by the courts, the vessel and cargo sold, and the dollars that belonged to him and his crew were planked down in their two hands. Knowing that it would take time to go through all these formalities, Marcy Gray asked for a leave of absence, which Beardsley granted according to promise, and in less than half an hour after the *Osprey* was hauled alongside the wharf, her disgusted young pilot, wishing from the bottom of his heart that she might sink out of sight before he ever saw her again, left her and went home as fast as the cars could take him. When we last saw him he had reached his mother's house, and was reading a letter from his cousin, *Rodney, the Partisan*, a portion of which we gave to the reader at the close of the first volume of this series.

"Rodney is full of enthusiasm, isn't he?" exclaimed Marcy, when he had finished reading the letter. "He says he looks for 'high old times' running the Yankees out of Missouri, but I am afraid he'll not enjoy them as much as he thinks he will. Perhaps the Yankees are not good runners. But Rodney has been true to his colors and I have not. I said I never would fight against the Union, but I have stood by and seen a gun fired at the old flag; and I have no doubt that the skipper of the *Hollins*, when he saw me aboard the privateer, took me for as good a rebel as there was in the crew. Perhaps he will see his mistake some day. I shall have to accept my share of the prize money, for if I don't Beardsley's suspicions will be aroused; but I'll put it away and send it to the master of the *Hollins* the first good chance I get. Has Wat Gifford been here since I went to sea? You know he warned me of two secret enemies I would have to look out for, and hinted that he would some day tell me who the rest are." ["But I think

I know already," added Marcy mentally.] While he was at sea he had had ample leisure to think over the situation, and had made up his mind that he knew right where the most serious danger that threatened him and his mother was coming from.

"Walter has been here," replied Mrs. Gray, "and I understand that he has since gone back to the army, his furlough, which was a short one, having expired. I was glad to see Walter, for it was a very great relief to visit with some one to whom I knew I could talk freely; but I must say he left a very unpleasant impression on my mind. He told me, in so many words, that we are suspected of being traitors at heart, and that there are but few of our neighbors we can trust."

"And who are they?" inquired Marcy. "When we know who our friends are, it will be no trouble for us to pick out our enemies."

"I asked Walter that very question, and after some hesitation he was obliged to confess that he could not name a single person. There are some who denounce secession in the very strongest terms, but that doesn't prove anything, for Walter has often done the same thing himself, and he is a rebel soldier," said Mrs. Gray sadly. "Only think of it, Marcy! To not one of the many who were our warm friends in times past, can we go for advice and sympathy, now that trouble is coming upon us. Is it not dreadful?"

"Who cares for advice or sympathy?" exclaimed the boy wrathfully. "We've got each other and Jack to go to when the pinch comes, and outsiders can just mind their own business and live to themselves, and let us do the same. Traitors! That word doesn't apply to us, mother."

"I know it doesn't; but for all that I am afraid that the 'outsiders,' as you call them, will not let us live to ourselves. Young Gifford almost as good as told me that some of our near neighbors intend to keep themselves posted in regard to our movements."

"The—the impudence of the thing!" exclaimed the young pilot, pounding his knees with his clenched hands. "Who's going to keep them posted? Where do they expect to get their information? Through the over-seer?"

"Through the overseer," whispered Mrs. Gray, in reply.

"Are you afraid to speak the words out loud?" cried Marcy, who had seldom been so excited as he was at that moment. "Great Moses! Have things come to such a pass that we dare not talk in our ordinary tones in our own house, but must carry on our conversation in whispers?"

"I was in hopes that my letters would prepare you for something like this," said his mother slowly.

"Well, they didn't. Of course I knew I should find things changed, but I never thought we should be spied upon in our own house," answered Marcy. "Traitors, are we, when we haven't done the first thing to deserve the name! But is there no way in which that villain Hanson can be got rid of?"

"There is but one way that occurs to me now," was the reply. "When his contract expires we can tell him that we do not intend to employ an overseer any longer."

"And that will be almost a year from now," groaned Marcy. "How can we live for so many months, knowing all the while that our every movement is watched, and that some one is constantly trying to catch every word we say? I don't believe I can stand it. Did Gifford say anything about——"

Marcy paused, got upon his feet, and opened quickly, but silently, one after another, all the doors that led from the room in which he and his mother were sitting. There were no eaves-droppers among the servants *yet*, but that was no sign that there wouldn't be some to-morrow or next day. An overseer who was left as much to himself as Hanson was, held great power in his hands; and some negro servants are as open to bribery as some white people are. Having made sure that there was no one listening at the door, Marcy drew his chair close to his mother's side before he spoke again.

"Did Gifford say anything about the money—the thirty thousand dollars in gold you have hidden in the cellar wall?" he asked, in suppressed tones.

"He did, and it troubles me more than anything else he said during his visit," replied Mrs. Gray, glancing nervously around the room, as if she feared that there might be a listener concealed behind some of the chairs or under the sofa. "In spite of my utmost care, that matter, which I hoped to keep from the knowledge of even the most faithful among the servants, has become known. I cannot account for it. It fairly unnerves me to think of it, for it suggests a most alarming possibility."

"Did Gifford say, in so many words, that you were known to have money in the house?"

"He did not. He said it was suspected."

"And what is the alarming possibility you just spoke of?" continued Marcy.

"Why, I am afraid that there is some trusted person nearer to me than the overseer is—some one right here in the house who has been watching me day and night," answered his mother, shivering all over and drawing nearer to her sturdy son, as if for protection. "You don't know how it makes me feel, or how keenly I have suffered since young Gifford's visit."

"I wish he had stopped away," said Marcy, almost fiercely.

"I don't," replied his mother. "He meant it for the best, and wouldn't have told me a word if I had not insisted. You must not blame Walter. It is best that I should understand the situation; and Marcy, you know *you* would not have told me a word of all this if Gifford had told it to you."

"Perhaps he did say something to me about it," answered the boy, with an air which said that his mother had not been telling him anything he did not know before. "But I have been more careful of your feelings than Gifford was."

"And did you mean to leave me all in the dark and utterly ignorant of the perils that surround us?" said Mrs. Gray reproachfully. "Do you think that would have been just to me? Don't imagine, because you are my protector and the only one I have to depend on while Jack is at sea, that you have all the courage there is between us. I know you would shield me entirely if you could, but it is impossible; and you must let me bear my part. I shall have to whether you consent or not. But you haven't yet told me where you have been, how you captured that vessel, what the captain said about it, or—or anything," she added, with a feeble attempt to bring the boy's usual smile back to his face. " Remember, I am deeply interested in all that you do."

" Well, you wouldn't be if you had seen the cowardly work I helped Beardsley carry out," replied Marcy. "In the first place, Crooked Inlet is buoyed in such a way that the stranger who tries to go through it will run his vessel so hard and fast aground that she will be likely to stay there until the waves make an end of her, or the shifting sands of the bar bury her out of sight."

" That's murderous," exclaimed Mrs. Gray, with a shudder. " Is Captain Beardsley about to turn wrecker ? "

" He means to wreck any war vessel that may give chase to his schooner," answered Marcy. " If we are pursued, I can take the *Osprey* through all right; but if the man-of-war attempts to follow us, and allows herself to be guided by the buoys, she'll stick. Oh, it's lovely business—a brave and honorable business," exclaimed the boy, running his hands through his hair and tumbling it up as he used to do at school when he found anything in his books that was too hard for him. "I have the profoundest contempt for the villain who brought me into it, and despise myself for yielding to him."

"But, Marcy, what else could you have done? Gifford assured me it was the only course open to you, and that by shipping as pilot on board that privateer you have somewhat allayed suspicion."

"Mother," said Marcy, placing his arm around her neck and whispering the words in her ear, "Captain Beardsley doesn't need a pilot any more than he needs some one to command his piratical craft. I suspected as much all the while, and the minute we got up to Crooked Inlet I knew it. He can tell you more about the coast in five minutes than I could in an hour."

"Of course, a trader——" began Mrs. Gray.

"Mother," repeated Marcy, "Lon Beardsley is not and never has been a trader. He's a smuggler between this country and Cuba. He says himself that he never made a voyage farther away from home than the West Indies. He knows every inch of the coast like a book."

"Then what does he want of you?" inquired Mrs. Gray, with a look of surprise. "Why can he not permit you to stay at home in peace, as he knows I want you to do? Do you still think he wants to test your loyalty to the South?"

"That's just what he is up to," replied Marcy. "He came here in the hope that I would refuse his offer, so that he would have an excuse for getting me into trouble."

Yes, that was one object Captain Beardsley had in view when he proposed to make Marcy Gray pilot of the privateer, but there was another behind it, and one that was much nearer to the smuggler's heart. As Marcy had told his friend Wat Gifford, on the day the two held that confidential conversation in front of the Nashville post-office, Beardsley wanted to marry Mrs. Gray's plantation; and when

he found that he must give up all hope in
that direction, like the poor apology for a
man that he was, he hit upon a plan for
taking vengeance upon Marcy's mother. If
she proved, when the test was applied, to be
friendly to the South and its cause, he would
not dare lift a finger against her or her
property, for he knew that if he did his
neighbors would quickly interest themselves
in the matter ; but if she would only refuse
to permit Marcy to ship on board the privateer, then he would have a clear field for
his operations. He could accuse Marcy's
mother of being a Yankee sympathizer, and
that would turn the whole settlement against
her at once, because she was already suspected of Union sentiments, and some of her
nearest neighbors were so certain that she
was loyal to the old flag and opposed to
secession, that they thought it their duty to
cease visiting her. It would be no trouble
at all, Beardsley thought, to arouse public
feeling against her ; but unfortunately for
the success of his plans, Mrs. Gray did not
refuse her consent ; the boy took the posi-

tion offered him on the *Osprey*, made one
voyage at sea, and did his duty as faithfully
as any other member of the crew.

"I know Beardsley wanted to find out
where I stood," repeated Marcy. "He expected and hoped that I would refuse to accept his proposition so that he would have
an excuse for persecuting us; but being disappointed there, he intends to work in another direction. He means to make trouble
on account of the money you have in the
cellar."

"But what business—what right has he with
it ?" said Mrs. Gray indignantly. "It's ours."

"I know it, and we're going to keep it;
but if Beardsley can make sure that you
went to Richmond, Wilmington, and Newbern for *money*—and I think you will find
that he looks to Hanson, the overseer, to
furnish him with the proof, and bring a
gang of longshoremen up here from Plymouth some dark night——"

"Oh, Marcy !" cried Mrs. Gray, starting
from her chair and clasping her hands in
alarm, "don't speak of it !"

"I wish from the bottom of my heart that I need not have told you of it," said the boy, getting upon his feet and pacing the floor with restless, angry strides. "But Wat Gifford believes that something of the sort is going to happen, and so do I. Wat didn't say so, but I am sure that is what he would have told me if he had found me at home when he came here. You knew there was danger in every one of those gold pieces you brought home with you; else why did you take so much pains to put them where you thought no one would be likely to find them?"

"It is true I did know it, and was afraid that if the news got abroad in the settlement, some of our poor neighbors might be tempted to commit crime," answered Mrs. Gray. "We never had so large an amount of money in the house before, and its presence troubles me greatly; but I never dreamed that we had anything to fear from an organized band of freebooters."

"And the fear of what Beardsley will do, if he finds out that the money is really in the house, is what troubles me," said the young pilot dolefully. "That man is capable of any desperate deed when he thinks he has the power on his side. I know you never thought of such a thing at the time, but your trips about the country, which Wat Gifford says could not have been made without an object of some sort, have excited a good deal of talk among the neighbors. Captain Beardsley posted Hanson, and Hanson, so Wat told me, is more to be feared than any one else, for he is right here on the place. These secret enemies will drive us both crazy."

"We'll not give them the satisfaction of knowing that they can trouble us in the least," replied his mother, with dignity. "Now we will dismiss them entirely from our minds, while you tell me all the interesting things that happened during your cruise."

"There isn't a thing to tell," was Marcy's answer. "We sighted the *Hollins* inside Diamond Shoals, threw a couple of shrapnel at her and she came to ; that's all there was of it. Her skipper was a sailorman all over, and plucky, too ; and if he had had anything to fight with, he would have made things lively for us. I never before felt so sorry for anybody as I did for him; but of course I didn't have a chance to tell him so. I may some day meet him under different circumstances."

When the boy said this he did not really believe that such a thing ever could occur, but nevertheless it did. Strange things happen in this world sometimes, and in process of time it came about that the young pilot again stood face to face with the master of the *Mary Hollins*, no longer a prisoner pleading with Captain Beardsley that his men might not be ironed like felons, but standing free on the quarter-deck of an armed vessel, with a hundred blue-jackets ready to do his bidding, and the Stars and Stripes waving proudly and triumphantly above him. And Beardsley—he was there, too; and perhaps we shall see what sort of heart he kept up when he found himself thrust into the "brig" so quickly that he did not have time to tell what his name was.

"How long does your leave of absence extend?" inquired Mrs. Gray, after a little pause.

"Until I am ordered to report," replied Marcy, with a laugh. "Perhaps the captain didn't know I wrote it out that way, but that isn't my fault. It was his business to read the paper before signing it. If he wants me he will have to send for me. You ought to have heard that Newbern mob whoop and yell when the crew of the *Hollins* were marched off to jail. They called them 'Abolitionists' and 'nigger-lovers'; but the prisoners kept their eyes straight to the front, and marched on as though they didn't hear a word of it. It was a shame to treat brave men that way."

Just as the young pilot ceased speaking there was a gentle knock at the door; and so sudden and unexpected was it, that it brought both him and his mother to their feet in a twinkling. How long had the person who gave that knock been within reach of the door, was the first thought that arose in the mind of each. Had some one crept along the hall and listened at the key-hole in the hope of hearing some of their conversation?

"If that is the case," Marcy whispered to his mother, "she has had her trouble for her

pains. We haven't said a dozen words that
could have been heard the length of this room.
'Come in!'"

The door opened to admit one of the numerous female house servants, who announced
that there was a gentleman on the gallery who
had called to see Mrs. Gray on very important
private and particular business.

"She looks innocent enough," thought
Marcy, who could not bring himself to believe,
as his mother evidently did, that some of the
domestics were watching their movements and
reporting the result of their observations to
the overseer. "I don't think she heard a
word, and she certainly could not have seen
anything." And then, finding that his mother
was looking at him as if she meant him to
understand that she knew what the visitor's
business was, and desired him to take it off
her hands, he said, aloud: "Who is the gentleman, and do you know what he's got to say
that is so very important and particular?"

"I don't know, sah, what he want to speak
about," answered the girl, "but de man is
Mr. Kelsey."

Marcy could hardly keep back an exclamation of disgust, and in an instant he was on his guard. The man's name and the message he had sent in warned him to be on the lookout for treachery. Kelsey was one of Beardsley's "renters"—that is to say, he hired from the captain a few acres of ground, on which he managed to raise enough corn and potatoes to keep his family from absolute want, and a little log cabin in which he found shelter when he was not absent on his hunting and thieving expeditions. Marcy had not seen him since his return from Barrington, but he had heard of him as a red-hot Confederate who went about declaring that hanging was too good for Yankees and their sympathizers. When Marcy heard of this, he told himself that the man was another Bud Goble, who, when the pinch came, would take to the woods and stay there as long as danger threatened.

"I'll be with him directly," he said, addressing himself to the girl, who went out, closing the door behind her.

"What in the name of wonder can that worthless man want with me?" whispered

Mrs. Gray, when she thought she had given the domestic time to get out of hearing. "He has never been in this house before except to beg."

"And he wouldn't be here now if he hadn't been sent," replied the boy.

"Oh, Marcy!" said his mother.

"That is just what I mean. It isn't old clothes or grub that he is after this time."

"But Beardsley couldn't have put him up to anything. He is in Newbern."

"No odds. He left plenty of friends behind to do his dirty work, and this fellow, Kelsey, is one of them. It will take a sharper man than he is to pull the wool over my eyes."

"Don't be over-confident, my son. He is not too insignificant—no one is too insignificant these times to do us some terrible injury. Be careful how you treat him and what you say to him. It might be dangerous to make him angry, for he has powerful friends behind him. Don't be gone long, for I shall be uneasy until you return."

"I'll be right back," promised Marcy ; and, giving his mother a reassuring kiss, he left the

room and went out on the porch to see what
Beardsley's friend and spy wanted.

The latter looked just as he did the last time
Marcy saw him—too lazy to take a long breath.
He was tall and lank, his hair fell down upon
his shoulders, his whiskers were as tangled
and matted as a little brush heap—in short, he
was as fine a specimen of a poor white as one
could find anywhere in the seceded States.
He looked stupid as well as shiftless, but the
young pilot knew he wasn't. He was as sly as
a fox and as cunning as well, and Marcy con-
fessed to himself that he stood more in fear of
him than he did of Captain Beardsley. When
the man heard Marcy's step upon the porch,
he tried to assume the servile air which was
characteristic of poor Southern whites before
the war; but he did not succeed very well.
His manner seemed to say that he knew he was
dealing with one he could crush whenever he
felt like it, and of whom he need not stand in
fear; and Marcy was quick to notice it.

"Sarvent, sah," said Kelsey, rising to his
feet and taking off his tattered hat, which,
however, he almost instantly replaced. "I

heared that you had got back again from sea,
an' that you had whopped the Yankees first
time tryin', same as our fellers done down to
Charleston."

"Yes, sir," replied Marcy, seating himself,
and depositing his feet on the railing, as if to
indicate that he was quite at the service of his
friend Kelsey as long as the latter wanted to
talk to him. "We whipped them, and we
could do the same thing again." ["And that's
nothing but the truth," he added, to himself.
"When an armed vessel meets one that's not
armed, the helpless one is bound to go under
every time."]

It is hard to tell just what Kelsey expected
the boy to say in response to his greeting, but
in spite of his usual self-control his face
showed that he had not looked for any such
answer as this. Marcy spoke and acted as if
he were delighted with the success that had
attended the *Osprey's* first cruise at sea, and
proud of being able to say that he was one of
her crew.

"You sent in word that you desired to see
my mother on very particular business," con-

tinued Marcy. "She doesn't feel like seeing anybody to-day—upset by the war news, you know—and I am here to speak for her. It's nothing bad, I hope?"

Kelsey straightened up on his seat and assumed a business air, as if these words had suggested an idea to him.

"Yes, it's kinder bad," said he. "We uns know that you are true blue, fur if you wasn't you wouldn't be on that privateer; an' if your maw wasn't true blue, she wouldn't a let you go."

["That sounds exactly like Beardsley," said Marcy, to himself.] "Well, what of it? Didn't I do my duty faithfully?"

"I ain't sayin' nothing agin that," replied the man hastily. "But—you're fur Jeff Davis, ain't you?"

Instead of answering in words, Marcy pulled down the corner of his right eye and looked at Kelsey as if to ask him if he saw anything green in it.

"What do ye mean by them movements?" demanded the visitor.

"I mean that I am not going to talk politics

with you," was the reply. "This settlement is full of traitors, and I'm going to hold my tongue unless I know who I am talking to. If I do that, I shan't get into trouble by speaking too freely in the hearing of a Yankee spy."

"But look a-here, Mister Marcy," protested Kelsey.

"If you came to pry into our private affairs, you might as well jump on your mule and go home, for you'll not get a word from me. I ought to put the dogs on you, for if all I hear is true you're the worst kind of a traitor." ["And so you are," thought Marcy, closely watching the effect of his words, although he did not seem to be doing so; "you're a traitor to the old flag."]

The visitor was astonished beyond measure, and it was fully a minute before he could collect his wits sufficiently to frame a reply.

CHAPTER II.

HIDING THE FLAGS.

" I THINK I have taken the right course,"
soliloquized the young pilot, who mentally congratulated himself on the ease with
which he had "got to windward" of this
sneaking spy. "If I fight him with his own
weapons I shall probably get more out of him
than I could in any other way."

"You heared that I was a traitor?" exclaimed Kelsey, as soon as he could speak.
"Mister Marcy, the man who told you that
told you a plumb lie, kase I ain't. I whooped
her up fur ole Car'liny when she went out, I
done the same when our gov'ner grabbed the
forts along the coast, an' I yelled fit to split
when our folks licked 'em at Charleston. Any
man in the settlement or in Nashville will tell
ye that them words of mine is nothing but the
gospel truth."

Marcy knew well enough that his visitor's

26

words were true, but he shook his head in a doubting way, as he replied :

"That may all be ; but *I* didn't hear you whoop and yell, and you must not expect me to take your word for it. You must bring some proof before I will talk to you."

"Why, how in sense could ye hear me whoop an' yell, seein' that you was away to school in the first place, an' off on the ocean with Beardsley in the next?" exclaimed Kelsey. "Ask Dillon, an' Colonel Shelby, an' the postmaster, an' see if they don't say it's the truth."

"You have mentioned the names of some of our most respected citizens," said Marcy slowly, as if he were still reluctant to be convinced of the man's sincerity. "And if they, or any of them, sent you up here to talk to my mother—why, then, I shall have to listen to you ; but mind you, if you are trying to play a game on me——"

"Mister Marcy," said Kelsey solemnly, "I ain't tryin' to come no game. Them men done it sure's you're born."

"Did what?"

"Sent me up here this mawnin'."

"That's one point gained, but won't mother be frightened when she hears of it?" thought Marcy, leaning his elbows on his knees and covering his face with his hands so that his visitor could not see it. "Some of the best men in the country have so far forgotten their manhood, and the friendship they once had for our family, that they can send this sneaking fellow here to worm something out of us."

"I don't believe a word of it," he cried, jumping to his feet and confronting his visitor.

"Ye—ye don't believe it?" faltered Kelsey, springing up in his turn. "Well, I—I—look a-here, Mister Marcy, mebbe this is something else you don't believe. Them men whose names I jest give you, say that you an' your maw an' all the rest of the Gray family is Union. What do ye say to *that?*"

"I say that they had better attend to their own business and let me attend to mine," answered Marcy. "Are Colonel Shelby and the rest of them for the Union?"

"Not much ; an' nuther be I."

"Are you in favor of secession?"

"I reckon," replied Kelsey earnestly ; and Marcy knew all the while that he could not have told what the word secession meant.

"Then why don't you prove it—you and Colonel Shelby, and the rest of the neighbors who are saying things behind my back that they don't care to say to my face? Why don't you prove your loyalty to the South by shouldering a musket and going into the army?"

"Why, we uns has got famblies to look out fur," exclaimed the visitor, who had never had this matter brought squarely home to him before.

"That makes no difference," answered the boy, who wondered if Kelsey's family would fare any worse while he was in the army than they did now, while he was out of it. "Every man in this country must show his good will in one way or another. And there's that loud-mouthed fellow Allison, who went out of his way to insult me in the post-office just before I went to sea. Nashville is full of such braggarts as he is. When they can't find anything

else to talk about they talk about me; and
I have smelt powder while they haven't."
["No odds if it was our own powder and the
wind blew the smoke into my face," he said to
himself.]

By this time Marcy had the satisfaction of
seeing that he had taken the wind completely
out of Kelsey's sails, and that the man who
had come there to trouble him was troubled
himself. He even began to fear that he had
gone too far, and that if he did not change his
tactics the visitor would go away without giving a hint of the errand that had brought him
to the house; for Kelsey picked up the hat
he had placed upon the floor beside his
chair, put it on his head and leaned forward
with his hands on his knees, as if he were
about to get upon his feet. That wouldn't do
at all. There was something in the wind—
something that Captain Beardsley, aided by
Colonel Shelby and others, had studied up on
purpose to get Marcy into a scrape of some
kind, and Marcy was very anxious to know
what it was.

"You hinted a while ago that Colonel

Shelby had sent you here to tell me some bad news," said the young pilot, in a much pleasanter tone of voice than he had thus far used in addressing his visitor. "Are you ready now to obey orders and tell me what it is?"

"Well, I dunno. I reckon mebbe I'd best ride down an' see the colonel first," replied the man. But his actions said plainly that he *did* know, and that he had no intention of facing his employer again until he could tell him that his instructions had been carried out.

"Of course, you must do as you think best about that; but if it is anything that concerns my mother or myself——"

"I should say so," exclaimed Kelsey. "I don't reckon it'll do any harm to tell you—but ain't there anybody to listen? It's very important an' private."

"I think you may speak with perfect freedom; but in order to make sure of it——" Marcy finished the sentence by getting up and closing both the doors that opened upon the veranda. "Now we're safe," said he; whereupon Kelsey revealed the whole plot in less than a score of words.

"Mebbe you don't know it," said he, in a whisper which was so loud and piercing that it could have been heard by an eavesdropper (if there had been one) at least fifty feet away, "but you are harboring a traitor right here on the place."

"Who is it?"

"Your mean sneak of an overseer."

It was now Marcy's turn to be astonished. He knew that there was not a word of truth in what the man said, and that if the overseer really was a Union man the planters round about would have sent a person of more influence and better social standing than Kelsey to tell him of it; but after all the plot was not as simple as it looked at first glance.

"Where's your proof?" was the first question he asked.

"Well, Hanson has been talkin' a heap to them he thought to be Union, but it turned out that they wasn't. They was true to the flag of the 'Federacy."

"What do Colonel Shelby and the rest want me to do?" inquired Marcy, catching at an idea that just then flashed through his mind.

"If they will write me a note stating the facts of the case and asking me to discharge Hanson, I will attend to it before the sun goes down."

"Well, you see they don't keer to take a hand in the furse at all, seein' that there's so many Union folks in the settlement," said Kelsey. "They've got nice houses an' nigger quarters, an' they don't want 'em burned up."

"But they are willing that I should get into trouble by discharging Hanson, and put myself in the way of having my house and quarters destroyed, are they?" exclaimed the boy, his face growing red with indignation, although, as he afterward told his mother, there wasn't really anything to arouse his indignation. "You may tell those gentlemen that if they want the overseer run off the plantation, they can come here and do it. If the Union men are as vindictive as Colonel Shelby seems to think they are, I don't care to get them down on me."

"But the Union folks won't pester you uns," said Kelsey, speaking before he thought.

3

"Ah! Why won't they?"

"Kase—kase they think you're one of 'em."

"I don't see how they can think so when they know that I belong to a Confederate privateer."

"Them men, whose names I give ye a minute ago, thought that mebbe you'd be willing to turn Hanson loose when you heared how he had been swingin' his tongue about that there money."

Kelsey had come to the point at last. He looked hard at Marcy to see what effect the words would have upon him, and Marcy returned his gaze with an impassive countenance, although he felt his heart sinking within him.

"What money?" he demanded, in so steady a voice that the visitor was fairly staggered. The latter believed that there was rich booty hidden somewhere about that old house, and he hoped in time to have the handling of some of it.

"I mean the money your maw got when she went to Richmon' an' around," replied the man, who, in coon hunters' parlance, began to wonder if he wasn't "barking up the wrong tree."

"Can you prove that she brought any money back with her?"

"No, I can't," answered Kelsey, in a tone which said as plainly as words that he wished he could. "I—me—I mean that the neighbors suspicion it."

"Oh, that's it. Let those officious neighbors keep on talking; and when they have talked themselves blind, you may tell them, for me, that what money we have is safe," said Marcy, with a good deal of emphasis on the adjective. "If you want to see what mother brought back from the city, go and look at the servants. Every one of them is dressed in a new suit. Now go on and tell me the bad news. I'm getting impatient to hear it."

"Heavings an' 'arth! Haven't I told it to ye already?" Kelsey almost shouted. "I think it is bad enough when you an' your maw are keepin', right here on the plantation, a man who is all the time waitin' an' watchin' fur a chance to do harm to both of ye. If you don't think so, all right. I was a fule fur

comin' here, an' I reckon I'd best be lumberin'.
If anything happens to ye, bear in mind that
I give ye fair warnin'."

"I will," answered Marcy. "And in the
mean time do you bear in mind that I am ready
to discharge Hanson at any time Colonel Shelby
proves to my satisfaction that he is a dangerous man to have around ; but I shall make no
move unless the colonel says so, for I don't
want to get into trouble with my neighbors."
["I wonder if I have done the right thing,"
thought Marcy, as the visitor mounted his
mule and rode out of the yard. "The next
plotter I hear from will be Hanson himself."]

The boy remained motionless in his chair
until Kelsey disappeared behind the trees that
bordered the road, and then got up and walked
into the sitting-room, where he found his
mother pacing the floor. Her anxiety and
her impatience to learn what it was that
brought Kelsey to the house were so overpowering that she could not sit still.

"Another plot to ruin us," whispered the
boy, as he entered the room and closed the
door behind him.

"Oh, Marcy, it is just what I was afraid of," replied Mrs. Gray. "Who is at the bottom of it this time?"

"The same old rascal, Lon Beardsley ; but he's got backing I don't like. There's Colonel Shelby for one, the postmaster for another, and Major Dillon for a third."

"The most influential men in the neighborhood," gasped Mrs. Gray, sinking into the nearest chair. "And the best."

"They used to be the best, but they are anything but that now. When men will stoop as low as they have, they are mean enough for anything. I suppose you ought to hear what that fellow said to me, but I don't know how I can tell it to you."

"Go on," said his mother, trying to bear up bravely. "I must hear every word."

Marcy knew that it was right and necessary that his mother should be kept fully informed regarding the plots that were laid against them, and that she should know what the planters were thinking and saying about her ; for if she were kept in ignorance, she would be at a loss how to act and speak in a sudden emergency.

She might be surprised into saying something in the presence of a secret enemy that would be utterly ruinous. So he drew a chair to her side and told her everything that had passed between Kelsey and himself. He did not try to smooth it over, but repeated the conversation word for word ; and when he came to the end, his mother was as much in the dark as Marcy was himself. She said she couldn't understand it.

"There are but two things about it that are plain to me," answered Marcy, "perhaps three. One is that the house is watched by somebody, and that the neighbors knew I was at home almost as soon as you knew it yourself. Another is that the suspicions aroused in the minds of some of our watchful neighbors are so strong that they amount to positive conviction. They are as certain that there is money in this house as they would be if they had caught you in the act of hiding it."

"Doesn't that prove that the overseer is not the only spy there is on the place?" said Mrs. Gray. "And I was so careful."

"I never will believe that anybody watched

you at night," said Marcy quickly. "The neighbors saw you when you went away and came back."

"But I brought goods with me on purpose to allay their suspicions."

"I am really afraid you didn't succeed. The other thing I know is, that you need not think yourself safe out of Captain Beardsley's reach even when he is at sea. As I said before, he has friends ashore to work for him while he is absent."

"What can we do? What do you advise?" asked his mother, after she had taken time to think the matter over.

"There is but one thing we can do, and that is to wait as patiently as we can and see what is going to happen next. This last plot is not fully developed yet, and until it is we must not make a move in any direction. I am as impatient as you are, and so I think I will ride out to the field and give the overseer a chance to say a word if he feels in the humor for it."

"Be very cautious, Marcy," said Mrs. Gray.

The young pilot replied that sleeping or waking he was always on the alert, and went

out to the little log stable, which did duty as
a barn, to saddle his horse. A long lane led
through the negro quarter to the field in which
the hands were putting in the time in clearing
out fence corners and burning brush, while
waiting for the early crops to get high enough
for hoeing. The overseer's mule was hitched
to the fence, and the overseer himself sat on a
convenient stump, watching the hands at their
work, and whittling the little switch that served
him for a riding-whip. The man was almost a
stranger to Marcy. The latter had seen and
spoken to him a few times since his return from
Barrington, but of course he did not like him,
for he could not forget that his mother was
afraid of him, and would be glad to see him
leave the place. He liked him still less two
minutes later, for, as he drew rein beside the
overseer's perch, threw his right leg over the
horn of his saddle and nodded to the man, the
latter said, first looking around to make sure
that none of the blacks were within hearing:

"I was sorry to see that man ride away from
the big house a while ago."

"What man?" inquired Marcy.   He looked

over his shoulder and saw that the front of the
house was entirely concealed from view, and
that the road that ran before it was shut out
from sight by the trees and the whitewashed
negro quarter. It followed then, as a matter of
course, that Hanson could not have seen anybody ride away from the house. He was deep
enough in the plot to know that if mother and
son had not had a visitor, they ought to have
had one.

"I suspicioned it was that shiftless, do-
nothing chap, Kelsey," replied the overseer.
" Looked sorter like his mu-el."

" Oh, yes ; Kelsey has been up to see us,"
answered Marcy. And then he tapped his boot
with his whip and waited to see what was
coming next. If the overseer wanted to talk,
he might talk all he pleased ; but Marcy was
resolved that he would not help him along.
Hanson twisted about on the stump, cleared his
throat once or twice, and, seeing that the boy
was not disposed to break the silence, said, as
if he were almost afraid to broach the subject :

"Have much of anything to talk about ?"

"He talked a good deal, but didn't say much."

"Mention my name?"

"Yes. He mentioned yours and Shelby's and Dillon's and the postmaster's."

"Say anything bad about us?" continued the overseer, after waiting in vain for the boy to go on and repeat the conversation he had held with Kelsey.

"Not so very bad," answered Marcy, looking up and down the long fence to see how the work was progressing.

"Look a-here, Mister Marcy," said Hanson desperately. "Kelsey told you I was Union, didn't he? Come now, be honest."

"If by being honest you mean being truthful, I want to tell you that I am never any other way," said the boy emphatically. "What object could I have in denying it? I don't care a cent what your politics are so long as you mind your own business, and don't try to cram your ideas down my throat. But I'll not allow myself to be led into a discussion. Kelsey did say that you are Union; and if you are, I don't see why you stay in this country. You can't get out any too quick."

"Are you going to discharge me?"

"No, I am not; and I sent word to Shelby and the rest that if they want you run off the place, they can come up here and do it. I shall have no hand in it."

Marcy could read the overseer's face a great deal better than the overseer could read Marcy's; and it would have been clear to a third party that Hanson was disappointed, and that there was something he wanted to say and was afraid to speak about. That was the money that was supposed to be concealed in the house.

"Was that all Kelsey said to you?" he asked, at length.

"Oh, no. He rattled on about various things —spoke of the ease with which the *Osprey* captured that Yankee schooner, and let fall a word or two about the battle in Charleston harbor."

"Is *that* all he said to you?"

"I believe he said something about being a good Confederate, and I asked him why he didn't prove it by shouldering a musket. I

don't go about boasting of the great things I
would do if I were only there. There's no need
of it, for I have been there." ["But it was
because I couldn't help myself," he added
mentally.]

"But folks say you're Union, all the same,"
said Hanson.

"What folks? Are they soldiers?"

"No. Citizens."

"Then I don't care that what they say,".
replied Marcy, snapping his fingers in the air.
"When they put uniforms on and show by
their actions that they mean business, I will
talk to them, and not before."

Marcy waited patiently for the overseer to
say "money," and the latter waited impatiently for Marcy to say it; and when at last
the boy made up his mind that he had heard
all he cared to hear from Hanson, he brought
his leg down from the horn of his saddle,
placed his foot in the stirrup, and gathered up
the reins as if he were about to ride away.

"Kelsey didn't say nothing to get you and
your maw down on me, did he?" inquired
Hanson, when he observed these movements.

"I shouldn't like for to lose my place just because I am strong for the Union and dead against secession."

"If you lose your place on that account, it'll be because Colonel Shelby and his friends will have it so," answered Marcy. "You are hired to do an overseer's work; and as long as you attend to that *and nothing else*, you will have no trouble with me. You may depend upon that."

"But before you go I'd like to know, pine-plank, whether you are friendly to me or not," continued Hanson, who was obliged to confess to himself that he had not learned the first thing, during the interview, that could be used against Marcy or his mother.

"I am a friend to you in this way," was the answer. "If I found you out there in the woods cold and hungry, and hiding from soldiers who were trying to make a prisoner of you, I would feed and warm you; and I wouldn't care whether you had a gray jacket or a blue coat on."

"He's a trifle the cutest chap I've run across in many a long day," muttered the overseer, as Marcy turned his filly about and rode away. "I couldn't make him tell whether he was Union or secesh, although I give him all the chance in the world, and he didn't say "money" a single time. Now, what's to be done? If the money is there and Beardsley is bound to have it, he'd best be doing something before that sailor gets back, for they say he's lightning and will fight at the drop of the hat. I reckon I'd better make some excuse to ride over town so't I can see Colonel Shelby."

"I think I have laid that little scheme most effectually," was what Marcy Gray said to himself as he rode away from the stump on which the overseer was sitting. "They haven't got a thing out of me, and I have left the matter in their own hands. If there is anything done toward getting Hanson away from this country (and I wish to goodness there might be), Shelby and his hypocritical gang can have the fun of doing it, and shoulder all the responsibility afterward."

But what was the object of the plot? That was what "banged" Marcy, and he told his mother so after he had given her a minute de-

scription of his brief interview with the overseer. Was it possible that there were some
strong Union men in the neighborhood, and
that Beardsley hoped Marcy would incur their
enmity by discharging Hanson on account of
his alleged principles? Marcy knew better
than to believe that, and so did his mother.

"I'll tell you what I think to be the most
reasonable view of the case," said the boy,
after taking a few turns across the floor and
spending some minutes in a brown study.
"Beardsley knows there is no man in the family; that we'd be only too glad to have somebody to go to for advice ; and he hoped we
would take that ignorant Hanson for a coun-
selor, if he could make us believe that he was
really Union. But Hanson didn't fool me, for
he didn't go at it in the right way. He's
secesh all over. The next thing on the pro-
gram will be something else."

"I trust it will not be a midnight visit from
a mob," said his mother, who trembled at the
bare thought of such a thing.

"So do I ; but if they come, we'll see what
they will make by it. They might burn the

house without finding anything to reward them
for their trouble."

"Oh, Marcy. You surely don't think they
would do anything so barbarous."

"They might. Think of what that Commit-
tee of Safety did at Barrington."

"But what would we do?"

"Live in the quarter, as Elder Bowen and
the other Union men in Barrington did after
their houses were destroyed. And if they
burned the servants' homes as well as our own,
we'd throw up a shelter of some sort in the
woods. I don't reckon that Julius and I have
forgotten how to handle axes and build log
cabins. The practice we have had in building
turkey traps would stand—— Say," whispered
Marcy suddenly, at the same time putting his
arm around his mother's neck and speaking
the words close to her ear, "if a mob should
come here to-night and go over the house, we'd
be ruined. There are those Union flags, you
know."

"I never once thought of them," was the
frightened answer. "Suppose I had had a
mob for visitors while you were at sea? Our

home would be in ashes now. Those flags are
dangerous things, and must be disposed of
without loss of time. I am sorry you brought
them home with you. Don't you think you
had better destroy them while you have them
in mind ?"

"Of course I will do it if you say so, and
think it will make you feel any safer; but I
was intending—you see——"

His countenance fell, and his mother was
quick to notice it. "What did you intend to
do with them ?" she asked.

"One of them used to float over the
academy," replied Marcy. "Dick Graham, a
Missouri boy, than whom a better fellow never
lived, stole it out of the colonel's room one
night because he did not want to see it insulted
and destroyed, as it would have been if Rodney
and his friends could have got their hands
upon it. He gave it to me because he knew it
would some day be something to feel proud
over, and said he hoped to hear that it had
been run up again."

"But, Marcy, you dare not hoist it here,"
exclaimed Mrs. Gray.

4

"Not now; but there may come a time when I shall dare do it. The other flag—well, the other was made by a Union girl in Barrington, who had to work on it by stealth, because her sister, and every other member of her family except her father, were the worst kind of secesh. Rodney thought sure he was going to put the Stars and Bars on the tower when the Union colors were stolen, but our fellows got mine up first, and would have kept it there if they had had to fight to do it. But I'll put them in the stove if you think best."

"You need not do anything of the kind," said Mrs. Gray, whose patriotism had been awakened by the simple narrative. "I shall not permit a party of beardless boys to show more loyalty than I am willing to show myself."

"Bully for you, mother!" cried Marcy. "We'll see both of them in the air before many months more have passed over our heads. Now, think of some good hiding place for them, and I'll put them there right away. Not in the ground, you know, for if the Union troops should ever come marching through here, we should want to get them out in a hurry."

"How would it do to sew them up in a bed-quilt?" said Mrs. Gray, suggesting the first "good hiding place" that came into her mind.

"That's the very spot," replied Marcy. "Put them in one of mine, and then I shall have the old flag over me every night."

No time was lost in carrying out this decision, and in a few minutes mother and son were locked in the boy's room, and busy stitching the precious pieces of bunting into one of the quilts. It never occurred to them to ask what they would do or how they would feel if some half-clad, shivering rebel should find his way into the room and walk off with that quilt without so much as saying "by your leave." Probably they never dreamed that the soldiers of the Confederacy would be reduced to such straits.

CHAPTER III.

NEVER before had the hours hung as heavily upon Marcy Gray's hands as they did at the period of which we write. There was literally nothing he could do—at least that he *wanted* to do. He did not care to read anything except the newspapers, and they came only once a day; he had never learned how to lounge around and let the hours drag themselves away; he very soon grew weary of sailing about the sound in the *Fairy Belle* with the boy Julius for a companion ; and so he spent a little of his time in visiting among the neighboring planters, and a good deal more in " pottering" among his mother's flower beds. Visiting was the hardest work he had ever done ; but he knew he couldn't shirk it without exciting talk, and there was talk enough about him in the settlement already.

52

To a stranger it would have looked as though he had nothing to complain of. He was cordially received wherever he went, often heard himself spoken of as "one of our brave boys" (although what he had done that was so very brave Marcy himself could not understand), and visitors at Mrs. Gray's house were as numerous as they ever had been; but Marcy and his mother were people who could not be easily deceived by such a show of friendship. Some of it, as they afterward learned, was genuine; while the rest was assumed for the purpose of leading them on to "declare" themselves. It was a mean thing for neighbors to be guilty of, but you must remember that, like Rodney Gray when he wrote that mischievous letter to Bud Goble, they did not know all the time what they were doing. Of course the high-spirited Marcy grew restive under such treatment; and when, after long waiting, the postmaster handed him a letter from Captain Beardsley, ordering him to report on board the *Osprey* without loss of time, he did not feel as badly over it as he once thought he should. On the contrary, he appeared to be very jubilant when he showed the letter to Allison and half a score of other young rebels who were always to be found loafing around the post-office at mail time.

"I'm off to sea again," said he. "Now the Yankees had better look out."

"It must be an enjoyable life, Marcy," replied Allison. "You see any amount of fun and excitement, draw big prize-money in addition to your regular wages, and, better than all, you run no sort of risk. It may surprise you to know that I have been turning the matter over in my mind a good deal of late, and have come to the conclusion that I should enjoy being one of a privateer's crew. What do you think about it?"

"I am not acquainted with a single fellow who would enjoy it more," answered Marcy, who told himself that Allison was just coward enough to engage in some such disreputable business. "You are just the lad for it. It is such fun to bring a swift vessel to and haul down the old flag in the face of men who are powerless to defend it."

Sharp as Marcy Gray was, his strong love for

the Union and his intense hatred for the business in which he was perforce engaged, sometimes led him to come dangerously near to
betraying himself. Allison looked sharply at
him, but there was nothing in Marcy's face to
indicate that he did not mean every word he
said.

"I am heartily glad I am going to sea again,"
continued the latter; and he told nothing but
the truth. The companionship of the ignorant
foreigners who composed the *Osprey's* crew
was more to his liking than daily intercourse
with pretended friends who were constantly
watching for a chance to get him into trouble.

"Do you think I could get on with Captain
Beardsley?" inquired Allison.

"You might. The crew was full when I left
the schooner, but I will speak to the captain, if
you would like to have me."

"I really wish you would, for I am anxious
to do something for the glorious cause of Southern independence. When do you sail?"

"I don't know. About all the captain says
in his letter is that he wants me to report immediately."

"Does he say whether or not the *Hollins* has been sold yet?"

"Oh, yes; he speaks of that, and congratulates me on the fact that I have eight hundred and seventy-five dollars more to my credit on the schooner's books than I did when I left her at Newbern."

"W-h-e-w!" whistled Allison. "How long did it take you to make the capture?"

"Four or five hours, I should say."

"Eight hundred and seventy-five dollars for four or five hours' work! Marcy, you have struck a gold mine. You will be as rich as Julius Cæsar in less than a year."

"How long do you suppose Uncle Sam will allow such—such work to be kept up?" exclaimed Marcy.

"Oh, no doubt he would be glad to stop it now if he could; but when he tries it, he will find that he's got the hardest job on his hands he ever undertook. There never was a better place for carrying on such business than the waters of North Carolina. Our little inlets are too shallow to float a heavy man-of-war."

"No matter how big the job may be, you will

find that these small-fry privateers" (it was right on the end of Marcy's tongue to say "pirates") "will be swept from the face of the earth in less than a year; so that I shall have no chance to get rich. But I'll have to be going, for I must start for Newbern this very night. I suppose you will all be in the army by the time I get back, so good-by."

Allison and his friends shook hands with him, wished him another successful voyage, and Marcy mounted and rode away, his filly never breaking her lope until she turned through the gate into the yard, and drew up before the steps that led to the porch. His mother met him at the door and knew as soon as she looked at him that he had news for her.

"Yes, I've got orders from Beardsley," said the boy, without waiting to be questioned. "And if Jack were only here, and I was about to engage in some honorable business, I should be glad to go. Mother, on the day we captured the *Hollins* we robbed somebody of fifty-six thousand dollars."

"Oh, Marcy, is it not dreadful!" said Mrs. Gray.

"It is, for a fact. We're having a bully time now, but the day will come when we'll have to settle with the fiddler. You will see. Yes, the vessel and her cargo sold for fifty-six thousand dollars. Half of it went to the government, and half of the remainder was divided among the three officers, Beardsley getting the lion's share, I bet you. The sixteen members of the crew get an equal share of the other fourteen thousand, the difference in rank between the petty officers and foremast hands being so slight that Beardsley did not think it worth while to give one more than another; but he hints that he has got something laid by for me."

"My son, it will burn your fingers," said Mrs. Gray.

"I can't help it if it does. I'll have to take all he offers me, but, of course, I don't expect to keep it. Now, mother, please help me get off. The longer I fool around home the harder it will be to make a start."

Marcy wanted to caution his mother to look out for Hanson while he was gone; but he did not do it, for he well knew that she had enough to trouble her already, and that the mention of the overseer's name would awaken all her old fears of spies and organized bands of robbers. He sent word to Morris, the coachman, to have the carriage brought to the door, loitered about doing nothing while his mother packed his valise, and in twenty minutes more was on his way to Newbern, which he reached without any mishap, not forgetting, however, to send a telegram on from Boydtown informing Beardsley that his orders had been received, and that the pilot was on his way to join the *Osprey*.

"And I wish I might find her sunk at her dock, and so badly smashed that she never could be raised and repaired," was what he thought every time he looked out of the car window and ran his eyes over the crowds of excited people that were gathered upon the platforms of all the depots they passed. "But, after all, what difference does it make? If I don't go to sea I shall have to live among secret enemies, and I don't know but one thing is about as bad as the other. If any poor mortal ever lived this way before, I am sorry for him."

Although Marcy was almost a stranger in Newbern, he had no difficulty in finding his vessel when he got out of the cars. He walked straight to her, and while he was yet half a block away, the sight of her masts told him that she was still on top of the water. She would soon be ready to sail, too, for her crew were rushing her stores aboard, while Captain Beardsley walked his quarter-deck smoking a cigar and looking on. His face seemed to say that he was a little surprised to see his pilot; but if he was he did not show it in his greeting.

"Well, there, you did come back, didn't you?" said he, extending his hand.

"Of course I came back," replied Marcy. "What else did you expect me to do? I was on the road in less than two hours after your order came to hand."

"That's prompt and businesslike," said the captain approvingly. "But I didn't look for you to appear quite so soon. How's everybody to home?"

"All right as far as I could see; and Allison wants to join your crew."

"The idea!" exclaimed Captain Beardsley. "Well, he can just stay where he is for all of me, hollering for the Confederacy and doing never a thing to help us gain our indep'ndence. His place is in the army, and I won't have no haymakers aboard of me. See any Union folks while you was to home?"

"I saw and talked with one man who said he was for the Union," answered the young pilot. He was prepared for the question, and positive that if he managed the matter rightly, Beardsley would soon let him know whether or not he was concerned in that little plot, as Marcy believed he was. But, as it happened, no management was necessary, for keeping a secret was the hardest work Beardsley ever did.

"Did, hey?" he exclaimed, throwing the stump of his cigar over the stern and looking very angry indeed. "I always suspected that man Hanson. You discharged him, of course."

"No, I didn't," replied Marcy. "It wouldn't have been safe. I told Kelsey that if the colonel and his friends desired that he should be run off the place, they could attend to the matter themselves. I wouldn't have the first thing to do with it. I was given to understand that there were many Union men in the settlement, and I didn't care to give them an excuse for burning us out of house and home."

"That was perfectly right. And what did Shelby say?"

"I didn't hear, for he sent no message to me."

"Did you say anything to Hanson about it?"

"I did, and told him that as long as he attended strictly to his business he would have no trouble with me."

Marcy had purposely avoided speaking Colonel Shelby's name and Hanson's, preferring to let Captain Beardsley do it himself. The latter walked squarely into the trap without appearing to realize that he had done it, and the young pilot was satisfied that his commander was the man who needed watching more than anybody else.

"I can't say that I hope Beardsley will be killed or drowned during the cruise," thought

Marcy. "But I do say that if he was out of the way I would have less trouble with my ·neighbors."

"Never mind," said Beardsley, after a little pause. "When I get home I will ask Shelby and Dillon to tell me all about it; and if that overseer of yourn is really Union, perhaps I can make him see that he had better go up to the United States, where he belongs."

The captain took a turn or two across the deck, looked up at the topmasts as he might have done if the schooner had been under way and he wanted to make sure that everything was drawing, and then he leaned up against the rail.

"Oh!" said he, as if the thought had just come to him, "what do you think of your good fortune? Eight hundred dollars don't grow in every boy's dooryard, I tell you. And, Marcy," he went on in a lower tone, "I've got as much more laid by for you. I told you I would do the fair thing, and I meant every word of it. You're pilot, you know."

"Thank you, sir," replied the boy—not because he felt grateful to Captain Beardsley for giving him nearly nine hundred dollars of another's man's money, but because he knew he was expected to say it.

"Seventeen hundred dollars and better will keep your folks in grub and clothes for quite a spell, won't it?" the captain continued. "But law! what am I saying? It ain't a drop in the bucket to such rich people as you be."

Marcy listened, but said nothing. He thought he knew what Beardsley had on his mind.

"Some folks pertend to think we're going to have the very toughest kind of a war, but I don't," said the latter. "The Yankees don't come of fighting stock, like we Southern gentlemen do; but if a war should come, I suppose your folks are well fixed for it?"

"About as well fixed as most of the planters in the settlement," answered the pilot. "You know we've had the best of crops for a year or two back."

"But I mean—you see—any money?" inquired the captain cautiously—so very cautiously that he thought it necessary to whisper the words.

"Oh, yes ; we have money. How could we live without it ?"

"That's so ; how could you ? I reckon you've got right smart of a lot, ain't you ?"

"Mother has some in the bank at Wilmington, but just how much I don't know. I never asked her."

The young pilot's gaze was fastened upon the men who were at work getting the provisions aboard, but for all that, he could see that Beardsley was looking at him as if he meant to read his most secret thoughts.

"I don't believe there's no money in that there house," was what the captain was saying to himself.

"Sly old fox," thought Marcy. "I knew he would betray his secret if I only held my tongue and gave him a chance to do it." And then he asked the captain when he expected to get the schooner ready for sea, and whether or not any prizes had been brought into port during his absence.

"There's been one prize brought in worth ten thousand dollars more'n our'n, dog-gone it all—there she is right over there—and there's

5

been three blockade-runners went out and two come in," was the captain's answer. " I didn't see why they should call 'em blockade-runners when we didn't think there was a blockade at all, excepting the paper one that appeared in Lincoln's proclamation ; but seeing that the brig *Herald* ain't been heard from since she run out of Wilmington, I begin to mistrust that there's war vessels outside, and that the *Osprey* may have a chance to show her heels. If that happens we'll make the best time we know how for Crooked Inlet, and trust to you to bring us through."

"You won't need any help from me," was what the boy said to himself. " I'll bet my share of that prize-money, that if we get into trouble with a Union cruiser you will take command of the schooner yourself and sail her through Crooked Inlet as slick as falling off a log."

" The folks around here and Wilmington have been hoping that the *Herald* might be captured, and that the United States people will have the backbone to hold fast to her," added Captain Beardsley.

"Why do they hope for any such bad luck as that?" inquired Marcy, considerably surprised.

"May be it wouldn't be bad luck. You see she is a Britisher, the *Herald* is, and her cargo was consigned to an English house all fair and square. A blockade, to be legal and binding upon foreign nations, must be effectual," said the captain, quoting the language his agent had often used in his hearing. "A paper blockade won't do; and if the Yankees can't send ships enough here to shut up our ports completely, any Britisher or Frenchman can run in and out as often as he feels like it, and the Yankees dassent do a thing to him. If the *Herald* has been captured she will have to be given up."

"But suppose Uncle Sam won't give her up?"

"We are hoping he won't, for that will get the British folks down on him; and between the two of us we'll give him such a licking that he'll never get over it. See?"

Yes; Marcy saw, now that the situation had been explained to him, but it was something he had never thought of before. Almost the first lesson he learned in history was that England had no love for the United States, and if she took a hand in the war that was surely coming, why then——

"Why, then, France may help Uncle Sam," exclaimed Marcy. "She has always been friendly to us, and didn't she send troops here during our Revolutionary war to help us whip the English?"

"She did ; but what was the reason she sent them troops over here?" demanded the captain, who had heard this question discussed a good many times while Marcy was at home on his leave of absence. "Was it because she had any love for republican—republican—ah—er—institutions? No, sir. It was because she wanted to spite the English for taking Canady away from her. France won't lift a hand to help the Yankees if we get into a row with them."

Beardsley took another turn about his quarter-deck, lighted a fresh cigar, and became confidential.

"Something tells me that this business of

privateering ain't a going to last long, and so
I think some of dropping it and starting
out in another," said he. "Any idea what
it is ?"

Marcy replied that he had not.

" Well, it's trading—running the blockade."

"To what ports ?" asked the boy.

"I can't rightly tell till I get some word
from them vessels that's just went out," was
the answer. "But it'll be Nassau or Havana,
one of the two. I'll take cotton out—cotton
is king, you know, and must be had to keep
all them working people in England from
starving—and bring medicine back. Medicine
is getting skurse and high-priced already.
And percussion caps. They're the things you
can make money on. Why, I have heard it
said that there wasn't enough gun caps in the
Confederacy to fight a battle with till Captain
Semmes made that tower of his through the
Northern States, buying powder and bullets,
and making contracts with the dollar-loving
Yankees to build cannon to shoot their own
kin with. But I want to see how the land lays
before I go into the business of running the

blockade. If there's big risk and little profit I ain't in."

"What port will you run out of?" was Marcy's next question ; and when the captain said it would probably be Wilmington, the boy was delighted, for he expected to hear him announce that after he gave up privateering and took to blockade-running he would no longer need the services of a pilot. But if such a thought came into Beardsley's mind he did not speak it aloud. Just then he was called to another part of the deck and Marcy picked up his valise and went below.

"Beardsley doesn't mean to let me go," he soliloquized, as he tossed the valise into his bunk and opened the locker in which he had stowed his bedding for safe-keeping. "He's got me fast, and there's no chance for escape as long as the *Osprey* remains in commission. Well, there's one comfort : Beardsley is not a brave man, and he'll make haste to lay the schooner up the minute he has reason to believe that it is growing dangerous outside."

Marcy went on deck again, and having nothing to do with the loading of the vessel, sauntered around with his hands in his pockets. He fully expected that Beardsley would have something more to say about the money that was supposed to be hidden in Mrs. Gray's house ; but he didn't, for the captain had almost come to the conclusion that there was no money there. If there was, Marcy could not be surprised into acknowledging the fact, and so Beardsley thought it best to let the matter drop until he could go home and hold a consultation with the overseer.

Bright and early the next morning the privateer cast off her fasts and stood down the river, reaching the sound in time to catch the flood tide that hurried her up toward Crooked Inlet. It was now the middle of July, and the Union and the Confederacy stood fairly opposed to each other. The Confederate Government, having established itself at Richmond, had pushed its outposts so far to the north that their sentries could see the dome of the Capitol across the Potomac. There were nearly eight hundred thousand square miles in the eleven seceded States, and of this immense territory all that remained to the Union

were the few acres of ground enclosed within
the walls of Fortress Monroe and Forts Pickens,
Taylor, and Jefferson.   Loyal Massachusetts
men had been murdered in the streets of Baltimore ; battles of more or less importance had
been fought both in the East and West, and
on the very day that Marcy joined the privateer, the future leader of the Army of the
Potomac won a complete victory over the rebel
forces at Rich Mountain.   The Richmond papers had very little to say about this fight,
except to assure their readers that it was a
matter of no consequence whatever ; but they
had a good deal to say concerning the "gallant
exploit" that Captain Semmes had performed
a few days before at the passes of the Mississippi.   Well, it *was* a brave act—one worthy
of a better cause—to run the little *Sumter* out
in the face of a big ship like the *Brooklyn*, and
when Marcy read of it he recalled what his
Cousin Rodney had once said to him while
they were talking about sailor Jack, who was
then somewhere on the high seas :

"He may never get back," said Rodney.
"We'll have a navy of our own one of these

days, and then every ship that floats the old flag will have to watch out. We'll light bonfires on every part of the ocean."

That was just what Captain Semmes intended to do, and history tells how faithfully he carried out the instructions of the Richmond Government.

Somewhat to Marcy's surprise, Captain Beardsley turned the command over to him when the schooner reached Crooked Inlet, and Marcy took her safely through and out to sea. If there were any war ships on the coast—and it turned out that there were, for the brig *Herald* had been captured and taken to a Northern port—they were stationed farther down toward Hatteras Inlet, and the schooner's lookouts did not see any of them until she had been some hours at sea. At daylight on the morning of the third day out the thrilling cry from the crosstrees "sail ho!" created a commotion on the privateer's deck, and brought Marcy Gray up the ladder half dressed.

"Where away?" shouted Captain Beardsley.

"Broad on our weather beam and standing

straight across our bows," was the encouraging response from aloft.

"Can you make her out?" asked the captain, preparing to mount to the crosstrees with a spy-glass in his hand. "You're sure she isn't a cruiser?"

"No, sir. She's a brig, and she's running along with everything set."

"Then we must cut her off or she'll get away from us. Put a fifteen-second shell in that bow gun, Tierney! Stand by the color halliards, Marcy!"

These orders were obeyed with an "Ay, ay, sir," although the brig was yet so far away that she could not be seen from the deck; but as the two vessels were sailing diagonally toward each other, she did not long remain invisible. The moment Marcy caught sight of her top-hamper, and while he stood with the halliards in his hand waiting for the order to run up the Stars and Stripes, Captain Beardsley began swearing most lustily and shouting orders to his mates, the sheets were let out, the helm put down, and the privateer fell off four or five points. Marcy knew the meaning of this before the excited and angry Beardsley yelled, at the top of his voice:

"The rascal is trying to dodge us. He's got lookouts aloft. Run up that flag, Marcy, and see if that won't quiet his feelings. Them war ships down to Hatteras have posted him, and if we don't handle ourselves just right we'll never bring him within range."

Marcy lost no time in running up the old flag; but if the master of the brig saw it he was not deceived by it. He showed no disposition to run back to Hatteras, and put himself under protection of the war ships there, as Marcy thought and hoped he would, but put his vessel before the wind, squared his yards, and trusted to his heels. It looked to Marcy like a most desperate undertaking, for you will remember that the schooner was far ahead of the brig, and that the merchant captain was about to run by her. It didn't seem possible that he could succeed, but the sequel proved that he knew just what his vessel was capable of doing. She came up at a "hand gallop," and finally showed herself from water-line to main-truck in full view of the privateer's crew. Her canvas loomed up like a great white cloud, and her low, black hull, by comparison, looked no bigger than a lead pencil. She went like the wind, and Marcy Gray told himself that she was the most beautiful object he had ever seen.

"I hope from the bottom of my heart that she will get away," was the one thought that filled his mind.

Perhaps the wish would have been even more fervent if he had known who was aboard that brig.

CHAPTER IV.

TWO NARROW ESCAPES.

"ANOTHER Cuban trader," shouted Captain Beardsley, standing erect upon the crosstrees and shaking his eye-glass in the air. "She's worth double what the *Hollins* was, dog-gone it all, and if we lose her we are just a hundred thousand dollars out of pocket. Pitch that shell into her, Tierney. Take a stick out of her and I'll double your prize money. Run up our own flag, Marcy. May be it will bring him to his senses."

The howitzer's crew sprang at the word. The canvas covering was torn off the gun and cast aside, the train-tackles were manned, and a minute afterward a fifteen-second shrapnel went shrieking toward the brig, all the privateer's men standing on tiptoe to watch the effect of the shot. To Marcy's great delight the missile struck the water far short of the mark, *ricocheted* along the surface a few hundred yards farther, and finally exploded, throwing up a cloud of spray, but doing no harm to the brig, which never loosened tack or sheet, but held gallantly on her way. A moment after the shrapnel exploded, her flag—the old flag—fluttered out from under the lee of her spanker, and little puffs of smoke arose from her port quarter. Some of her crew were firing at the privateer with rifles. Of course, the distance was so great that they never heard the whistle of the bullet, but it was an act of defiance that drove Captain Beardsley almost frantic.

"When we catch her I'll hang the men who fired those shots," he shouted, jumping up and down on his lofty perch. "What are you standing there gaping at, Tierney? Give that gun more elevation and try her again."

"I had her up to the last notch in the rear sight, sir," replied Tierney. "I can't give the gun any more elevation. The cascabel is down to the bottom of the screw now. I can't reach the brig into an eighth of a mile."

"Try her again, I tell you," roared the enraged captain. "Are you going to stand chinning there while a hundred thousand dollars slips through our fingers?"

The captain continued to talk in this way while the howitzer was loaded and trained for the second shot; but he might as well have saved his ammunition, for this shrapnel, like the first, did no harm to the brig. It didn't frighten her company, either, for they set up a derisive yell, which came faintly to the ears of the privateer's crew.

"*Oh*, how I'd like to get my hands on that fellow!" shouted Captain Beardsley. "I'd learn him to insult a Confederate government vessel. I'd——"

Marcy Gray, who stood holding fast to the halliards, looking aloft and listening to what Beardsley had to say, saw the lookout, who had remained at his post all this time, touch the captain on the shoulder and direct his gaze toward something in the horizon. Marcy looked, too, and was electrified to see a thick, black smoke floating up among the clouds. Could it be that there was a cruiser off there bearing down upon them? He looked at Captain Beardsley again, and came to the conclusion that there must be something suspicious about the stranger, for the captain, after gazing at the smoke through his glass, squared around and backed down from aloft with much more celerity than Marcy ever saw him exhibit before.

"It is a cruiser," thought the young pilot, when the captain assumed charge of the deck and ordered the schooner to be put about and headed toward Crooked Inlet. "She has heard the sound of our guns and is coming up to see what is the matter."

Marcy couldn't decide whether the captain's pale face and excited, nervous manner were occasioned by the fears that had been conjured up by the sudden appearance of that strange vessel in the offing, or by the rage and disappointment he felt over the loss of the valuable prize he had so confidently expected to capture. He hauled down the schooner's flag, packed it away in the chest where it was usually kept, and then had leisure to take a look at the crew. Could they be the same men who had so valiantly fired into that unarmed brig a short half hour before?

"It *is* a cruiser," repeated Marcy, turning to the side to conceal the look of exultation which he knew the thought brought to his face. "It can't be anything else, for the whole ship's company are scared out of their boots. We were so busy with the brig that we never saw her until she got so close on to us that she is liable to cut us off from the Inlet. If she comes within range of us Captain Beardsley will find that there is a heap of difference between shooting and being shot at. I hope——"

Marcy was about to add that he hoped the on-coming war ship would either capture or sink the *Osprey*, and so put a stop to her piratical career ; but if she did, what would become of him ? If one of those big shells came crashing into the schooner, it would be as likely to hit him as anybody else, and if the privateer were cut off from the Inlet and captured, he would be taken prisoner with the rest of the crew and sent to some Northern prison. Of course, Marcy could not make the captain of the war ship believe that he did not ship on the privateer of his own free will, and that he was strong for the Union ; and indeed it would be danger-

6

ous for him to try, for the folks at home would be sure to hear of it sooner or later, and then what would happen to his mother? As the young pilot turned these thoughts over in his. mind, he came to the conclusion that he would feel a little safer if he knew that the schooner would reach the Inlet in advance of the steamer, but he was obliged to confess that it looked doubtful. She was coming up rapidly, land was a long way off, and it would be many hours before darkness came to their aid.

"That rain squall out there is our only salvation," Marcy heard the captain say to one of the mates. "When it comes up we'll haul our wind and run for Hatteras. The cruiser will hold straight on her course, and if the squall lasts long enough we may be able to run her out of sight."

Although Captain Beardsley was frightened at the prospect of falling into the hands of those whose flag he had insulted, he did not lose his head. The plan he had suddenly adopted for eluding the steamer proved that he could take desperate chances when it was necessary. By hauling his wind (which in this case meant shaping the schooner's course as near as possible toward the point from which the wind was blowing), he would be compelled to pass within a few miles of the steamer, and if the rain-cloud, under cover of which he hoped to escape, lifted for the space of one short minute, he was almost certain to be discovered. The squall came up directly behind the steamer, and in about half an hour overtook and shut her out from view.

"Now's our time," exclaimed Beardsley. "Flatten in the fore and main sails and give a strong pull at the headsail sheets. Tierney, go to the wheel."

Marcy lent a hand, and while the orders were being obeyed was gratified to hear one of the crew remark that the squall was something more than a squall; that it was coming to stay, and that they would be lucky if they saw the end of it by sunrise the next morning. If that proved to be the case they would have nothing to fear from the steamer. All they would have to look out for was shipwreck.

Half an hour was all the time that was necessary to prove that the sailor knew what he was talking about. The wind blew a gale and the rain fell in torrents. Just before the storm reached them, Captain Beardsley thought it would be wise to shorten his canvas, but all he took in were the gaff-topsails and fore-topmast staysail. Shortly afterward it became necessary to reef the sails that were left, and when that had been done the captain declared that he wouldn't take in anything else, even if he knew that the wind would take the sticks out of the schooner by the roots. He would rather be wrecked than go to prison any day.

Things could not have worked more to Beardsley's satisfaction if he had had the planning of the storm himself. The privateer's crew never saw the steamer after the rain and mist shut her out from view; and when the sun arose the next morning, after the wildest night Marcy Gray ever experienced on the water, there was not a sail in sight.

"I wish it was safe for us to stand out and try our luck again," said Captain Beardsley, who had been aloft sweeping the horizon with his glass. "But the Yankee war ships are getting too thick for comfort."

"Don't you expect to find some of them about Hatteras?" inquired Marcy.

"Of course I do. I believe the one that was chasing us yesterday came from there, and that that brig we lost held some communication with her before she sighted us. If she hadn't been warned by somebody, what was the reason she began dodging the minute she saw us? I hope to slip in between them, or at least to get under the protection of the guns of the forts at the Inlet before any of the cruisers can come within range. Privateering is played out along this coast. As soon as we get into port I shall tear out the bunks below, reduce my crew, and go to blockade running."

"But you'll run the same risk of capture that you do now," Marcy reminded him.

"But I won't be captured with guns aboard of me," said Beardsley, with a wink that doubtless meant a great deal. "Perhaps you don't know it, but I gave orders, in case that steamer sighted us again, to throw everything in the shape of guns and ammunition overboard. Then they couldn't have proved a thing against us."

"The size of your crew would have laid you open to suspicion," replied Marcy.

"Yes; but suspicion and proof are two different things," was the captain's answer. "But I am afraid of them howitzers, all the same, and am going to get shet of them the minute we get to Newbern. I don't reckon I can give you a furlong to go home this time, 'cause it won't take two days to get the schooner ready to take out a load of cotton."

"But you'll not need a pilot any longer," said Marcy, who was very much disappointed.

"What's the reason I won't? Do you reckon I'm going to run out of Hatteras in the face of all the war ships that are fooling around here? Not much. And I'm not going to hug the coast, neither. I'll make Crooked Inlet my point of departure, like I always have done, and then I'll stand straight out to sea till I get outside the cruisers' beat. See? Then I'll shape my course for Nassau. It'll give us a heap of bother and we'll go miles out of our way; but we'll be safe."

"But suppose we are captured after all your precautions; what then?"

"Well, if we are we'll lose our vessel and be sent to jail; but we'll not be treated as pirates, don't you see? The Northern folks are awful mad 'cause our President has issued letters of mark-we and reprisal, and their papers demand that every one of us who is taken shall be hung to the yardarm. To tell you the honest truth, that kinder scared me, and that's one reason why I want to get out of the business of privateering."

"And you think you will still need a pilot?"

"Can't you see it for yourself from what I have told you?" asked Beardsley, in reply. "And, Marcy, you'll make more money with less risk than you do in this business. It ain't to be expected that men will run the risk of going to jail for regular foremast hands' wages. They want more money, and it's right that they should have it. Why, them blockade-runners I told you about paid their hands five hundred dollars apiece for the run to Nassau and back. What do you think of that?"

"I think it is good wages," replied Marcy. ["If the business was only safe and honorable," he added, to himself.]

"Of course it is good wages. I don't expect to get a crew for any less; but, as I said before, I'll do the fair thing by you. If you go home you will have to enlist—I've heard the folks say that everybody had got to show his hand one way or the other—and then you would get only twelve or thirteen dollars a month. Think of that!"

Marcy was right when he told himself that the captain had him fast, and that there was no release for him as long as the *Osprey* remained in commission. It was a gloomy outlook, but the only thing he could do was to make the best of it.

As soon as the captain thought it safe to do so every inch of the privateer's canvas was given to the breeze, and she made good headway toward her destination. That day and the ensuing night passed without excitement of any sort, and at sunrise the next morning two objects were in plain sight from the schooner's deck. One was the entrance to Hatteras Inlet, and the other was a large steamer in the offing. The two vessels had been in view of each other ever since daylight. They were both headed for the same point—one making the most desperate efforts to place herself under cover of the guns of the forts, and the other making equally desperate efforts to bring the schooner within range of her bow-chaser before she could get there. It was a close and exciting race, and the crews of both vessels watched it anxiously. The black smoke rolled in thick clouds from the steamer's funnels, and the privateer's topmasts snapped and bent like fishing-rods, while her white-faced captain paced his quarter-deck, dividing his attention between his imperilled top-hamper and the pursuing steamer, and rubbing his hands nervously. At last the climax came. A puff of white smoke arose from the steamer's bow, and a shell from an old-fashioned smooth-bore thirty-two pounder dropped into the water about half way between her and the flying schooner. If that same steamer had had for a bow-chaser the heavy rifled gun she had a few months later, the result would have been different. As it was, Captain Beardsley gathered courage, and the anxious look left his face.

"If that's the best he can do we're all right,"

said he gleefully. "If this breeze holds half an hour longer we'll show him our flag."

"Shall we give him an answer from one of the howitzers, sir?" inquired Tierney.

"Not for your life!" replied Beardsley, quickly. And then he added in a lower tone, addressing himself to Marcy, who stood near, "That would be a bright idea, wouldn't it? This breeze may die away any minute, and we don't want to do anything to make them Yankees madder at us than they be now. Another thing, we mustn't give 'em anything to remember this schooner by. We may be caught when we try to run the blockade with our cargo of cotton, and we don't want anybody to recall the fact that we once had guns aboard. See?"

It was a long time before Marcy Gray could make up his mind how the chase was going to end, although he noticed when it first began that there were two things in the schooner's favor. One was that she was so far out of range that her pursuer could not cripple her, and the other was, that the wind that was favorable to her was unfavorable to the steamer, so

that the latter could not use her sails. He
also took note of the fact that Beardsley hugged
the shore pretty closely, and this made it evi-
dent that he intended to beach the schooner
rather than permit her to fall into the hands of
the Yankees. But he was not driven to such
extremity. The breeze held out, and although
the steamer continued to fire her bow-chaser at
intervals, the privateer rounded the point un-
harmed ; while the pursuer, not caring to trust
herself within range of the rifled guns on shore,
veered around and stood out to sea. A look
through his glass showed Beardsley that the
half-finished batteries had been manned in
readiness to give the war ship a warm reception
if she had ventured to follow the privateer
through the Inlet.

"Marcy, run up the flag so that our friends
in the forts can see who we are !" commanded
Beardsley. "The last time we sailed through
here we had a prize following in our wake, and
we would have had a more valuable one to-day
if that brig hadn't been warned by them
Yankees outside."

The Confederate emblem proved to be as

good as a countersign, and Captain Beardsley was permitted to sail on through the Inlet without going ashore to give an account of himself. As soon as he was safe inside the bar he directed his course toward Newbern, which he reached without any more adventures; but there were no cheers to greet him as his schooner was pulled into the wharf. Beardsley's agent, who was the first to spring over the rail, looked very much disgusted.

"Why, Captain, how is this?" were the first words he uttered. "I didn't expect to see you come back empty handed."

"No more did I expect to come back that way," was the captain's reply. "But we can't always have luck on our side. There is too many cruisers out there."

"Did you see any of them?"

"Well, I reckon. We had a race with two of them, and I ain't going privateering no more."

"Scared out, are you?" said the agent, with some contempt in his tones. "Well, it may interest you to know that while you were fooling around out there, doing nothing, we have fought the battle that will bring us our independence."

"*You* did ?" exclaimed Beardsley, who knew that the agent thought he had played the part of a coward in making such haste to get back to port. "You didn't have nary hand in it. You stay around home, yelling for the Confederacy, and flinging your slurs at we uns who have been under the fire of a Yankee war ship, but you ain't got the pluck to go into the service yourself. We didn't see but one merchantman while we was gone and she was a brig ; and as she carried three times the canvas we did she had the heels of us, and besides she wouldn't let us come within range. It was all we wanted to do to get into Hatteras, on account of the cruiser that fired on us. What battle was it that gained us our independence ?"

"Bull Run," replied the agent.

"Where's that ?"

"Somewhere up in Virginia. We had thirty-five thousand men and the Yankees more than twice as many ; but we threw them into a panic and run them clear into Washington. I

expect our army has got the city by this
time.''

"I didn't think the Yankees would fight,"
said the captain reflectively. "Then the war
is just as good as over.''

"That's what the Richmond papers say.''

"And it won't be no use for me to go blockade running?''

"Oh, yes it will. Peace hasn't been declared
yet, and you had better make money at something while you can. After all, I don't know
that I blame you for coming back. We've lost
two blockade-runners and one privateer since
you went out.''

"There, now''; exclaimed Beardsley. "And
I'd have lost my own vessel if I hadn't had
the best of luck. What you sneering at me
for?''

"Well, you see you were safe outside, and I
was sure you would come back with a prize. I
was disappointed when I saw you coming up
the river alone.''

"Not more disappointed than I was myself,''
answered the captain. "That brig was worth
a power of money, and I might have been

chasing her yet if that man-of-war hadn't hove in sight."

This was all the conversation Marcy over-heard between Beardsley and his agent, for the two drew off on one side and talked earn-estly in tones so low that he could not catch a word they said. It was plain that they came to an understanding on some point, for shortly afterward they went into the cabin, and Marcy was commanded to station himself at the head of the companion ladder and pass the word for the crew as fast as their names were called. He could see that the schooner's books and papers had been placed upon the cabin table, and that led him to believe that the reduction of the crew was to begin immediately. When the first man who was sent below came on deck again with his wages in his hand, Marcy whis-pered :

"What did the captain say when he paid you off ?"

"He didn't say he was gallied," replied the sailor, with a knowing look, "but I'll bet he is. The booming of that war ship's guns was too much for his nerves, and he's going to quit pirating and go to blockade running. I don't see but that one is about as dangerous as the other."

One by one the members of the crew were sent into the cabin, and as fast as they received their money and their discharges they bundled up their clothes and bedding and went ashore. At last there were only six foremast hands left, including Marcy Gray, and these were summoned into the cabin in a body to listen to what Captain Beardsley had to propose to them. He began with the statement that privateering was played out along that coast, because numerous cruisers were making it their business to watch the inlets and warn passing vessels to look out for themselves. It was no use trying to catch big ships that would not let him come within range, and so he had decided to put his howitzers ashore, tear out the berths and gun decks fore and aft, and turn the *Osprey* into a freighter. He would change her name, too, give her another coat of paint, and take the figures off her sails, so that she could not be recognized from the description the *Hollins's* men would give of her when they went North.

"I have kept you men because you are the best in the crew," said Beardsley in conclusion, "and of course I want none but good men and true aboard of me ; but you needn't stay if you don't want to. I want you to understand that blockade running is a dangerous business, and that we may be captured as others have been ; but if you will stand by me, I'll give you five hundred dollars apiece for the run— one hundred to spend in Nassau, and the balance when you help me bring the schooner safe back to Newbern. What do you say?"

The men had evidently been expecting something of this sort, for without a moment's hesitation Tierney, speaking for his companions, replied that the captain's liberal offer was accepted, and they would do all that men could do to make the *Osprey's* voyages profitable. Marcy said nothing, for Beardsley had already given him to understand that he was to be one of the blockade-runner's crew. He was the only native American among the foremast hands, and the only one who could sign his name to the shipping articles, the others being obliged to make their marks. When

7

this had been done the men returned to the deck, and the agent went ashore to make arrangements for landing the guns, to hunt up a gang of ship carpenters, and find a cotton-factor who was willing to take his chances on making or losing a fortune. He worked to such good purpose that in less than an hour two parties of men were busy on the schooner —one with the howitzers and the other with the bunks below—and a broker was making a contract with Beardsley for taking out a cargo of cotton. When the broker had gone ashore Beardsley beckoned Marcy to follow him into the cabin.

"The schooner owes you seventeen hundred dollars and better," said he, as he closed the sliding door and pointed to a chair. "It's in the bank ashore, and you can have it whenever you want it. Would you like to take out a venture?"

It was right on the point of Marcy's tongue to reply that he would be glad to do it; but he checked himself in time, for the thought occurred to him that perhaps this was another attempt on the part of Captain Beardsley to

find out something about the state of his
mother's finances. So he looked down at the
carpet and said nothing.

"There's money in it," continued Beardsley. "Suppose you take out two bales of
cotton, sell it in Nassau for three times what
it was worth a few months ago, and invest the
proceeds in quinine ; why, you'll make five
hundred per cent. Of course I can't grant all
the hands the same privilege, so I will make
the bargain for you through my agent, and
Tierney and the rest needn't know a thing
about. What do you say ?"

"I don't think I had better risk it," answered Marcy.

"What for ?" asked Beardsley.

"Well, the money I've got I'm sure of, am
I not ?"

"Course you are. Didn't I say you could
have it any minute you had a mind to call
for it ?"

"You did ; but suppose I should put it into
cotton, as you suggest, and the *Osprey* should
fall into the hands of one of those war ships
outside. There'd be all my money gone to the

dogs, or, what amounts to the same thing, into the hands of the Yankees. I may want to use that money before the war is over."

"But didn't you hear the agent say that we ain't going to have any war? We've licked 'em before they could take their coats off."

"But perhaps they'll not stay whipped. My teachers at the academy were pretty well posted, and I heard some of them say that a war is surely coming, and in the end the Southern States will wish they had never seceded."

"Well, them teachers of yourn was the biggest fules I ever heard tell of," exclaimed Beardsley, settling back in his chair and slamming a paper-weight down upon the table. "Why, don't I tell you that we've got 'em licked already? More'n that, I don't mean to fall into the hands of them cruisers outside. I tell you that you'll miss it if you don't take out a venture. And as for your mother needing them seventeen hundred dollars to buy grub and the like, you can't pull the wool over my eyes in no such way as that. She's got money by the bushel, and I know it to be a fact."

"Then you know more than I do," replied Marcy, his eyes never dropping for an instant under the searching gaze the captain fixed upon him. "Now, I would like to ask you one question: You have money enough of your own to load this vessel, have you not?"

"Why, of course I—that's neither here nor there," replied Beardsley, who was not sharp enough to keep out of the trap that Marcy had placed for him. "What of it?"

"I know it to be a fact that you could load the schooner with cotton purchased with your own money if you felt like it," answered the young pilot, "but you don't mean to do it. You would rather carry cotton belonging to somebody else, and that is all the proof I want that you are afraid of the Yankees. If you want to do the fair thing by me, why do you advise me to put my money into a venture, when you are afraid to put in a dollar for yourself?"

"Why, man alive," Beardsley almost shouted, "don't I risk my schooner? Every nigger I've got was paid for with money she made for me by carrying cigars and such like between Havana and Baltimore."

"That's what I thought," said Marcy, to himself. "And you didn't pay a cent of duty on those cigars, either."

"I do my share by risking my schooner," continued the captain. "But I want somebody to make something besides myself, and if you don't want to risk your money, I reckon I'll give the mates a chance. That's all."

"What in the name of sense did I go and speak to him about them cigars for?" he added, mentally, as the pilot ascended the ladder that led to the deck. "I think myself that there's a war coming, and if we get licked I must either make a fast friend of that boy or get rid of him; for if he tells on me I'll get into trouble sure."

It looked now as though Marcy might some day have it in his power to make things very unpleasant for Captain Beardsley.

CHAPTER V.

A CAT WITHOUT CLAWS.

"I REALLY believe I've got a hold on the old rascal at last," said Marcy to himself, as he leaned against the rail and watched the men, who, under direction of the mates, were hard at work getting the howitzers ashore. "From this time on he had better be careful how he treats my mother, for he may fall into the hands of the Yankees some day; and if that ever happens, I will take pains to see that he doesn't get back to Nashville in a hurry. I'll go any lengths to get a letter to the Secretary of the Treasury, telling him just who and what Beardsley is, and then perhaps he will stand a chance of being tried for something besides piracy and blockade running."

Marcy's first care was to write to his mother. While omitting no item of news, he took pains to word the letter so cautiously that it could not be used against him in case some of his secret enemies in and around Nashville, the postmaster and Colonel Shelby, for instance, took it into their heads to open and read it instead of sending it to its address. They had showed him that they were quite mean enough to do it. Then he went ashore to mail the letter and take notes, and was not long in making up his mind that he was not the only one who thought there was going to be a war. Although the Newbern people were very jubilant over the great victory at Bull Run, they did not act as though they thought that that was the last battle they would have to fight before their independence would be acknowledged, for Marcy saw infantry companies marching and drilling in almost every street through which he passed, and every other man and boy he met was dressed in uniform. As he drew near to the post-office he ran against a couple of young soldiers about his own age, or, to be more exact, they ran against him ; for they were coming along with their arms locked, talking so loudly that they could have been heard on the opposite side of the street, and when the *Os-*

prey's pilot turned out to let them pass, they tried to crowd him off into the gutter. But Marcy, beside being a sturdy fellow, knew how to stand up for his rights. He braced his foot firmly against the curbstone and met the shock of the collision so vigorously that those who would have sent him headlong into the street were sent backward themselves, and came very near going head first down the stairs that led into a basement restaurant.

"Don't you think I ought to have a little of this sidewalk?" he asked good-naturedly, as the two straightened up and faced him with clenched hands and flashing eyes.

"Then put on a uniform and you can have as much of it as you want," said one, in reply.

"How long have you had those good clothes of yours?" inquired Marcy. "Were they in the fight at Bull Run?"

"Of course not. We only enlisted a week ago, but we show our good will and you don't."

"Then you have never smelled powder or heard the noise of the enemy's guns?"

"It isn't likely, for there's been no fighting

around here," said the same speaker, who began to wonder if he and his companions hadn't made a mistake.

"Then go and get some experience before you take it upon yourselves to shove a veteran into the ditch," said Marcy loftily. "I've been in the service ever since President Davis issued his call for privateers. You've heard of the *Osprey*, haven't you? Well, I belong to her."

"Is that so?" exclaimed the other, extending his hand, which the pilot was prompt to accept. "I am sorry we insulted you and beg your pardon for it. But you ought to wear something to show who you are, for the folks around here don't think much of citizens unless they have declared their intention of enlisting as soon as they can get their affairs in shape."

"I knew why you bumped up against me, and that was the reason I didn't get mad at it," answered Marcy. "You don't seem to have much to do; and if you will walk up to the post-office with me, I'll show you over the *Osprey*, if you would like to take a look at her. But we'll have to be in a hurry if we want to see her with the guns aboard, for she is being changed into a blockade-runner."

"Ah! That's the money-making business," said one of the recruits with enthusiasm. "I wish I knew something about boats, so that I could go into it myself. What wages do you get?"

"Five hundred dollars for the run to Nassau and back."

The eyes of Marcy's new friends grew to twice their usual size. They looked hard at him to see if he was really in earnest, and then whistled in concert.

"It's worth it," continued Marcy, "and I don't believe you could get men to go into it for less. From the time we leave the protection of the forts at Hatteras to the time we get back, we shall be in constant fear of capture. We know something of the dangers of the business, for we had two narrow escapes during our last cruise."

Of course the recruits wanted to know all about it, and as they faced around and walked with him, Marcy gave them a short history of what the schooner had done since she went into commission. When he told how neatly that Yankee brig had slipped through Captain Beardsley's fingers, his companions looked at him in surprise.

"What a pity," said one. "And yet you talk as if you were glad of it."

"I talk as if it was a brave and skilful act, and so it was," answered Marcy. "You would say the same if you had been there and seen it done."

"No, I wouldn't. The Yankees are not brave and skilful, and they can't do anything to make me think they are. How will they feel when they see our President sitting in the White House, dictating terms of peace to them? I hope our company will be there to witness the ceremony."

This was a point Marcy did not care to discuss with the two recruits, for fear he might say something to arouse in their minds a suspicion that he was not intensely loyal to the Confederacy, even if he did sail under its flag; so he inquired if there were anything else but drilling and marching going on in Newbern.

"Not much else in the city," replied one of the young soldiers. "But there's a heap going on about five miles below. There's a corps of engineers down there laying out a system of fortifications which are to be a mile long. It will take eight or nine thousand men to garrison them, and they will be defended by thirty-one guns."

"But I don't see any sense in it," said the other, who seemed to think he had learned considerable of the art of war since he put on his gray jacket. "A Yankee army will never come so far south as Newbern, and their gunboats can't get past the forts at Hatteras."

But, all the same, the Confederate authorities thought the works ought to be pushed to completion, and so they were ; but they did not amount to much, for Burnside's troops captured them after a four hours' fight, with the loss of only ninety-one men killed, the garrison retreating to Newbern and taking the cars for Goldsborough. When Marcy heard of it a few months later, he wondered if his new acquaintances were in the fight, and if they still held to the opinion that the Yankees were not brave.

After leaving the post-office they spent an hour on board the *Osprey*, and parted at last well pleased with the result of their meeting, and fully satisfied in their own minds that the Yankees had been so badly whipped at Bull Run that they would never dare face the Confederate soldiers again. At least the two recruits were satisfied of it; but Marcy thought he knew better.

On the morning of the next day but one, a tug came alongside and towed the schooner up to a warehouse, where there was a load of cotton waiting for her; and for want of something better to do, Marcy hunted up a cotton-hook and assisted in rolling the heavy bales on board. The little vessel was so changed in appearance that a landsman would hardly have recognized her. The treacherous figure "9," which Beardsley had caused to be painted on her sails, in the hope that merchant vessels would take her for a harmless pilot-boat, was not to be seen; all the black paint about her, from the heel of her bowsprit to the crosstrees, had given place to a bluish-white; and on both sides of her bow and over her cabin door the name *Hattie* appeared in large gilt letters.

"Now, when them *Hollins* men get home and try to give the war ships a description of the privateer that captured them, they will be mighty apt to shoot wide of the mark, won't they ?" said Captain Beardsley, who was much pleased with the work the painters had done under his instructions. "There ain't the first thing aboard of us to show that we used to be engaged in the privateering business. Oh, I'm a sharp one, and it takes something besides a Yankee to get the start of me."

Beardsley was so impatient to get to sea, and so very anxious to handle the fortune he was sure he was going to make by his first attempt at blockade running, that he employed all the men that could be worked to advantage, and took on board every bale he could possibly find room for. The deck load was so large that it threatened to interfere with the handling of the sails! and when a tug pulled the schooner's head around till it pointed down the river, she set so low in the water that she could not show her usual speed, even with the

tide in her favor, and Tierney said in Marcy's
hearing that he believed he could hoist a sail
in a washing-tub and reach Nassau before the
schooner could leave the sand dunes of Hatteras out of sight. But the captain did not
seem to think he had made any mistake in loading his vessel, although he did show some
anxiety for her safety ; for when she reached
Crooked Inlet he walked aft and took charge
of the wheel himself, and without saying one
word to the young fellow whom he called his
pilot, until he saw the latter looking at him as
if he wanted to know what Beardsley meant
by such work.

"There, now," said the captain, by way of
explanation, "I thought you was below; I did
for a fact. And so I said to myself that I
wouldn't bother you, but would try and take
her through without your help, just to see if
I could do it, you know. Supposing you was
the only one aboard who knew the channel,
and something should happen to you, and I
should want to come through here in a hurry
to get out of the way of a war ship that was
close in my wake ; wouldn't I be in a pretty

fix? Now stand by, so 't you can give me a word in case I don't hold her just right."

"You old hypocrite," thought Marcy. "If that was the first lie you ever told it would choke you. So he thinks something is going to happen to me, does he? Now what does he mean by that?"

Captain Beardsley had done nothing more than Marcy expected him to do, but he did not have a word of fault to find with it, as a regular pilot would have done when he saw his business taken out of his hands in so unceremonious a fashion. If the skipper was willing to pay him five hundred dollars for doing nothing, the boy didn't think he ought to complain. He took his stand close by the captain's side, but he did not touch the wheel, nor did he so much as look at the black and red buoys that marked the channel. He was turning these words over in his mind : "Suppose something should happen to you!" Was he to understand that Beardsley had made up his mind to get rid of him in some way?

"If that is what he wants, why didn't he

8

pay me off while we were in Newbern ? " was
the question Marcy asked himself. " But for
some reason or other it doesn't suit him to
have me at home with mother ; and that
makes me think that there's going to be an
attempt made to steal the money she has hidden in the cellar wall. Oh, how I wish Jack
was at home."

When the schooner was clear of the Inlet,
Beardsley gave the boy a wink as if to say, " I
did take her through, didn't I ? " held a short
consultation with the mates, during which the
course was determined upon, then mounted to
the cross trees with his glass in his hand ; and
after sweeping it around the horizon, gave the
cheering information to those below that there
was nothing in sight. But there was something in sight a few hours later—something
that put Beardsley in such a rage that he did
not get over it for a day or two. It was a
schooner a little larger than his own, and she
was standing directly across the *Hattie's* bows.
She did not show any disposition to " dodge "
as the brig had done, but held straight on her
course, and this made Captain Beardsley sus-

pect that there might be a cruiser following in her wake to see that she did not get into trouble. But if there was, his glass failed to reveal the fact, and this suggested an idea to him. When the stranger's topsails could be seen from the *Hattie's* deck he shouted down to his mate :

"Say, Morgan, I'll tell you what's the matter with that fellow. He don't know that there's such things as privateers afloat, and he ain't seen nary cruiser to warn him. That's why he don't sheer off."

"I reckon you're right, cap'n," replied the mate. "It's plain that he ain't afraid of us."

"Well, if I am right," continued Beardsley, "it proves that the war ships off Hatteras have went off somewheres, and that the coast below is all clear ; don't you think so ? What do you say if we make a straight run for our port ? We'll save more than a week by it."

"I'm agreeable," answered the mate, who, upon receiving a nod from the captain, gave the necessary orders, and in a few minutes the *Hattie* was close-hauled and running in such a direction that if the two vessels held on their way, they would pass almost within hailing distance of each other. Of course the captain of the stranger must have witnessed this manœuvre, but he did not seem to be surprised or troubled by it; for he kept straight on and in another hour dashed by within less than a quarter of a mile of Captain Beardsley, who lifted his hat and waved it to a small party of men, her officers probably, who were standing on her quarter-deck. In response to the salutation the Stars and Stripes were hoisted at her peak.

"If she had done that three weeks ago wouldn't I have brought that flag down with a jerk?" exclaimed Beardsley angrily. "Did anybody ever hear of such luck? Why didn't she show up when we had them howitzers aboard? They don't know what to make of us, for I can see two fellows with glasses pointed at us all the time. Run up that Yankee flag, Marcy."

The latter was prompt to obey the order, and he was quite willing to do it, since it was not in Beardsley's power to do any harm to the handsome stranger. After being allowed

to float for a few minutes the two flags were
hauled down and stowed away in their respective chests, and the little vessels parted company without either one knowing who the
other was.   But there was an angry lot of men
on board the *Hattie.*   Beardsley showed that
he was one of them by the hard words he used
when he came down from aloft and sent a
lookout up to take his place, and Tierney,
after shaking his fist at the Yankee, shut one
eye, glanced along the rail with the other, as
he had glanced through the sights of the howitzer he once commanded, and then jerked
back his right hand as if he were pulling a
lock-string.   Marcy Gray was the only one
aboard who carried a light heart.

After the schooner's course was changed
there was a good deal of suppressed excitement among the crew, for Captain Beardsley was about to take what some of them
thought to be a desperate risk.   Probably
there were no cruisers off Hatteras when that
merchant vessel passed, but that was all of
fifteen or twenty hours ago, and they had had
plenty of time to get back to their stations.

So a bright lookout was kept by all hands, and Beardsley or one of the mates went aloft every few minutes to take a peep through the glass. Marcy thought there was good cause for watchfulness and anxiety. In the first place, the Bahama Islands, of which Nassau, in the Island of New Providence, was the principal port, lay off the coast of Florida, and about five hundred miles southeast of Charleston. They must have been at least twice as far from Crooked Inlet, so that Captain Beardsley, by selecting Newbern as his home port, ran twice the risk of falling into the hands of the Federal cruisers that he would if he had decided to run his contraband cargo into Savannah or Charleston.

"It seems to me that the old man ought to have learned wisdom after living for so many years in defiance of the law," thought Marcy, when it came his turn to go aloft and relieve the lookout. "Of course a smuggler has to take his chances with the revenue cutters he is liable to meet along the coast, as well as with the Custom House authorities, and I should think that constant fear of capture would have

made him sly and cautious ; but it hasn't."—
"Nothing in sight, sir," he said, in answer to an
inquiry from the officer who had charge of the
deck.

And this was the report that was sent down
by every lookout who went aloft during the
next four days ; and what a time of excitement and suspense that was for Marcy Gray
and all the rest of the *Hattie's* crew. Perhaps there was not so much danger of being
run down at night by some heavy vessel as
there would have been a few months before,
but Marcy's nerves thrilled with apprehension
when he stood holding fast to the rail during
the lonely mid-watch, and the schooner, with
the spray dashing wildly about her bows and
everything drawing, was running before a
strong wind through darkness so black that
her flying-jib-boom could not be seen, and
there was no light on board except the one in
the binnacle.

"I know it's dangerous and I don't like it
any better than you do," Beardsley said to
him one night. "But think of the money
there is in it, and what a fule you were for not

taking out a venture when I gave you the chance. I bought four bales apiece for the mates, and they will pocket the money that you might have had just as well as not."

"But I want to use my seventeen hundred dollars," replied Marcy ; and so he did. He still clung to the hope that he might some day have an opportunity to return it to the master of the *Hollins*, and that was the reason he was unwilling to run the risk of losing it.

"Go and tell that to the marines," said Captain Beardsley impatiently. "They'll believe anything, but I won't. You don't need it ; your folks don't, and I know it. Keep a bright lookout for lights, hold a stiff upper lip, and I will take you safely through."

And so he did. Not only were the Federal war ships accommodating enough to keep out of the way, but the elements were in good humor also. The schooner had a fair wind during the whole of her perilous journey, and in due time it wafted her into the port of Nassau. Although Marcy Gray had never been there before, he had heard and read of New Providence as a barren rock, with scarcely soil enough to produce a few pineapples and oranges, and of Nassau as a place of no consequence whatever so far as commerce was concerned. It boasted a small sponge trade, exported some green turtles and conch-shells, and was the home of a few fisherman and wreckers; this was all Marcy thought there was of Nassau, and consequently his surprise was great when he found himself looking out upon the wharves of a thriving, bustling little town. The slave-holders' rebellion, "which brought woe and wretchedness to so many of our States, was the wind that blew prosperity to Nassau." When President Lincoln's proclamation, announcing the blockade of all the Confederate ports was issued, Nassau took on an air of business and importance, and at once became the favorite resort of vessels engaged in contraband trade. There were Northern men there too, and Northern vessels as well; for, to quote from the historian, "The Yankee, in obedience to his instincts of traffic, scented the prey from afar, and went there to turn an honest penny by assisting the Confederates to run the blockade." The supplies which the Confederates had always purchased in the North, and of which they already began to stand in need, were shipped from Europe in neutral vessels; and being consigned to a neutral port (for Nassau belonged to England), they were in no danger of being captured by our war ships during the long voyage across the Atlantic. It was when these supplies were taken from the wharves and placed in the holds of vessels like the *Hattie* that the trouble began, and men like Captain Beardsley ran all the risk and reaped the lion's share of the profits. Almost the first thing that drew Marcy's attention was the sight of a Union and Confederate flag floating within a few rods of each other.

"What's the meaning of that?" he asked of Beardsley, as soon as he found opportunity to speak to him. "We don't own this town, do we?"

"No; but we've got a Consulate here," was the reply. "I don't know's I understand just what that means, but it's some sort of an officer that our government has sent here to look out for our interests. If a man wants to go from here to our country, he must go to that Consulate and get a pass before any blockade-runner will take him. Now don't you wish you had took my advice and brought out a venture?"

"It's too late to think of that now," answered Marcy. "And your own profits are not safe yet. It must be all of a thousand miles from here to Newbern, and perhaps we'll not have as good luck going as we did coming. I am to have a hundred dollars to spend here, am I not?"

"Course. That's what I promised before you and the rest signed articles. I'll give it to you the minute this cotton is got ashore and paid for. What you going to do with it?"

"I thought I would invest it in medicine."

"Your head's level. You couldn't make bigger money on anything else."

"And as it is my own money and the captain of the *Hollins* has no interest in it, I shall feel quite at liberty to spend it as I choose," soliloquized Marcy, as the captain turned away to meet the representative of the English house to which his cargo of cotton was consigned. "Besides, I must keep up appearances, or I'll get into trouble."

"Turn to, all hands, and get off the hatches," shouted one of the mates. "Lively now, for the sooner we start back the sooner we'll get there."

Marcy did not know whether or not he was included in this order addressed to "all hands," but as the officer looked hard at him he concluded he was. At any rate he was willing to work, if for no other purpose than to keep him from thinking. Somehow he did not like to have his mind dwell upon the homeward run.

CHAPTER VI.

RUNNING THE BLOCKADE.

THE gang of 'longshoremen, which was quickly sent on board the *Hattie* by the Englishman to whom we referred in the last chapter, worked to such good purpose that in just forty-eight hours from the time her lines were made fast to the wharf, the blockade-runner was ready for her return trip. Meanwhile Marcy Gray and the rest of the crew had little to do but roam about the town, spending their money and mingling with the citizens, the most of whom were as good Confederates as could have been found anywhere in the Southern States. Marcy afterward told his mother that if there were any Union people on the island they lived in the American Consulate, from whose roof floated the Stars and Stripes. Marcy was both astonished and shocked to find that nearly every one with whom he conversed believed that the Union was already a thing of the past, and that the rebellious States never could be whipped. One day he spoke to Beardsley about it, while the latter was pacing his quarter-deck smoking his after-dinner cigar.

"If those English sailors I was talking with a little while ago are so very anxious to see the Union destroyed, I don't see why they don't ship under the Confederate flag," said he. "But what has England got against the United States, anyway?"

"Man alive, she's got everything against 'em," replied the captain, in a surprised tone. "Didn't they lick old England twice, and ain't the Yankee flag the only one to which a British army ever surrendered? You're mighty right. She'd be glad to see the old Union busted into a million pieces; but she's too big a coward to come out and help us open and above board, and so she's helping on the sly. I wish the Yankees would do something to madden her, but they're too sharp. They have give up the *Herald*—the brig I was telling you about that sailed from Wilmington just before you came back from your furlong.

She was a Britisher, you know, and a war ship took her prisoner ; but the courts allowed that Wilmington wasn't blockaded at all, except on paper, and ordered her to be released. I only wish the Yankees had had the pluck to hold fast to her.''

Marcy's thoughts had often reverted to the capture of the brig *Herald* and to Captain Beardsley's expressed wish that the act might lead to an open rupture between the United States and England, and he was glad to learn that there was to be no trouble on that score. But England could not long keep her meddlesome fingers out of our pie. She did all she dared to aid the Confederacy, and when the war was ended, had the fun of handing over a good many millions of dollars to pay for the American vessels that British built and British armed steamers had destroyed upon the high seas.

"I saw you bring aboard some little bundles a while ago," continued Beardsley. "What was in 'em?"

"One of them contained two woolen dresses I bought for mother, and in the others there was nothing but medicine," said Marcy. "Woolen goods will be worth money by and by."

"Oh, yes; they'll run up a little. Things always do in war times. The money them medicines cost, you will be able to turn over about three times when we get back to Newbern. You'll clear about three hundred dollars, when you might just as well have made five thousand, if you'd took my advice and put in your seventeen hundred, as I wanted you to do."

Marcy made no reply, for he had grown weary of telling the captain that he intended to use that money for another purpose.

During the two days they remained in port two large steamers came in, and on the way out they passed as many more, both of which showed the English colors when Marcy, in obedience to Beardsley's orders, ran the Confederate emblem up to the *Hattie's* peak.

"Everything that's aboard them ships is meant for us," said Captain Beardsley. "I know it, because there never was no such steamers sailing into this port before the war.

Them fellows over the water are sending in goods faster'n we can take 'em out.   Go aloft, Marcy, and holler the minute you see anything that looks like a sail or a smoke."

When the pilot had been discharged and the schooner filled away for home, her crew settled down to business again, and every man became alert and watchful. Those dreadful night runs on the way down Marcy always thought of with a shiver, and now he had to go through with them again ; and one would surely have ended his career as a blockade-runner, for a while at least, had it not been for the credulity or stupidity of a Union naval captain. This particular night, for a wonder, was clear ; the stars shone brightly, and Marcy Gray, who sat on the crosstrees with the night-glass in his hand, had been instructed to use extra vigilance. There was a heavy ground swell on, showing that there had recently been a blow somewhere, and the schooner had just breeze enough to give her steerage way, with nothing to spare. Marcy was thinking of home, and wondering how much longer it would be necessary for him to

9 .

lead this double life, when he saw something that called him back to earth again. He took a short look at it through his glass, and then said, in tones just loud enough to reach the ears of those below :

"On deck, there."

"Ay, ay !" came the answer. "What's to do ?"

"Lights straight ahead, sir."

"Throw a tarpaulin over that binnacle," commanded Beardsley ; and a moment later Marcy saw him coming up. He gave the glass into his hands and moved aside so that the captain could find a place to stand on the cross-trees. Either the latter's eyes were sharper than Marcy's, or else he took time to make a more critical examination of the approaching vessel, for presently he hailed the deck in low but excited tones.

"I'm afraid we're in for it, Morgan," said he. "I do for a fact. Tumble up here and see what you think of her. I can make out that she is a heavy steamer," he added, as Marcy moved to the other side of the mast, and the mate came up and stood beside the captain, "and if she can't make us out, too, every soul aboard of her must be blind. Our white canvas must show a long ways in this bright starlight. What is she?"

"I give it up," replied the mate.

"She is coming straight for us, ain't she?"

"Looks like it. Suppose you change the course a few points and then we can tell for a certainty."

Captain Beardsley thought this a suggestion worth acting upon. He sent down the necessary orders to the second mate, who had been left in charge of the deck, and in a few minutes the schooner was standing off on the other tack, and rolling fearfully as she took the ground swell almost broadside on. Then there came an interval of anxiety and suspense, during which Marcy Gray strained his eyes until he saw a dozen lights dancing before them instead of two, as there ought to have been, and at last Captain Beardsley's worst fears were confirmed. The relative position of the red and green lights ahead slowly changed until they were almost in line with each other, and Marcy was sailor enough to know what that meant. The steamer had caught sight of the *Hattie*, was keeping watch of her, and had altered her course to intercept her. Marcy began to tremble.

"I know how a prison looks when viewed from the outside," he said to himself. "And unless something turns up in our favor, it will not be many days before I shall know how one looks on the inside."

It was plain that his two companions were troubled by the same gloomy thoughts, for he heard Beardsley say, in a husky voice:

"She ain't holding a course for nowhere, neither for the Indies nor the Cape; she shifted her wheel when we did, and that proves that she's a Yankee cruiser and nothing else. See any signs of a freshening anywhere?"

"Nary freshening," replied the mate, with a hasty glance around the horizon. "There ain't a cloud as big as your fist in sight."

Of course Beardsley used some heavy words —he always did when things did not go to suit him—and then he said, as if he were almost on the point of crying with vexation:

"It's too bad for them cowardly Yankees to

come pirating around here just at this time when we've got a big fortune in our hands. Them goods we've got below is worth a cool hundred thousand dollars in Newbern, if they're worth anything, and my commission will be somewhere in the neighborhood of twenty-five per cent.; dog-gone it all. Can't we do nothing to give her the slip? You ain't fitten to be a mate if you can't give a word of advice in a case like this."

"And if I wanted to be sassy I might say that you ain't fit to command a ship if you can't get her out of trouble when you get her into it. There can't no advice be given that I can see, unless it be to chuck the cargo over the side. I reckon that would be my way if I was master of the *Hattie*."

"But what good would that do?" exclaimed Beardsley. "Where are my dockyments to prove that I am an honest trader? And even if I had some, and the cargo was safe out of the hold and sunk to the bottom, I couldn't say that I am in ballast, because I ain't got a pound of any sort of ballast to show. Oh, I tell you we're gone coons, Morgan. Do the Yankees put striped clothes on their prisoners when they shove 'em into jail, I wonder?"

The mate, who had come to the wise conclusion that the only thing he could do was to make the best of the situation, did not answer the captain's last question. All he said was:

"If you dump the cargo overboard the Yankees won't get it!"

"But they'll get my schooner, won't they?" Beardsley almost shouted. "And do you reckon that I'm going to give them Newbern fellows the satisfaction of knowing that I saved their goods by sending them to the bottom? Not by a great sight. If that cruiser gets my property she'll get their'n, too. I don't reckon we'd have time to clear the hold anyway."

Marcy Gray had thought so all along. The lights were coming up at a hand gallop, and already they were much nearer than they seemed to be, for the shape of the steamer could be made out by the unaided eye. When Beardsley ceased speaking, the sound of a gong was clearly heard, and a minute later the steamer blew her whistle.

"What did I tell you, Morgan?" whined the captain. "She's slowing up, and that whistle means for us to show lights. The next thing we shall see will be a small boat coming off. I hope the swell'll turn it upside down and drown every mother's son of her crew that—. On deck, there," he shouted, in great consternation. "Get out lights, and be quick about it. She'll be on top of us directly."

"She can see us as well without lights as she can with 'em," growled the mate, as he backed down slowly from the crosstrees. "I don't care if she cuts us down. I'd about as soon go to the bottom as to be shut up in a Yankee prison."

Marcy Gray was almost as badly frightened as Beardsley seemed to be. The steamer was dangerously near, and her behavior and the schooner's proved the truth of what he had read somewhere, that "two vessels on the ocean seemed to exercise a magnetic influence upon each other, so often do collisions occur when it looks as though there might be room for all the navies of the world to pass in review." So it was now. The two vessels drifted toward each other, broadside on, and the breeze was so light that the *Hattie* was almost helpless ; but the stranger was well handled ; her huge paddle wheels, which up to this moment had hung motionless in the water, began to turn backward, and presently Marcy let go his desperate clutch upon the stay to which he was clinging, and drew a long breath of relief. Whatever else the cruiser might do to the *Hattie*, she did not mean to send her to the bottom.

"Schooner ahoy ! " came the hail.

"On board the steamer," answered Captain Beardsley, who had been allowed a little leisure in which to recover his wits and courage.

" What schooner is that? "

" The *Hattie* of New York," shouted Beardsley. " Homeward bound from Havana with a cargo of sugar. Who are you ? "

" The United States supply steamer *Adelaide*. What are you doing a hundred miles eastward of your course, and showing no lights? " asked the voice ; and Marcy fully expected that the next words would be, "I'll send a boat aboard of you."

"I'm afraid of privateers," was Beardsley's response. "I heered there was some afloat, and I can't afford to fall in with any of 'em, kase everything I've got on 'arth is this schooner. If I lose her I'm teetotally ruined."

"Well, then, why don't you hold in toward Hatteras, where you will be safe? There's a big fleet in there, and in a few days there'll be more."

"You don't tell me! Much obleeged for the information! I will put that way as fast as this breeze will take me. Seen anything suspicious? No? Then good-by and farewell."

Beardsley shouted out some orders, the schooner filled away so as to pass under the steamer's stern, and to Marcy's unbounded astonishment she was permitted to go in peace. The stranger's gong sounded again, and she also went on her way. There was scarcely a word spoken above a whisper until her lights had disappeared; then the schooner's own lanterns were hauled down, her head was turned to the point of the compass toward which it had been directed when the steamer was first discovered, and Captain Beardsley was himself again.

"By gum!" said he, striding up and down the deck, pausing now and then to go through the undignified performance of slapping his mates on the back. "*By* gum, I done it, didn't I! What sort of a Yankee do you reckon I'd make, Marcy? I talked just like one—through the nose, you know. Pretty good acting; don't you think so?"

"It was good enough to save the schooner," replied Marcy.

"And that was what I meant to do if I could. I wouldn't have give a dollar for my chances of getting shet of that steamer till she began to back away to keep from running us down, and then something told me that I'd be all right if I put a bold face on the matter. And that's what I done. Oh, I'm a sharp one, and it takes a better man than a Yankee to get ahead of me. I was really much obliged to him for telling me of that blockading fleet at Hatteras, for now I'll know better than to go nigh that place. Hold the old course, Morgan, and that will take us out of the way of coasters and cruisers, both. I'll go below and turn in for a short nap."

"If I should follow this business until I am gray-headed I don't think I should ever again have so narrow an escape," said Marcy to himself, as he too went below to take a little needed rest. "Why, it seems like a dream ; and somehow I can hardly bring myself to believe it really happened. If the Yankees talk the way Captain Beardsley did, all I can say for them is that they are queer folks."

It seemed as though the schooner's crew could never get through talking about their short interview with the supply steamer, for every one of them had given up all hope of escape, and looked for nothing else but to see an armed boat put off to test the truth of Captain Beardsley's statements regarding the *Hattie* and her cargo. The mate, Morgan, was completely bewildered. He could not understand how a man who had showed a disposition to cry when he saw his vessel in danger, could be so cool and even impudent when the critical moment came.

In due time all thoughts of the enemy they had left astern gave way to speculations concerning those they might find before them.

The latitude of Hatteras Inlet was thought to be particularly dangerous ; but that was passed in the night and Marcy breathed easily again, until Beardsley began to take a slant in toward the shore, and then there was another season of suspense. But the day drew to a close without bringing any suspicious smoke or sail to add to their fears, and when darkness came Crooked Inlet was not more than thirty miles away. If the strong and favoring wind that then filled the schooner's sails held out, her keel would be plowing the waters of the Sound by midnight or a little later, and Captain Beardsley's commission would be safe. At least that was what the latter told Marcy ; and, while he talked, he jingled some keys in his pocket with as much apparent satisfaction as though they were the dollars he hoped to put there in a few days more. But the old saying that there is many a slip came very near holding true in Beardsley's case. The latter was so certain that he had left all danger behind him, and that he had nothing more to do but sail in at his leisure and land his cargo when he got ready, that he did not think it

worth while to man the crosstrees after night-
fall; consequently there was no watchful lookout to warn him of the suspicious looking
object that moved slowly out of the darkness a
mile or so ahead, and waited for him to come
up. About eleven o'clock Marcy Gray strolled
forward and climbed out upon the bowsprit to
see if he could discover any signs of the land,
which, according to his calculations, ought not
to be far distant.

"I might as well be out here as anywhere
else," he thought, pulling out the night-glass,
which he had taken the precaution to bring
with him. "Of course the skipper will run
her through without any aid from me, as he
did before, and so—what in the world is that?
Looks like a smooth round rock; but I know
it isn't, for there's nothing of that sort about
this Inlet."

Marcy took another look through the glass,
then backed quickly but noiselessly down from
his perch and ran aft to the quarter-deck.
The captain was standing there joking with
his mates, and congratulating them and himself on the safe and profitable run the *Hattie*

had made ; and as Marcy came up he threw
back his head and gave utterance to a hoarse
laugh, which, in the stillness of the night,
could have been heard half a mile away.

"Captain ! Captain ! " exclaimed Marcy,
in great excitement, "for goodness' sake don't
do that again ! Keep still ! There's a ship's
long boat filled with men right ahead of us."

It seemed to Marcy that Beardsley wilted
visibly when this astounding piece of news
was imparted to him. His hearty laugh was
broken short off in the middle, so to speak,
and when turned so that the light from the
binnacle shone upon his face, Marcy saw that
it was as white as a sheet.

"No ! " he managed to gasp.

" Why, boy, you're scared to death," said
one of the mates, rather contemptuously.
" Where's the ship for the long boat to come
from ? "

"I don't know anything about that," answered Marcy hurriedly. " I only tell you
what I saw with my own eyes. Here's the
glass, Captain. Go for'ard and take a look
for yourself."

The captain snatched the glass with almost frantic haste and ran toward the bow, followed by the mates and all the rest of the crew, with the exception of the man at the wheel. With trembling hands Beardsley raised the binoculars, but almost immediately took them down again to say, in frightened tones :

"For the first time in my life I have missed my reckoning. We're lost, and the Yankee fleet may be within less than a mile of us. Take a look, Morgan. I never saw that rock before."

"But I tell you it isn't a rock," protested Marcy. "It is a boat, and she's lying head on so that she won't show as plainly as she would if she lay broadside to us. Do you see those long black streaks on each side ? Those are oars, and they were in motion when I first saw them."

The mate was so long in making his observations that Marcy grew impatient, and wondered at his stupidity. He could see without the aid of a glass that it was a boat and nothing else ; and more than that, the schooner had by this time drawn so near her that he could make out two suspicious objects in her bow—one he was sure was a howitzer, and the other looked very like the upright, motionless figure of a blue-jacket, awaiting the order from the officer in command to pull the lockstring. An instant later a second figure arose, as if from the stern-sheets, and the command came clear and distinct:

"Heave to, or we'll blow you out of the water!"

"Now I hope you are satisfied!" exclaimed Marcy.

He expected to see Beardsley wilt again; but he did nothing of the sort. It required an emergency to bring out what there was in him, and when he saw that he must act, he did it without an instant's hesitation.

"Lay aft, all hands!" was the order he gave. "Marcy, stand by to watch the buoys in the Inlet. Morgan, go to the wheel and hold her just as she is. Don't luff so much as a hair's breadth. We'll run them Yankees down. It's our only chance."

"And a very slim one it is," thought Marcy,

as he took the glass from the mate's hand and
directed it toward the point where he thought
the entrance of the Inlet ought to be. "The
cruiser to which this boat belongs can't be far
away, and she will come up the minute she
hears the roar of the howitzer."

"Heave to, or we'll sink you!" came the
order, in louder and more emphatic tones.

"Starboard a spoke or two. Steady at
that," said Beardsley, turning about and addressing the man who had been stationed in
the waist to pass his commands. "Ten to one
they'll miss us, but all the same I wish I knew
how heavy them guns of their'n is."

"They have but one," replied Marcy, wondering at the captain's coolness. "Can't you
see it there in the bow?"

"Well, if it's a twenty-four pounder, like
them old ones of our'n, and they hit us at the
water-line, they'll tear a hole in us as big as a
barn door."

All this while the schooner had been bearing
swiftly down upon the launch, and when the
officer in command of her began to see through
Beardsley's little plan, he at once proceeded
10

to set in motion one of his own that was calculated to defeat it. His howitzer was loaded
with a five-second shrapnel, and this he fired
at the schooner at a point-blank range of less
than a hundred yards. He couldn't miss
entirely at that short distance, but the missile
flew too high to hull the blockade-runner. It
struck the flying jib-boom, breaking it short
off and rendering that sail useless, glanced and
splintered the rail close by the spot where
the captain and his pilot were standing, went
shrieking off over the water, and finally ex-
ploding an eighth of a mile astern. The skipper and Marcy were both prostrated by a
splinter six feet long and four inches thick
that was torn from the rail; but they
scrambled to their feet again almost as soon as
they touched the deck, and when they looked
ahead, fully expecting to find the launch under
the schooner's fore-foot and on the point of
being run down, they saw an astonishing as
well as a most discouraging sight. The boat
was farther away than she was before, and
her whole length could be seen now, for not
only was she broadside on, but the darkness

CAPTAIN BEARDSLEY SURPRISED.

above and around her, which had hitherto
rendered her shape and size somewhat indistinct, was lighted up by a bright glare that
shot up from somewhere amidships, and the
sound of escaping steam could be plainly
heard.

"Oh, my shoulder! Dog-gone it all, my
shoulder!" cried Beardsley, placing the in-
step of his left foot behind his right knee and
hopping about as if it were the lower portion
of his anatomy that had been injured instead
of the upper. " She's got a steam ingine aboard
of her, and them oars of her'n was only meant
for snooping up and down the coast quiet and
still' so't nobody couldn't hear 'em. We're
gone this time, Morgan; and I tell you that
for a fact!"

The moment Marcy Gray recovered his feet
he made an effort to pick up the glass that had
fallen from his grasp, but to his surprise, his
left hand refused to obey his will. When he
made a second attempt, he found that he could
not move his hand at all unless he raised his
arm at the shoulder. He was not conscious of
much pain, although he afterward said that his

arm felt a good deal as it did when Dick Graham accidentally hit his biceps with a swiftly pitched ball. But his right hand was all right, and with it he snatched up the glass and leveled it at the Inlet, which to his great delight he could plainly see straight ahead.

"Mind what you are about, Captain," said he, as soon as he could induce the man to stand still and listen to him. "That first buoy is a black one, and you want to leave it to port. If you keep on as you are holding now you will leave it to starboard, and that will run you hard and fast aground."

"Don't make much odds which way we go," whined Beardsley, holding fast to his elbow with one hand and to his shoulder with the other. "Just look what them Yankees is a doing!"

The captain became utterly disheartened when he saw that his plan for sinking the launch and making good his escape into the Inlet was going to end in failure, and Marcy did not blame him for it. The officer in command of the small boat, whoever he might be, was a determined and active fellow; his crew were picked men; his little craft was a "trotter," and he knew how to handle both of them. He had been sent out by one of the blockading squadron to patrol the coast and watch for just such vessels as the *Hattie* was, and although he had steam up all the while, he used his twenty-four muffled oars, twelve on a side, as his motive power; and this enabled him to slip along the coast without making the least sound to betray his presence. As luck would have it, he had not discovered Crooked Inlet. If he had, he would have lifted the buoys, and it might have led to extra watchfulness on the part of the blockading fleet. But he had discovered the *Hattie*, and his actions proved that he did not mean to let her escape if he could help it.

CHAPTER VII.

THE MATE'S LUCKY SHOT.

"JUST look what them Yankees is a doing now," repeated Captain Beardsley; and when Marcy turned his eyes from the warning buoy to the launch, he saw that the latter was scuttling rapidly out of harm's way; that her bow was swinging around so that she would pass by within less than a hundred feet of the schooner; that the oars had been dropped overboard, and were dragging alongside by the lanyards that were fastened to them; that some of the crew had arisen to their feet and stood facing the *Hattie;* and that the rest were busy with the howitzer in the bow.

"Heave to, or we'll cut you all to pieces!" shouted the officer in command; and Marcy could see him plainly now, for he stood erect in the stern-sheets with a boat-cloak around him. "We'll send canister and rifle balls into you next time, and they'll come so thick that they won't leave so much as a ratline of you. Heave to, I say!"

At this juncture a rifle or pistol shot, Marcy could not tell which it was, sounded from the schooner's quarter-deck, and the plucky officer was seen to throw his hands above his head, grasp wildly at the empty air for a moment, and then disappear over the side of the launch. In an instant all was confusion among the blue-jackets. The coxswain, who of course was left in command, shouted to the engineer to shut off steam, to the crew to drop their muskets and pick up their oars, and to the captain of the howitzer to cut loose with his load of canister.

"Lay down, everybody," cried Beardsley, who plainly heard all these orders; and suiting the action to the word, he quickly stretched himself upon the deck. Marcy had barely time to follow his example before the howitzer roared again, and the canister rattled through the rigging like hail, tearing holes in the canvas, splintering a mast here and a boom there, but never cutting a stay or halliard. If a topmast had gone by the board, or a sail come down by the run, the schooner would have been quite at the mercy of the launch ; for the latter could have carried her by boarding, or taken a position astern and peppered the *Hattie* with shrapnel until Captain Beardsley would have been glad to surrender. The captain did not see how his vessel could escape being crippled, and he would have surrendered then and there if any one in the launch had called upon him to do so ; but when he got upon his feet and saw that every rope held, and that the schooner was just on the point of entering her haven of refuge, he took heart again.

"Marcy, go aft and tell Morgan that that buoy ahead is a black one," said he, as soon as he had taken time to recover his wits. "Lay for'ard some of us and cut away this useless canvas. The *Hattie* ain't catched yet, doggone it all. I tell you, lads, it takes somebody besides a plodding, dollar-loving Yankee to get to windward of Lon Beardsley."

"The captain desired me to remind you that that buoy is a black one, and you want to leave it to port," said Marcy, taking his stand beside the man at the wheel. "Who fired that shot? It came from this end of the vessel."

"The second mate fired it," replied Morgan, "and he done it just in the nick of time. The killing of that officer was all that saved our bacon."

"Oh, I hope he wasn't killed!" exclaimed Marcy.

"You do, hey? Well, I don't. I'd like to see the last blockader on this coast tumbled into the drink in the same way. What did the old man say about it?"

"Not a word. I think he was too surprised to say anything."

"Was anybody hurt by that shell?" continued Morgan. "I seen the jib flying in the wind and the rail ripped up, and you and the old man was standing right there."

."Something or other knocked both of us flatter than pancakes," answered Marcy. "The captain must have been hit all over; but I was struck only on the arm, and I don't seem to have much use of it any more."

"You can go for'ard and look out for the buoys, can't you? All right. Sing out whenever you see one, and I will stay here and take her through while the cap'n gets that head-sail out of the way."

Before obeying this order Marcy stopped long enough to level the glass toward the place where he supposed the launch to be. Having worked the water out of the cylinders the engineer had shut off the stop-cocks so that she could not be heard, and as there was no flame shooting out of her smoke-stack, she could not be seen; but she was still on top of the water, and eager to do mischief. While Marcy was moving his glass around trying to locate her, the howitzer spoke again; but as the schooner took the wind free after rounding the first buoy, her course was changed, so that the shell passed behind her, and exploded far ahead and to the right.

"You've got your wish," said Morgan. "That shot means that they have picked up their cap'n, and that he's as full of fight as ever. Well, let him bang away, if he wants to. He can't hurt the sand-hills, and this channel is so crooked that he won't hit us except by accident."

"But he will follow in our wake, won't he?"

"Who cares if he does so long as he don't sight us? We'll dodge him easy enough after we get into the Sound. Now toddle for'ard and look out for me."

["It's an ill wind that blows nobody good," thought the boy, as he leaned his uninjured arm upon the splintered rail and brought the glass to his eye. "This night's work will put an end to the *Hattie's* blockade-running. If that fellow astern don't catch us, he will surely find and pull up the buoys, and then we can't follow the channel except by sending a boat on ahead with a lead-line. That might do when we were going out, but it wouldn't work running in if there was an enemy close behind us. Another thing, this Inlet will be watched in future. Now you mark my words."] "Red buoy on the starboard bow," he called out to the man at the wheel.

Morgan repeated the words to show that he understood them, and just then Beardsley came up, having seen the useless jib brought on deck and stowed away.

"Be careful and make no mistake, Marcy," said he. "It's a matter of life and death with us now—and money."

"I can call off the color of every buoy between here and the Sound," replied the pilot confidently. "I took particular pains to remember the order in which they were put out. Where are you hurt, Captain?" he added, seeing that the man had let go of his shoulder and was now holding fast to both elbows.

"I'm hurt in every place; that's where I am hurt," said Beardsley, looking savagely at Marcy, as if the latter was to blame for it. "Something hit me ker-whallop on this side, and the deck took me ker-chunk on the other; and I'll bet there ain't a spot on ary side as big as an inch where I ain't black and blue. You wasn't touched, was you? But I thought I seen you come down when I did."

"I went down fast enough," answered Marcy. "I bumped my head pretty heavily on the deck, but the worst hurt I got was right here. And I declare, there's a bunch that don't belong to me. Is it a fracture of the humerus, I wonder?"

"A which?" exclaimed the puzzled captain.

"I really believe the bone of my upper arm is broken," replied Marcy, feeling of the bunch to which he had referred. "It doesn't hurt much except when I touch it. It only feels numb."

Just then the howitzer spoke again, and another shrapnel flew wide of the schooner and burst among the sand dunes. Another and another followed at short intervals, and then the firing ceased. The launch had given it up as a bad job; the pursuit was over and Marcy and the captain were the only ones injured.

"She has either run hard and fast aground, or else she is amusing herself with them buoys of our'n," said Beardsley, when he became satisfied that the launch was no longer following in the schooner's wake. "Now, where's that good-looking son of mine who fired the lucky shot that tumbled that Yankee officer overboard? Whoever he is, I'll double his wages. He ought to have it, for he saved the vessel and her cargo. Let him show up."

The second mate obeyed the order, exhibiting the revolver that had fired the shot, and the captain complimented him in no measured terms. Marcy could not help acknowledging to himself that their escape was owing entirely to the prompt action the mate had taken without waiting for orders; but all the same he was sorry for that Federal officer.

Less than an hour's run sufficed to take the schooner out of the Inlet and into the Sound, and when Beardsley had given out the course and seen the sails trimmed to suit it, he went into his cabin, from which he presently issued to pass the word for Marcy Gray. When the boy descended the ladder he found the first mate and two foremast hands there besides the captain; and on the table he saw two pieces of thin board, and several strips of cloth that had evidently been torn up for bandages. He noticed, too, that the atmosphere was filled with the odor of liniment.

"What are you going to do?" he asked, in some alarm.

"We're going to set that—that—what-do-you-call-it of your'n," replied the captain cheerfully. The name that Marcy had given to the bone of his upper arm was too much for him. He could not remember it.

The boy knew that all sea captains have more or less knowledge of medicine and surgery. It is necessary that they should have, for sailors are often seized with illness, or meet with serious accidents when their ship is at sea, and so far from a doctor that without immediate aid from some source they would surely lose their lives. Marcy had read of a whaling captain, one of whose men was jerked overboard from his boat by a wounded whale, dragged for six hundred feet or more through the water with frightful speed, and who was finally released by his leg giving way to the strain. The captain saw that that leg must be attended to or the man would die. His crew were too badly frightened to help him, so he amputated the injured member himself; and all the surgical instruments his ship afforded were a carving-knife, a carpenter's saw, and a fish-hook. But he saved the man's life. Marcy thought of this and shuddered at the thought of submitting himself to Beardsley's rude surgery.

"I believe I would rather wait until we get to Newbern," said he doubtfully.

"Why, man alive, we may not see port for a week," answered the captain. "How do we know but what there are a dozen or more steam launches, like the one we've just left astern, loafing about in the Sound waiting for us? If there are, we'll have to get shet of 'em somehow, and that will take time. If we don't 'tend to your arm now, it may be so bad when the doctor sees it that he can't do nothing with it without half killing of you. Take off his coat and vest, men ; and Morgan, you roll up his sleeve. There is folks around home who think you are for the Union, and that you ain't secesh, even if you do belong to my vessel. If you run foul of one of 'em while you are gone on your furlong, just point to your arm and tell him to hold his yawp."

"Are you going to give me a leave of absence?" asked Marcy, who was so delighted at the thought that he could scarcely keep from showing it.

"I reckon I'll have to. I ain't got no use for a one-handed man ; but I'll keep your place open for you, never fear. Just see that, now. Ain't that a pretty looking arm for a white boy to carry around with him? It makes me hate them Yankees wusser'n I did before."

The wounded arm was already becoming inflamed, and it was painful, too ; and although Beardsley's assistants were as careful as they could be, Marcy winced while they were helping him off with his coat and vest and rolling up his sleeve. When this had been done one of the men, in obedience to a slight nod from the captain, seized Marcy around the chest under his arms, the mate by a movement equally quick grasped his left wrist, and both began pulling in opposite directions with all their strength, while Beardsley passed his huge rough hands up and down over the "bunch" until he was satisfied that the protruding bone had been pulled back to its place. The operation was a painful one, and the only thing that kept Marcy from crying out was the remembrance of Beardsley's words "I ain't got no use for a one-handed man." That broken arm would bring him a furlough.

"There, now ; that'll do. 'Vast heaving,"
11

said the captain, at length. "Put some of the stuff in that bottle on one of them bandages and hand it over here. Pretty rough way of getting to go home, but better than none at all, and I reckon your maw will be just as glad to see you as she would if you had two good arms. Don't you reckon she will?"

After his arm had been bandaged and placed in a sling, Marcy was quite willing to go into the forecastle and lie down in his bunk; and there he stayed until the schooner entered the Neuse River and a tug came alongside to tow her up to the city. This time there were plenty of cheers to welcome her, the first coming from the working parties who were building the fortifications, and the next from the soldiers and loafers who were assembled upon the wharf to which she was made fast, and who howled themselves hoarse when they caught sight of the holes in her sails, her broken bowsprit, and . her splintered rail.

"I see that blockade running has its dangers as well as privateering," said Beardsley's agent, as he sprang over the rail and seized the captain's hand. "The *Hattie* is cut up pretty badly, but the *Osprey* was never touched. Been in a fight?"

"Well, no, not much of a fight, because we uns didn't have nothing to fight with. But the schooner ran through a pretty tol'able heavy fire, I tell you."

It was all over now, and Beardsley could afford to treat the matter with indifference; but Marcy remembered that when that splinter knocked him down, the captain was the worst frightened man in the crew. However, Beardsley was not as badly hurt as he thought he was. When he came to make an examination of his injuries, all he could find was a black and blue spot on one of his shoulders that was about half as large as his hand; but he made more fuss over that than Marcy Gray did over his broken arm.

"Anybody shot?" continued the agent.

"Well, yes; two of us got touched a little, but not enough to growl over. You see it was this-a-way——"

"I suppose I may go ashore now and hunt up a surgeon, may I not?" Marcy interposed.

He thought from the way Beardsley settled

himself against the rail that he was preparing
for a long talk with the agent, and that it
would be a good plan to have his own affairs
settled before the captain became too deeply
interested in his narrative to listen to him.
There was little to detain him in Newbern.
On the way up the river Beardsley had given
him a written leave of absence for ninety days,
and a check on the bank for his money ; and
all he had to do besides presenting that check
was to have his arm examined by a surgeon.

"Of course you can go," replied Beardsley.
"And if I don't see you when you come back
for your dunnage, don't forget them little messages I give you for the folks at home, nor
them letters ; and bear in mind that I want
you back as soon as ever you can get well."

Marcy promised to remember it all, and the
captain went on to say :

"He's the bravest lad that ever stepped in
shoe leather. When them Yankees sent that
shell into us and knocked him and me down
and smashed his arm *all* to flinders, he stood in
the bow and piloted us through Crooked Inlet
as slick as falling off a log ; and there was his

arm broken all the while, and hanging by his side as limp as a piece of wet rope. Oh, he's a good one, and I don't for the life of me see how I am going to get on without him. I've said as much in them letters I wrote to the folks to home."

Under almost any other circumstances Marcy Gray would have been disgusted; but as it was, he was quite willing that Beardsley should talk about him in this strain as often as he felt like it.

"Perhaps it will help me with those secret enemies at home," he said to himself, as he stepped upon the wharf and forced his way slowly through the crowd, not, however, without being compelled to shake hands with a dozen or more who wanted to know when and where he got hurt and who did it, and all about it. "I should really like to see the inside of the letters the captain gave me to hand to Shelby and the rest. I wonder if he thinks I am foolish enough to open and read them? He'll not trap me that way; but I wouldn't trust any letters to him that I didn't want him to read, I bet you."

Arriving at a drug store which bore the name of a medical man upon one of its doorposts, Marcy entered and asked where he could find somebody to tell him whether or not his broken arm had been properly set and cared for.

"Step right this way, and I will tell you in less than five minutes," said the man who stood behind the counter. "How did you break it?"

"I was knocked down," replied Marcy.

"Who knocked you down?"

"A Yankee!"

"Hey day! Bull Run?"

"No, sir; Crooked Inlet."

"Well, I thought you looked like a sea-faring man. What vessel do you belong to?"

"The blockade-runner *Hattie*. She used to be the privateer *Osprey*."

"Were you one of the brave fellows who captured the *Mary Hollins*?" exclaimed the surgeon, giving Marcy a look of admiration. "It was a gallant deed."

"I was there when she was taken," answered the boy, while the doctor was helping him off with his coat. "Do you know what become of her crew?"

"They were paroled and sent North long ago. We didn't want such folks among us."

"But they are not prisoners of war."

"That doesn't matter. They had to promise that they would not take up arms against us until they were regularly exchanged; and if they do, and we find it out, they will stand a fine chance of being strung up. You've got a pretty good surgeon aboard your ship, and he has made a good job of this. I wonder if I know him. Is he a Newbern man?"

"No, sir; he hails from up toward Plymouth. And he isn't a doctor, either. He's the captain."

"Oh, ah!" said the surgeon, who was very much surprised to hear it. "I see, now that I come to look at it closely, that it is not quite as straight as I thought it was. It sticks out a little on this side, and your arm will always be more or less crooked. It is unfortunate that you did not have a surgeon aboard; but we will have to let it go."

"Of course I can't do duty with one hand, said Marcy, "and so the captain has given me leave to go home for awhile. I can travel on the cars, I suppose ? "

" There's nothing in the world to hinder it," replied the medical man, who seemed on a sudden to have lost all interest in Marcy and his injured arm. "I will do it up again and give you a little medicine, and you will get along all right. It's a mere trifle."

When Marcy asked what his bill was, he told himself that he made a mistake when he said it was the captain and not a doctor who set his arm, for the surgeon charged him a good round price for his trouble, as well as for the little bottle of tonic he wrapped up for him ; and when he went to the telegraph office, the operator who sent off a dispatch to his mother made no distinction between him and a citizen. The dispatch ran as follows :

Arrived from Nassau this morning with a valuable cargo after a running fight with the Yankees. Had two men slightly injured. Will leave for Boydtown by first train.

" After mother reads that she will not be so very much shocked when she sees me with my arm in a sling," was what he told himself as he passed the dispatch over to the operator.

"Did you have a fight with one of the blockaders?" asked the latter carelessly. He had become accustomed to the sight of wounded men since the battle of Bull Run was fought, and did not take a second look at Marcy.

"It wasn't much of a fight, seeing that there was but one shot fired on our side," answered the pilot. "But that one shot was what brought us through. It wasn't a blockader, either, but a launch; and if you want to see what she did to us, step down to the wharf and take a look at the *Hattie*. One more round of canister would have made a wreck of us."

"And you happened to be one of the two who were wounded, I reckon," said the operator. "Fifty cents, please."

"The last time I sent off a dispatch from here you did not tax me a cent for it," Marcy reminded him. "Is your patriotism on the wane?"

"Not much; but you couldn't expect us to

keep up that thank-ye business forever, could you ? How would we run the line if we did ? We think as much of the brave boys who are standing between us and Lincoln's Abolitionists as we ever did ; but it takes the hard cash to pay operators and buy poles and wires."

Marcy had no trouble in getting his check cashed, and when he went back to the schooner after his valise and bundles, he had twenty-one hundred dollars in his pocket. But there were seventeen hundred dollars of it that did not belong to him. He was only keeping it until he could have opportunity to return it to the master of the *Mary Hollins*. He found that Captain Beardsley had gone ashore with his agent, and as Marcy had already said good-bye to him, it was not necessary that he should waste any valuable time in hunting him up. He took a hasty leave of his shipmates, hired a darkey to carry his luggage to the depot, and was in time to purchase his ticket for a train that was on the point of leaving for Goldsborough. He had hardly settled himself in his seat before he became aware that nearly all the passengers in the car were looking at him, and finally one of them came and seated himself by his side.

"You are not in uniform," said the passenger, "but all· the same I take it for granted that it was the Yankees who put your arm in a sling."

"Yes, sir ; they did it," answered Marcy.

"Well, now, I want to know if it's a fact that the Yankees outnumbered us two to one in that fight," continued the man.

"You refer to the battle of Bull Run, I suppose. I don't know. I wasn't there, and I don't hesitate to say that I am glad of it. One howitzer is as much as I care to face. I got this hurt while coming into Crooked Inlet on the schooner *Hattie.* She's a blockade-runner."

"Oh! well, if there's going to be a war, as some people seem to think, you blockade-runners will be of quite as much use to the Confederacy as the soldiers. We shall be dependent upon foreign governments for many things that we used to get from the North, and men like you will have to supply us. Was it much of a fight?"

Marcy briefly related the story, and when it was finished the man went back to his old seat; but during the journey the young pilot was obliged to tell more than a score of people that he was not present at the battle of Bull Run, and consequently could not have got his injury there. He kept his ears open all the way, and was gratified to learn that the Confederates had not followed up their victory, that they were not in Washington, and that there was no reason to suppose that they had any intention of going there immediately; and he thought he knew the reason why, when he heard one of the passengers say that a few more victories like Bull Run would ruin the Confederacy.

At an early hour the next morning Marcy stepped off the train at Boydtown and found Morris waiting for him. That faithful servitor's eyes grew to twice their usual dimensions when he saw his young master with his arm in a sling, and without waiting to learn the extent of his injuries, he broke out into loud lamentations, and railed at the Yankees in such a way that the by-standers were led to believe that old Morris was the best kind of a rebel.

"The Missus done tole me two men shot on the *Hattie*, and las' night I dreamed you one of 'em," said he.

"Silence!" whispered Marcy angrily; "can't you see that you are drawing the attention of all the people on the platform by your loud talking? I wasn't shot, either. Come to the carriage and I will tell you all about it."

Even after Morris had been assured that the young pilot had merely been knocked down by a splinter, Marcy didn't tell him that that "splinter" weighed between fifteen and twenty pounds, for he knew it would get to his mother's ears if he did ; and that his injuries were by no means serious ; the old slave was not satisfied, but continued to scold and fume at such a rate that Marcy was glad when the carriage whirled through the gate and drew up at the steps, at the top of which his mother stood waiting to receive him.

"Da' he is, Missus ; but the Yankees done kill him," exclaimed Morris, opening and shutting the carriage door with a bang, as if he hoped in that way to work off some of his excitement.

CHAPTER VIII.

A NOISE AT THE WINDOW.

MRS. GRAY'S countenance grew white with alarm. She flew down the steps, and throwing both her arms about her son's neck, hid her face on his shoulder and sobbed violently. Marcy put his uninjured arm around her, and his mother leaned so heavily upon it that the boy thought she was going to faint.

"Now see what you have done, you black rascal, by wagging your tongue so freely," said Marcy angrily. "I've the best notion in the world to have you sent to the field."

"But, moster," protested the frightened coachman, "de Yankees did shoot——"

"Hold your tongue! If you lisp another word I will have you sent to the overseer as sure as you are a living darkey. Now take those things out of the carriage and put them in my room; and when you have done that, go

174

off somewhere and spend an hour or two every day telling the truth, so that you will get used to it.   Come into the house," he added gently, leading his mother up the steps, "and I will tell you all about it.   I wasn't shot.   I was struck by a splinter."

["Oh, Marcy," sobbed Mrs. Gray, "your face tells a different story.   You have suffered —you are suffering now ; and there isn't a particle of color in your cheeks.   Don't try to deceive me, for I must know the worst sooner or later."

" I am not trying to deceive you," answered Marcy, although he *was* trying to break the disagreeable news as gently as he could.   "I was knocked down by a splinter and my arm was broken."

"There now," began his mother.

" But it's all right," Marcy hastened to add. " Beardsley set the bone in less than three hours after it was broken, and the surgeon I consulted in Newbern said he made a good job of it.   I don't know what you think about it, but I am not sorry it happened."

" Oh, Marcy ! why do you say that ? "

"Because it gave me a chance to come home. To tell you the truth, blockade running is getting to be a dangerous business. We had four narrow escapes this trip. Beardsley's impudence and a Union captain's simplicity brought us out of the first scrape, a storm came to our aid in the second, sheer good luck and a favoring breeze saved us in the third, and a shot from the second mate's revolver brought us out of the fourth. We are liable to fall into the hands of the cruisers any day; and suppose I had been captured and thrown into a Northern prison! You might not have seen me again for a year or two; perhaps longer. Bring those bundles in here and take the valise upstairs," he added to the coachman, who just then passed along the hall with Marcy's luggage in his hands. "Open that bundle, mother. You need not be ashamed to wear those dresses, for they were bought in Nassau with honest money —money that I earned by doing duty as a foremast hand. I didn't pay any duty on them because no one asked me for it. And in fact I don't know whether there is a custom-house in Newbern or not. The box in the other bundle contains nothing but bottles of quinine."

"What induced you to get so much?" asked Mrs. Gray, who had wiped away her tears and was trying to look cheerful again.

"Captain Beardsley first called my attention to the fact that medicine had gone up in price, and I saw by a paper I got in Nassau that the rebels are already smuggling quinine across the Potomac," answered Marcy. "There's a good deal of ague about here, and we'd be in a pretty fix if we should all get down with it, and no medicine in the house to help us out." Here he got up and drew his chair closer to his mother's side, adding in a whisper, "I've twenty-one hundred dollars in gold in my valise, lacking what I paid for my railroad ticket, and nearly four hundred dollars of it belongs to me. The rest belongs to the captain of the *Hollins*."

"Do you still cling to the hope that you will some day meet him again?" asked his mother.

"I know it will be like hunting for a needle in a haystack, but if I don't find him I shall have the satisfaction of knowing that I tried

12

to, and that I haven't spent any of his money. I'll keep it locked in my trunk until my arm gets so that I can handle a spade, and then I'll hide it in one of the flower beds. Now, how is everything about home? Has Kelsey shown his ugly face here since I went away, or have you heard anything from those 'secret enemies' that Wat Gifford spoke of? How has Hanson behaved himself?"

Mrs. Gray's report was so satisfactory that Marcy was put quite at his ease. She had had nothing to worry over, she told him, except, of course, his absence and Jack's, and if she had not received so many warnings she would not have suspected that there were such things as secret enemies around her. But she had relaxed none of her vigilance, and was always on her guard when any of the neighbors came to see her. It was a dreadful way to live, but there was no help for it.

By the time Marcy had removed some of the stains of travel from his face and clothing, supper was announced; and as he had to talk about something during the meal, he entertained his mother with a minute description of

the exciting incidents that happened during
the *Hattie's* homeward run. He could talk of
these things in his ordinary tone of voice, and
he did not care who overheard him. More
than that, he was satisfied that every word he
uttered in the presence of the girl who waited
at table would go straight to Hanson's ears,
and he was really talking for Hanson's benefit.
He retired at an early hour, after his arm had
been bathed and bandaged again (his mother
could not keep back her tears when she saw
how inflamed and angry it looked), and left
his lamp burning, as he had done every night
since his friend Gifford dropped that hint
about a visit from an organized band of 'longshoremen. Before he got into bed he unlocked
his valise and took from it two things that his
mother knew nothing about,—a brace of heavy
revolvers,—which he placed where he could get
his hands upon them at a moment's warning.

"Thank goodness the old flag is above me
once more, and not that secession rag that
Beardsley seems to be so proud of," thought
Marcy, as he pounded his pillow into shape
and drew the quilts over his shoulders. "If

Colonel Shelby and the rest knew that there are two Union flags somewhere among these bedclothes, how long do you suppose this house would stand? If those men are such good rebels, I can't for the life of me understand why they don't go into the service, instead of staying at home and making trouble for their neighbors. I should think they would be ashamed of themselves."

There were plenty of such men all over the South, and Marcy Gray was not the only one who wondered why they did not hasten to the front, seeing that they were so very hostile to the Yankees and their sympathizers, and professed so much zeal for the cause of Southern independence. His cousin Rodney often asked himself the same question while Dick Graham was staying at his father's house, waiting for a chance to get across the Mississippi River. Tom Randolph, who could not forget that Captain Hubbard's Rangers had refused to give him the office he wanted, was Rodney's evil genius. Although Tom became in time commander of a small company of Home Guards, he could be for the old flag or against it, as

circumstances seemed to require. When the
Union forces took possession of Baton Rouge
and the gunboats anchored in front of the city,
Randolph sent more than one squad of Yankee
cavalry to search Mr. Gray's house for firearms, and took measures to keep Rodney,
Dick Graham, and the other discharged Confederates in constant trouble ; but when
General Breckenridge and his army appeared,
and it began to look as though the rebels were
about to drive the Union forces out and take
possession of Baton Rouge and the surrounding country, Tom Randolph gave his scouts
the names of all the Union men in Mooreville
and vicinity, and of course they did not escape
persecution. But Tom, sly as he was, could
not play a double part forever. His sin found
him out and his punishment came close upon
the heels of it. We shall tell all about it in
its proper place.

Having no watch to stand on this particular
night, and having no fear of capture by
cruisers or a fight with armed steam launches,
Marcy soon fell asleep, to be awakened about
midnight by a sound that sent the cold chills

all over him. He could not have told just what it was, but all the same it frightened him. He sat up in bed and pulled one of his revolvers from under his pillow. He listened intently, and in a few seconds the sound was repeated. Then he knew that it was made by a pebble which some one in the yard below had tossed against his window. It was a signal of some sort, but who made it, and why should the visitor, whoever he might be, seek to arouse him without disturbing his mother?

"By gracious!" thought Marcy, resting his revolver on his knee with the muzzle turned toward the window, as if he half expected to see some one try to force an entrance there. "What can it mean? It may be a dangerous piece of business to draw the curtain and open that window, for how do I know but that there's somebody below waiting for a chance to pop me over? How do I know but those 'longshoremen have come up——"

When this thought passed through the boy's mind his fear gave place to indignation; and hesitating no longer he threw off the bedclothes and advanced toward the window, just

as another pebble rattled against it. He
dashed the curtain aside, threw up the sash,
and thrust his head and his revolver out of the
window. The night was so dark that he could
not see a thing except the dark sky and the
darker shadows of the trees against it.

"Who's there?" he demanded. "Speak
quick."

> "The despot's heel is on thy shore ;
>   His torch is at thy temple door.
> Avenge the patriotic gore
>   That flecks the streets of Baltimore,
> And be the battle queen of yore—
>   Maryland ! my Maryland !"

That was the answer he received to his challenge. It was given in a voice that he had
never heard before, and Marcy was so utterly
amazed that he could not interrupt the speaker,
or say a word himself when the verse was concluded. It was part of a rebel song that had
recently become very popular in Baltimore,
but it had not yet reached North Carolina.
For only an instant, however, did Marcy stand
motionless and speechless, and then he pointed

his weapon in the direction from which the voice sounded, saying in steady tones:

"If you don't give me an answer that I can understand, I'll cut loose. Who are you?"

"I am a homeless, friendless smuggler," replied the voice; and at the same instant a familiar bark, followed by an impatient whine, told the astonished Marcy that his faithful watchman, Bose, was under the window with the stranger. The unexpected discovery made every nerve in his body tingle with excitement, and his next words were uttered in a husky and indistinct tone.

"Jack!" he exclaimed. "Oh, Jack! Is that you?"

"It's I," answered the visitor, speaking in his natural voice this time. "I'm here safe and sound, and none the worse for having been a prisoner in the hands of that pirate, Captain Semmes."

"Go round to the front door and I will be right down," said Marcy, in suppressed tones. He could not imagine why his brother should make his presence known in this guarded way instead of boldly demanding admittance at +'

door, but he knew that there was some reason for it and conducted himself accordingly. He moved about his room very quietly while he dressed himself as well as he could with only one hand to work with, and then he caught up the lamp, hurried downstairs and made his way to his mother's room. His low tap met with an instant response.

"Oh, mother," exclaimed Marcy, "Jack's come home, and he's Union."

"Of course he is for the Union," answered Mrs. Gray calmly, although she was almost as highly excited as Marcy was. "I have never thought of him as being a rebel."

"The rebels had him prisoner," added Marcy ; and with this bit of news to add to his mother's excitement, the boy ran to the front door. The moment he opened it a stalwart young fellow sprang upon the threshold with his arms spread out ; but he stopped suddenly when his eyes fell upon Marcy's white face and upon the sling in which he carried his left hand.

"What's happened to you?" he demanded, as soon as he could speak.

"I got that while helping Captain Beardsley run a cargo of contraband goods through Crooked Inlet," replied Marcy, laughing at the expression of surprise and disgust that came upon the young sailor's bronzed face as he listened to the words. "First I was a privateer and now I am a blockade-runner."

"There must be some good reason for it, because I know as well as you do that you do not belong on that side of the house," said the returned wanderer, closing and locking the door after beckoning to Bose, who was never permitted to enter the house except upon extraordinary occasions. "I had a fine chance to become a rebel pirate. When the prize-master who was put aboard of us after we were captured, found that I was from a seceded State, he promised if I would ship on the *Sumter* to ask Captain Semmes——"

Just at this point the young sailor looked over his brother's shoulder and saw his mother coming along the hall. A second later he held her clasped in his arms. She looked very small and frail while standing beside that tall, broad-shouldered son, who was as fine a speci-

men of an American sailor as could be found
anywhere outside of New England. Although
he was but three years older than Marcy, who
was by no means a puny fellow, he stood head
and shoulders above him, and was built like a
young Hercules. It was little wonder that
Mrs. Gray and Marcy had awaited his coming
with the greatest anxiety and impatience, or
that the former should say to himself : "From
this time on I can sleep in peace. Jack's got
home and mother's property is safe."

"Now that you have got through saying
'hallo,' I'd like to have you tell me why you
came home like a thief in the night instead of
knocking at the door," said Marcy. "I don't
know when I have been so frightened."

" Aha! That shows that I did not make a
mistake in going to so much trouble to be on
the safe side. You are afraid of the neighbors,
are you ? I read the papers when I could
get them, and among other things I learned
that the South is divided against itself, and
that few men know for certain who their friends
are. Let's go somewhere and sit down."

Jack led his mother into the sitting-room,

Marcy following with the lamp, and taking care to see that all the doors were closed before he seated himself.

"I should judge from your actions, Marcy, that this family is divided against itself, and that you are afraid to trust the servants," said Jack. "If that's the case, the papers told the truth. Now tell me how you got that bad arm. Were you shot?"

Marcy did not spend much time on his story, for he was impatient to learn when and where his brother had been captured, and how he had managed to escape after a prize crew had been thrown aboard his vessel. He simply told of his experience in the blockade-runner *Hattie*, leaving his exploits in the *Osprey* to be narrated at some future time.

"I am glad the *Hattie* got through the blockade all right seeing that you were aboard of her," said Jack, when Marcy brought his story to a close. "But if Uncle Sam doesn't do something to break up blockade-running, he'll have a war on his hands that will make him open his eyes. It will not take me five minutes to tell my story. I was a prisoner not

more than twelve hours, and during that time
not the first exciting thing happened. If it
hadn't been for the fact that there was a strange
officer in command of the brig, and that our
old man was walking around with his hands in
his pockets, saying nothing, we wouldn't have
known that we were prisoners at all."

With this introduction the returned sailor
settled into an easy position among the sofa
pillows and related his experience very nearly
as follows, with this exception : He quite for-
got to say that he was the one who first conceived the idea of taking the *Sabine* out of the
hands of the prize crew that Semmes had
placed aboard of her, and that, if it had not
been for his courage and prompt action, the
brig would either have been sold for the benefit of the Confederate Government, or burned
in the Caribbean Sea after her neutral cargo
had been put ashore.

It happened on the morning of July 4, and
the *Sabine*, in company with the brig *Herndon*,
was sailing along the southern coast of Cuba,
having recently left the port of Trinidad-de-
Cuba with a cargo of sugar and molasses, which

was consigned to an English port in the Island of Jamaica. Although there was some sea on and rain squalls were frequent, there was but little breeze, and consequently the *Sabine* could not have run into neutral waters even if second mate Jack Gray, who had charge of the deck, had known that the steamer that was bearing down upon her was the freebooter, *Sumter*.

"What do you mean by neutral waters?" Marcy wanted to know.

"Why, every country that owns a strip of seacoast owns also the waters for three miles out," replied Jack. "And inside of that marine league, as it is called, the cruisers of one nation mustn't trouble the ships of another with which it happens to be at war. For example, if two armed vessels belonging to two different nations who are at loggerheads, happen to sail into the same neutral port, they can't fight there, but must go outside; and if one of them runs out, the other must wait twenty-four hours before following her."

The coast of Cuba was in plain view when the *Sumter* was sighted, but as there was little breeze stirring, and the brigs could not escape, Captain Semmes was not obliged to resort to the cowardly trick he usually practiced—that is, hoisting the English ensign to quiet the fears of the crew of the unlucky vessels he intended to destroy. He began business at once ; and the first thing that drew the attention of second mate Jack Gray, as he planked the quarter-deck thinking of almost everything except Confederate war vessels, was the roar of a thirty-two pounder. Jack looked up to see a thick cloud of white smoke floating slowly away from the side of the steamer, and to take note of the fact that a peculiar looking flag floated from her peak. Jack had never seen it before, but he knew in a minute what it was. At the same time he noticed that the *Herndon*, which was half a mile or so in advance of the *Sabine*, had backed her main topsail and hoisted her own colors—the Stars and Stripes.

"Tumble up here, Captain," exclaimed Jack, rushing to the top of the companion-ladder. "There's a rebel steamer on the lee bow, speaking to us."

"I wondered what that noise was," said the captain, as he came up the ladder in two jumps, and saw that a boat had already been lowered from the steamer and was putting off to take charge of the *Herndon*.

The captain knew that there were rebel privateers afloat, for in a foreign port he had read of the escape of the *Savannah* from Charleston on June 2, and of the inglorious ending of her short career as a freebooter. The *Savannah* captured one merchantman with a cargo of sugar, and afterward gave chase to a brig, which turned out to be the man of war *Perry*. The *Savannah* was captured after a little race, and her crew were sent to New York as prisoners. But the captain of the *Sabine* never knew until that moment that the rebels had let loose steam vessels to prey upon the commerce of the Northern States. He looked at the "pirate," which, having sent off a boat to complete the capture of the *Herndon*, had put herself in motion again and was drawing closer to the *Sabine*, glanced up at the sails, and then turned his wistful eyes toward the Cuban coast line.

"There isn't the ghost of a chance," said Jack, who easily read the thoughts that were passing in the mind of his commander. "If we try to run and she doesn't feel like chasing us, she'll shoot us into little bits."

"She's got five guns," remarked the first mate, who was making a close examination of the steamer through the spyglass. "She's loading one of them, and it might be a good plan for us to come to and show colors."

These words brought the captain to his senses. He gave the necessary orders, and in a few minutes the brig's maintopsail had been backed and the Union emblem was floating from her peak. There were an astonished lot of men aboard of her, and they were so angry, too, that they could not stand still. They clenched their hands and gritted their teeth when they saw a boat filled with armed men put off from the steamer, and when the boarding officer came over the side and informed the captain of the *Sabine*, in courteous tones, that his vessel was a prize to the Confederate cruiser *Sumter*, they could scarcely control themselves.

13

"I suppose I shall have to give in," said the Yankee skipper. "But I tell you plainly that if I had five guns and as many men as you've got, one or the other of us would have been on his way to the bottom before this time."

"Oh, I don't doubt that you would make us plenty of trouble if you had the power," said the rebel officer, with a smile. "But, fortunately, you haven't got it. I shall have to ask you to get your papers and go off to the *Sumter* with me. What's your cargo, where from, and whither bound?" he added, turning to Jack, when the captain had disappeared in the cabin.

The second mate did not waste any time or words in giving the desired information.

"Ah! A neutral cargo bound. from one neutral port to another," said the officer. "I am sorry to hear that."

"Why are you?" inquired Jack.

"Because under the circumstances we cannot destroy your vessel."

"What's the use of being so mean just because you happen to possess the power?" said Jack.

"Young man," replied the officer sharply, "we are bound to harass you Yankees all we can and in every way we can. That's what your people are doing to us. But what else can we do? France and England have denied us the privilege of taking our prizes into any of their ports, and there's but one course left for us to pursue. But Spain has n't spoken yet, and perhaps we shall test her friendship for us by taking you into a Cuban port."

Things turned out just as the boarding officer thought they would. The captain of the brig was taken off to the *Sumter*, and after his papers had been examined he was sent back, and a prize crew, consisting of a midshipman and four sailors, was placed on board the brig. Both prizes were then taken in tow by the *Sumter*, which steamed away for the harbor of Cienfuegos, Captain Semmes laboring under the delusion that Spain would permit him to have his Yankee prizes condemned and sold in a Spanish port. The Confederate midshipman commanded the brig, the Yankee sailors sullenly performed the little work there was to be done, and the four Confederate sailors stood around and kept watch of them.

Only one thing that was worthy of note occurred during the day. The *Sumter* steamed slowly along the coast, making not more than five knots an hour, and the Yankee sailors, enraged over the loss of their vessel, and looking forward to nothing else but a long term of confinement in a Southern prison, were very uneasy, and naturally enough they wanted to exchange opinions on the situation ; but that was something the midshipman would not permit. He was vigilant, and would not allow the brig's crew to get together for fear that they might hatch up a plan for recapturing their property. If a couple of them got near enough together to whisper a few words to each other, he would call out roughly :

"What are you about, there ? Get farther apart, you two."

This state of affairs continued until night came and darkness settled down over the Caribbean Sea, and then Captain Semmes himself did something that caused the heart of every one of the *Sabine's* crew to beat high with hope.

CHAPTER IX.

THE "SUMTER" LOSES A PRIZE.

WHILE the majority of the *Sabine's* crew chafed and fretted like captive birds which beat their wings against the bars of their cage to no purpose, there were two who stood aloof from every one and from each other; who never spoke a word, but who nevertheless came to a perfect understanding through the interchange of frequent and expressive glances. They were the captain and Jack Gray. Each one knew as well as if the other had explained it to him, that both had resolved upon the same thing—that before the sun rose again the *Sabine* must be taken out of the hands of the prize crew, and her course shaped toward a Northern port, no matter what the risk might be.

"I knew, although I had no chance to speak to the old man about it, that our first hard work must be to disarm those five rebels," said

197

Jack, in telling his story. "I knew it would be easy enough to do that if we all moved together, for there was but one native American in the prize crew—the midshipman—and he was a little whiffet to be strangled with a finger and thumb. Even the fact that we were in the middle of the tow, the *Sumter* ahead and the *Herndon* behind, wouldn't have made any difference to us if we had had control of the brig, because a few lusty blows with an axe would have severed the two hawsers and the darkness would have aided us in making our escape; but the trouble was, the elements were against us. The wind would not come up, and of course it would be of no use for us to take the brig unless we had a breeze to help us draw off."

While the captain and his vigilant second mate were waiting and watching in the hope that something might unexpectedly turn up in . their favor, Captain Semmes came to their aid. The *Sumter*, with her heavy tow and little breeze to help her, was making headway altogether too slowly to suit him; and besides, it had occurred to him that it might be well to run ahead and find out what the authorities at

Cienfuegos thought of him and his government, and whether or not they would permit Yankee prizes to be condemned and sold in that port. The first intimation the brig's crew had that Captain Semmes was about to cast off his tow was a warning whistle from the *Sumter*. This was followed by a sudden slackening of the hawser, and a few minutes later the *Sumter's* black hulk showed itself on the starboard bow. She was backing water.

"*Sabine* ahoy!" came the hail.

"On board the *Sumter!*" replied the midshipman.

"Cast off the *Herndon's* hawser and stand by to pass it aboard of us."

The midshipman responded with an "Ay, ay, sir!" and ordered the brig's crew to lay aft and hold themselves in readiness to cast off when they received the word. It took half an hour to transfer the line from one vessel to the other (it was accomplished by the aid of a small boat), and then another order came to the prize-master of the *Sabine*.

"Haul in your own hawser and make sail and follow us into port," were the instructions he received, and which he at once proceeded to act upon. He did not notice, however, that the first man to seize the hawser and lay out his strength upon it with a "Heave yo! All together now," was the surly second mate, who seemed to take the loss of his vessel so much to heart that he hadn't said a word to anybody since the prize crew was put aboard of her. But Jack Gray was there with an object. When the end of the hawser had been wound around the capstan, and the bars were shipped, he took pains to place himself next to a couple of Green Mountain boys, whose courage had been proved in more than one trying ordeal.

"Heave yo! 'Round she goes. Strike up a song, somebody," shouted Jack; and then he leaned over and spoke so that not only the two men who were heaving at the bar with him but also the three who were on the bar in front could hear every word he said. "Listen, boys," said he earnestly. "We're going to take the ship out of the hands of these pirates. Put a handspike or an axe where you can get your hands on it, and be ready to jump the instant the old man or I make a move."

Jack could say no more just then, for in his progress around the capstan he came opposite the place where the midshipman was standing. He breasted the bar manfully and joined in the song, looking as innocent as though he had never thought of knocking the midshipman overboard if the latter gave him even the shadow of a chance to do it.

"I knew well enough that you cabin fellows would never let these villains get away with the brig," said the man on his left, as soon as it was safe for him to speak. "Jump as soon as you get ready and we'll be there. What was it you read to us from that Mobile paper you brought aboard at Rio—that one Southern gentleman is as good as five Northern mud-sills? We will give them a chance to prove it."

"Pass the word among the boys and tell them to stand by to bear a hand when the time comes," added the second mate. "But be sly about it, for we must not arouse the suspicions of these rebels. They are armed and we are not."

In due time the hawser was hauled aboard and stowed away, and then the midshipman prepared to make sail and follow the *Sumter*, which was by this time so far off that her lights could not be seen. It took a good while to do this, and once, while working on the fore-yard, Jack was delighted to find himself by his captain's side.

"I hope that rebel officer didn't see you come up," said Jack. "If he did he will be on his guard, and then good-by to all our chances of taking the ship."

"Do you take me for a dunce?" asked the captain, in reply. "I came up when he wasn't looking, because I wanted a chance to say a word to you."

"I know what you would say if you had time," was Jack's answer. "So do the men. They have all been posted, and are as eager to get the ship back as you can possibly be."

"Very good," said the captain, who was highly gratified. "Stand by the companion-ladder and watch all that goes on in the cabin."

Having seen the last sail sheeted home Jack obeyed the order to "lay down from aloft," and engaged the midshipman in conversation to give the captain a chance to gain the deck without being discovered. At the same time he noticed that the long wished for breeze was springing up, and that everything was beginning to draw beautifully. At this moment the steward came up from the cabin and approached the place where they were standing.

"You haven't had any supper, sir," said he, saluting the midshipman. "Won't you come down and drink a cup of coffee and eat an orange?"

Jack fairly trembled while he waited for the officer's reply. He was afraid he would decline the invitation—Jack knew *he* would have done so if he had been in the midshipman's place, and that nothing short of an overpowering force would have taken him from the deck so long as he was prize-master of the brig. But the young officer's fears had not only been lulled to sleep by the orderly conduct of the *Sabine's* crew, which led him to believe that they, like all the rest of their countrymen, were too cowardly to show fight under any circumstances, but he was tired and hungry, and he thought that a cup of coffee and something

good to eat would take the place of the night's
sleep which he knew he was going to lose. Accordingly he followed the steward toward the
cabin, and then Jack told himself that something was about to happen—that this was a
part of the captain's plan for seizing the vessel.
Jack had been instructed to stand at the top of
the companion-ladder and watch all that went
on below, and in order that he might carry out
those instructions without attracting the midshipman's attention, he quietly removed his
shoes and stood in his stocking feet. As he
was about to start for the post that had been
assigned him, he saw an opportunity to aid
the captain that was too good to be lost. Standing within less than ten feet of him was one of
the Confederate sailors. He was leaning over
the rail looking down into the water, evidently in a brown study. He held his musket
clasped in his arms in a position something
like "arms port," and Jack knew that
he carried his revolver on the right side,
that the butt was entirely out of the
holster, and that there was no strap to hold
the weapon in place. He had taken note of

these facts when the prize-crew first came on board.

Before attempting to carry out the desperate plan he had so suddenly conceived for securing this particular rebel, Jack swept a hasty glance over the deck to calculate his chances for success. They could not have been better. There was not another one of the prize-crew in sight; but just across from him, on the other side of the deck, stood Stebbins, one of the Green Mountain boys who had worked at the capstan with him. Other members of the crew were making a pretense of being busy at something in the waist, but they were one and all keeping a close watch on the second mate, and there were hand-spikes, axes, or belaying-pins within easy reach. Jack made a warning gesture to Stebbins, and the sailor at once reached for his capstan-bar. With two quick, noiseless steps Jack placed himself close behind the dreaming rebel, and thrusting his left arm over his shoulder seized his musket with a firm grasp, while at the same time, with his right hand, he deftly slipped the revolver from its holster.

"Not a word—not a whisper!" said Jack, placing the muzzle of the heavy Colt close to the rebel's head. "Let go that gun. Stebbins, take off his cutlass and buckle it around your own waist."

When the captive recovered himself sufficiently to look around, he was astonished to find that he was confronted by four of the brig's foremast hands, all of whom carried weapons of some sort, which they held threateningly over his head. There was no help for it, and he was prompt to obey both Jack's orders; that is to say, he gave up his gun and kept his lips closed.

"Lead him aft, Stebbins, and stand guard over him with your cutlass," commanded Jack. "If he tries to run or give warning to his companions, cut him down. Smith, take this musket and keep a sharp eye on me. The officer is in the cabin, and I don't think the old man means to let him come out very soon."

Stebbins moved off with his prisoner, Smith and the other two sailors stationed themselves where they could see everything the second mate did, and the latter advanced close to the companion-way so that he could look down and obtain a view of the interior of the cabin. At the very first glance he saw something to discourage him.

"The moment the old man told me to watch all that went on in the cabin, that moment I understood his plan," said Jack. "And when I afterward compared notes with him and the steward, I learned that I had made no mistake. The captain was not denied the privilege of going in and out of his cabin as often as he pleased, and that was one place where the midshipman, who was really a sharp officer, did wrong. Another wrong move he made was in scattering his men about the deck. If he had kept them close together, so that they could have helped one another, we never could have taken the brig."

It was during one of these visits to the cabin that the captain took his revolver from the place in which he had concealed it when he saw the prize-crew coming aboard, and put four pairs of hand-cuffs into his pockets; for when the rebel boarding officer hauled down his colors, he determined that at sunrise the

next morning the Stars and Stripes should
again float at his peak if he had to sacrifice
half his crew to get them there. His next
move was to order his steward to dish up
supper, and when it was ready he sent word
to the midshipman to come down and have a
bite ; but, although the brig was towing at the
stern of the *Sumter*, and there was not the
smallest chance for her to escape, the officer
would not trust himself within reach of the
skipper and his mates. However, he was not
afraid to go into the cabin alone, and when the
steward asked him, in Jack's hearing, to come
below and drink a cup of coffee and eat an
orange, he accepted the invitation ; but his
actions indicated that he was very suspicious.

"Sit down here, sir," said the steward,
drawing back the chair he had placed for
him.

"Well, hardly," replied the officer, glancing at the door behind him, which, by the
way, opened into the captain's state-room.
"Move that chair and plate to the other side
of the table."

"Certainly, sir," said the steward, in his

politest tones; and the command was promptly obeyed.

The first thing the midshipman did after he had taken his seat, was to draw his revolver from its holster and show it to the steward ; and then he placed it on the chair under his left leg.

"You will observe that I don't put it on the table and give you a chance to snatch it while I am in the act of drinking my coffee," said he blandly.

"Certainly, sir," said the steward again.

"You Yankees have the reputation of being pretty sharp people," continued the officer, "and I believe you are somewhat famous for the tricks you play upon unsuspecting strangers; but you will find that there are smarter men south of Mason and Dixon's line than there are north of it. Now, if we understand each other, trot out your grub."

The steward ran up the ladder, at the top of which he found the second mate, standing back out of the light so that the midshipman could not see him if he chanced to look toward the deck.

14

"Did you notice that he would not sit where I wanted him to?" whispered the steward. "The old man is in his state-room, waiting for a chance to rush out and grab him, but I am afraid that move on the Confederate's part will knock the whole thing in the head."

"Not by a long shot," replied Jack. "We've got firearms of our own now, and if the worst is forced upon us, we'll engage them in a regular battle. But we don't want to shoot if we can help it, for that might bring the *Sumter* upon us."

The steward vanished in the galley, and while he was gone Jack thought seriously of giving him the revolver he had taken from the captured rebel, and telling him to watch his chance to put it to the head of the midshipman while he was eating his supper, and demand his surrender on pain of death. That would have been just the thing to do, Jack thought, if he were only sure that the steward's courage would not fail him when the critical moment came; but unfortunately he was not quite positive on that point. He had never had an opportunity to see how the

steward would act in an emergency, and after
a little reflection he concluded that he had
better keep the weapon in his own possession.

In a few minutes the steward came out of the
galley, carrying a tray upon which he had
placed a tempting supper, and Jack saw him
descend into the cabin and put it on the table.

"Here, you fellow, that won't do," he heard
the midshipman exclaim. "Don't take quite
so much pains to get behind me, if *you* please.
Stand around on the other side of the table, so
that I can see everything you do."

"Certainly, sir," answered the steward, as
he hastened to take the position pointed out
to him.

If Jack Gray had been in the cabin at that
moment he would have seen that he did a wise
thing when he decided to hold fast to his revolver instead of handing it over to the steward
and depending upon him to capture the midshipman, for when the latter emphasized his
commands by pulling his six-shooter from
under his leg and raising and lowering the
hammer with one hand, keeping the muzzle
pointed toward the steward's head all the

while, the latter grew as white as a sheet and trembled in every limb. After he thought he had inflicted sufficient torture upon the timid fellow, the Confederate put up his weapon and demanded:

"What State are you from?"

"Massachusetts, sir."

"Are all Massachusetts men as great cowards as you are?"

"Certainly, sir," answered the steward, who was afraid to say anything else.

"Then we're going to have a walk-over, sure enough," said the rebel. "You Yankees are afraid to fight."

"Certainly, sir."

Every word of this conversation was overheard by a man who, but for a most unfortunate interruption, would have forced the Confederate officer to swallow his words almost as soon as they had left his lips. It was the skipper. He had come down from aloft and reached his cabin without being seen, and it was in obedience to his instructions that the prizemaster had been asked below to get some supper. His plan was to have the steward seat the

officer with his back to a certain state-room, so
that he could be seized from behind and choked
into submission before he knew that there was
a third party in the cabin; but that could not
be done now.   The rebel's suspicions led him
to change to the other side of the table, and he
now sat facing the state-room door, on whose
farther side stood the merchant captain with
rage in his heart and a cocked revolver in his
hand.   The captain knew that he was going to
put himself in danger when he attempted to
make a prisoner of the midshipman, but that
did not deter him.   When he heard that sweeping charge of cowardice made against the men
of his native State he could stand it no longer,
but jerked open the door and sprang into the
cabin.

Now came that unexpected interruption to
the skipper's plan of which we have spoken.
The steward heard the door of the state-room
creak softly behind him, and, knowing what
was coming, he made a quick jump to one side
to get out of the skipper's way and leave him
a clear field for his operations; but he was so
badly frightened that he hardly knew what he

was about, and consequently he did the very thing he tried to avoid. He sprang directly in front of his commander, and the two came together with such force that they measured their length on the cabin floor, the captain and his revolver being underneath. For one single instant the prize-master sat as motionless in his chair as if he had been turned into a block of wood; but it was for one instant only. He was quick to comprehend the situation, and equally quick to act. He sprang to his feet, and before either of the prostrate men could make a move he ran around the end of the table and covered them with his revolver.

"If you stir or utter a word I will shoot you as quickly as I would shoot a couple of dogs which disputed my right to use the highway," said he, in tones that could not have been steadier if he had been ordering the boatswain's mate of the *Sumter* to pipe sweepers. "Captain, drop that revolver on the floor without moving your hand a hair's-breadth."

"Let go your own revolver," said a voice in his ear; and to his infinite amazement the Confederate suddenly found himself in a grasp

JACK GRAY RECAPTURES THE BRIG.

so strong that it not only rendered him incapable of action, but brought him to his knees in a second. One vise-like hand was fastened upon the back of his neck and the other upon his wrist, turning the muzzle of the revolver upward, so that it pointed toward the roof of the cabin.

This is what we referred to when we stated that if it had not been for Jack Gray's courage and prompt action, it is probable that the brig would never have been recaptured. When the midshipman jumped from his chair and ran around the table, he turned his back toward the companion-way; and the moment he did so, Jack Gray, who saw that the critical time had come and that the next few seconds would decide who were to be masters of the brig, made a spring for the ladder. As he was in his stocking feet his movements were noiseless, and so rapid, too, that he had the Confederate prize-master in his grasp before the latter was fairly done speaking. Then he was powerless, for the second mate had a grip that few who knew him cared to contend against.

"Didn't you have the revolver you took

from the captured sailor in your pocket?" inquired Marcy, when Jack reached this point in his story.

"I did, but I didn't think it best to depend upon it, for this reason: Although the midshipman wasn't much to look at, he had showed himself to be possessed of any amount of pluck, and I was afraid that even if I succeeded in getting the drop on him he might shoot any way, for the double purpose of disabling me and calling his men to his assistance. So I made all haste to get a hold on him."

"Now that I think of it," continued Marcy, who was deeply interested in the narrative, "why did Captain Semmes keep the *Herndon* in tow when he cast off the *Sabine?* Why didn't he let both vessels go?"

"I have never been able to account for that except upon the supposition that he had more confidence in our prize-master than he had in the one he put aboard the *Herndon*," replied sailor Jack. "The *Herndon* was a heavy vessel, and had a much larger crew than we had; and perhaps that had something to do with it. I think we taught Semmes a lesson he will re-

member. I don't believe he will ever again
trust a Yankee prize and a Yankee crew out of
reach of his big guns."

The master of the brig and his frightened
steward got upon their feet as soon as they
could, and found that the Confederate officer
had been secured beyond all possibility of escape. The second mate had twisted his revolver from his grasp; Smith, the man to whom
Jack had given the captured musket, was holding a bayonet close to his nose, and another
sailor was threatening him with a handspike.

"Did you really think that nine Yankee
sailors would permit five traitors to work their
sweet will on them?" demanded the skipper,
as he let down the hammer of the officer's revolver and dropped the weapon into his own
pocket. "I think you will learn to your cost
that you have been very much mistaken in
the opinions you have formed of Northern
people. I shall have to ask you to go into my
state-room and remain there, leaving the door
open. Smith, stay here and watch him, while
the rest of us go on deck, and attend to the
other four."

"There are but three left, Captain," observed Jack. "One is already a prisoner, and Stebbins is keeping guard over him."

At that moment a body of men marched aft from the forecastle, came to a halt at the top of the ladder, and a hoarse voice hailed the cabin. It was the voice of the first mate.

"Tumble up, Cap'n," said the officer. "We've got the rest of 'em hard and fast. Tumble up and take command of your ship. She's your'n once more."

That was the most gratifying piece of news Jack Gray had ever heard.

CHAPTER X.

A COOL PROPOSITION.

ALTHOUGH the captain and Jack had not spoken to the first mate since the brig was captured, except it was in the presence of some member of the prize-crew, they had scowled and winked at him as often as the opportunity was presented, and the mate knew well enough what they meant by it and what they intended to do. He determined to do his part. He managed to exchange a few words with some of the brig's crew, whom he instructed to stand by him and be ready to lend a hand when the time came. He saw Jack make the first capture, with Smith's aid and Stebbins's, and by adroitly engaging the other three members of the prize-crew in conversation, it is probable that he kept them from taking note of what was going on in the waist. When he saw Jack make a rush for the companion-ladder, he seized the nearest Confederate, his men quickly overpowered the other two, and then he marched aft to tell his captain the good news. It was all done in less than two minutes, and Captain Semmes was none the wiser for it. The surprise was complete. There was not a shot fired, and the movements of the Yankee sailors were so rapid that resistance was useless.

"You've got the brig all to yourself again, Cap'n," said the mate. "What shall I do with these varmints?"

"Send them down here," was the reply. "And tell Stebbins to send his man down also."

As the four prisoners filed into the cabin, Jack was rather surprised to see that they did not appear to be at all cast down by the sudden and unexpected turn affairs had taken. Indeed, one of them, who spoke with a rich Irish brogue, boldly declared:

"Sure it's not mesilf that cares at all, at all. I've had enough of the bloody hooker."

"Have a care," whispered Jack, nudging him in the ribs with his elbow. "Your commanding officer is in that state-room. He can hear every word you say."

"Sorry a wan of me cares whether he can or not," replied the sailor. "We were promised big wages and prize-money by the bushel if we would help capture the Yankee ships on the high seas. We've took two prizes besides this wan, and the *Herndon*, but we put the torch to thim, and niver a cint of prize-money is there forninst the name of Paddy Scanlan on the books."

"Well, Paddy," said the captain, with a laugh, "you may abuse the rebels all you please, and no one aboard my vessel will say a thing to you. Now, will you give your word of honor that you will behave yourselves as long as you stay aboard of me?"

"Sure I will," replied the sailor earnestly.

"I mean all of you rebels," said the captain. "You treated us very civilly while we were your prisoners, and I want to treat you in the same way if you will let me. Let's have your promise."

It was given without a moment's hesitation, and was to the effect that as long as they re-

mained on the *Sabine* they would make no dis-
turbance, but would in all respects conduct
themselves with as much propriety as though
they had been regularly shipped as members
of her crew.

"As long as you stand to that agreement I
will allow you the liberty of the deck, beginning to-morrow morning," said the captain.
"But I tell you plainly that if you go back
from your word, I will have you in irons before
you know what is the matter with you. Smith,
stand at the foot of the ladder until you are
relieved. On deck the rest of us!"

Never had the *Sabine's* crew worked harder
than they did on this particular night to bring
their vessel about and get her on her course
again ; but this time the skipper did not intend
to make for the port to which his cargo was
consigned. He told his mates that as soon as
the brig rounded the western end of the island
of Cuba, he would fill away for Key West,
which was the nearest Federal naval station.

"I won't trust myself and my ship in these
waters an hour longer than I am obliged to,"
he declared. "How do I know but that there

may be a dozen or more vessels like the *Sumter* cruising about here, watching their chance to make bonfires of the defenseless merchant vessels? Now let this be a standing order: While we are under way we'll not speak a single ship, no matter what flag she floats. If you see a sail, run away from it.''

"And strict obedience to that order saved our bacon,'' said Jack, in conclusion. '' We got up to Key West without any mishap, turned our prisoners over to the commandant of the station, and then filled away for Boston, taking with us a cargo that ought to have gone another way. We were warned to look out for little privateers—sailing vessels with one or two guns aboard—and the navy fellows told us that the coasts of North and South Carolina were particularly dangerous; but our brig was a grayhound, the captain had the fullest confidence in her, and so he held his course. But we kept a bright lookout night and day, and were almost worn out with watching by the time we reached our home port.''

"You didn't see anything of those privateers, did you?'' said Mrs. Gray.

"Yes; we sighted one somewhere in the latitude of Sandy Point," answered Jack. "She fired a couple of shells at us, and tried to lay herself across our course; but she couldn't make it. We ran away from her as if she had been anchored."

"What sort of a looking craft was she?" exclaimed Marcy, starting up in his chair.

"Well, she was a fore-and-after and had figures painted on her sails to make us believe that she was a pilot boat," answered Jack, somewhat surprised at his brother's earnestness. "But she was about four times too big for a pilot boat. She hoisted Union colors, and when she found that she could not decoy us within range that way, she ran up the secession rag and cut loose with her bow-chaser; but she might as well have saved her ammunition, for she didn't come anywhere near us."

"And neither did the rifle-shots that you fired in return come anywhere near us," added Marcy.

"Anywhere near you?" exclaimed Jack, starting up in his turn. "What do you mean? What do you know about it?"

"I know all about it, for I was there," replied Marcy. "It was I who ran up those
flags, and although I didn't dream that you
were on the brig, you can't imagine how delighted I was when I saw that she was bound
to give us the slip. That privateer was Captain Beardsley's schooner, and I was aboard of
her in the capacity of pilot."

Sailor Jack settled back in his chair as if to
say that *that* was the most astounding thing
he had ever heard in his life.

"*Pilot!*" he exclaimed, at length. "Lon
Beardsley doesn't need a pilot on this coast.
He has smuggled more than one cargo of
cigars through these inlets."

"I know that. But you are aware that
Beardsley has been our enemy for years. He
couldn't find any way to take revenge until
this war broke out, and then he began troub-
ling us. He knew, and he knows to-day, that I
am Union all over, and down on secession and
all who favor it, and when he offered me the
pilot's berth and promised to do the fair thing
by me, he was in hopes that mother would refuse to let me go ; then, don't you see, he

15

would have had an excuse to set our rebel neighbors against us on the ground that we were traitors to our State."

"I always knew that Lon Beardsley was beneath contempt, but this rather gets ahead of me," said Jack hotly.

"But it so happened that we saw through his little game. Mother never said a word, and I shipped as pilot aboard the privateer *Osprey*," continued Marcy. "And, Jack (here he got up, moved his chair close to the sofa on which his brother was sitting and lowered his voice to a whisper), I was on her when she made her first and only capture, and upstairs in my valise I have seventeen hundred dollars in gold, my share of the money the *Mary Hollins* brought when she was condemned and sold in the port of Newbern."

"That would be a nice little sum of money if it had been earned in an honorable way," observed Jack.

"But it wasn't," said Marcy, "and consequently I don't intend to keep it. I'm going to give it back to the one to whom it belongs. Oh, you needn't laugh. I mean it!"

"I know you do, and I hope that you will some day find the man ; but I am afraid you won't.   Where is Beardsley now ? "

"I left him at Newbern.   The presence of the cruisers on the coast frightened him so that he gave up privateering—he didn't want to run the risk of being captured with guns aboard of him for fear that he might be treated as a pirate—and took to running the blockade. We made one successful trip, taking out cotton and bringing back an assorted cargo worth somewhere in the neighborhood of a hundred thousand dollars, and it was while we were trying to make Crooked Inlet on our way home that we came the nearest to being captured. We ran foul of a howitzer launch, which turned loose on us with shrapnel and canister, and gave me this broken arm and Beardsley a black and blue shoulder."

"I wish from the bottom of my heart that she had given him a broken head," said Jack. " Were you much hurt ? "

"I don't mind it in the least," answered Marcy.   " It has given me a chance to visit with mother and you.   But I don't quite understand why you came home as you did. What made you so sly about it? Go more into particulars, but don't talk too loud."

"Is it a fact that you are afraid to converse in ordinary tones in your own house?" said Jack, looking inquiringly at his mother.

"Marcy and I have been very cautious, for we don't know whom to trust," answered Mrs. Gray. "One of our principal sources of anxiety is the money we have hidden in the cellar wall——"

"Thirty thousand dollars!" whispered Marcy in his brother's ear. "Mother brought it home herself and spent three nights in fixing a place for it."

"Holy Moses!" said Jack under his breath. "Do the neighbors know it?"

"They suspect it, and that is what troubles us."

"I don't wonder at it. Why, mother, there are plenty of white trash about here who would rob you in a minute if they thought they could do it without bringing harm to themselves. I declare, I am almost afraid to leave home again."

"Oh, Jack!" said his mother, the tears starting to her eyes; "you surely will not leave me again."

"Not if you bid me stay, but I didn't think you would do it, knowing, as I did, that you are strong for the Union. That was the reason I came home in the night and threw stones at Marcy's window. I intended, after a short visit, to show my love for the old flag by making my way out to the blockading fleet, and shipping with the first commander who would take me. Consequently, I did not want to let any of the neighbors know that I came home at all. I was sure that there must be some Union people here, but of course I don't know who they are any more than I know who the rebels are; so I thought it best to keep my movements a secret. However, I might as well have saved myself the trouble," added Jack, while an expression of anxiety settled upon his bronzed features; "of course I can't keep out of sight of the servants, and if there are any treacherous ones among them, as you seem to think, they will blab on me to the first rebel they can find."

"They will tell the overseer of it," said Marcy. "He's a sneak and a spy as well as a rebel."

" Why do you keep him, then ? " demanded Jack. " Why didn't you kick him off the place as soon as you found out that he could not be trusted ? "

"I hired him for a year," answered Mrs. Gray. "And if I should discharge him on account of his political opinions, can you not see that I would give the rebels in the settlement the very opportunity that I believe they are waiting for—the opportunity to persecute me ? "

"Perhaps there is something in that," said Jack thoughtfully. " I must say that this is a nice way to live. But the Confederates can't say a word against you now, because Marcy sails under their flag."

" If anybody tells you that story don't you believe a word of it," said Marcy. "They know why I went aboard that privateer as well as if I had told them all about it. But, Jack, what did you mean when you told me that you were a homeless, friendless smuggler ? "

" I am not exactly homeless and friendless," replied the sailor, with a hearty laugh, "but it is a fact that I am a smuggler in a small way. When I found myself safe in Boston, the first thing I thought of was getting home. I first decided I would go to Washington and try to get a pass through the Union lines ; but I soon found that that wouldn't do, for I saw by the papers that the Federals were straining every nerve to close the Potomac against smugglers and mail-carriers, and that satisfied me that no passes were granted. My only hope then was to get here by water. I met my captain every day or two, and he helped me out by securing me a berth on the schooner, *West Wind*. He never said a word to me about the character of the vessel, although he must have known all about it and given me a good recommend besides, for the day after I went aboard, Captain Frazier called me into his cabin, and took me into his confidence.

" I thought the master of the *Sabine* was a strong Union man," said Marcy. "But this looks as though he was giving aid and comfort to the rebels."

"Well, no; he didn't mean it that way. He was giving aid and comfort to *me*, don't you see? He wanted to help me get home, and I assure you I was glad of the chance he gave me. Captain Frazier was an old friend of his. He happened to find out that Frazier was about to turn an honest penny by selling the Confederates medicine and other little things of which they stood in need, and instead of betraying him, he recommended me as a suitable man for second mate, for I was a tolerable sailor, and well acquainted with the coasts of the Carolinas. I accepted the position when it was offered me, and brought the *West Wind* through Oregon Inlet as slick as you please, although the channel doesn't run within a hundred yards of where it did the last time I went through there."

"Did you take out a venture?"

"Of course. I risked about two-thirds of my hard-earned wages."

"What did you buy?"

"Quinine, calomel, and about half a dozen different kinds of quack medicines in the shape of pills and tonics. But there was where I made a mistake. I ought to have put all the money in quinine. If I had, I would have made two or three hundred dollars more than I did. As it was I cleared about twelve hundred. And that reminds me that I left my grip-sack on the gallery."

He and Marcy went out to bring it in, and when they returned, Jack was slapping the side of the valise to make the gold pieces jingle.

"My son, I am very sorry you did it," said Mrs. Gray reproachfully. "Very sorry indeed."

"Why, mother, just listen to this," replied Jack, hitting the valise another sounding whack.

"I hear it," said his mother. "But when you brought those things down here and piloted that vessel through the blockade, didn't you violate the laws of your country? Did you not render yourself liable to arrest and imprisonment?"

"Well, to be honest, I did; but you see I was looking into the future. When I reached Newbern I wasn't home by a long shot.

There's a right smart stretch of country between that place and this. I walked nearly every step of the way from Boydtown, and every man I met was the hottest kind of a rebel, or professed to be. When questioned, as I often was, I could tell a truthful story about being second mate of a schooner that had slipped into Newbern with a lot of goods for the Confederacy, and furthermore, I had the documents to prove it," said Jack, drawing an official envelope from an inside pocket. "This is a strong letter from the captain of the *West Wind*, recommending me to any blockade-running shipmaster who may be in need of a coast pilot and second mate; but I never expect to use it. Here are some documents of an entirely different character," and as he said this, the sailor thrust his hand into the leg of his boot and pulled forth another large envelope. "This contains two letters, one from the master of the *Sabine*, and the other from her owners ; and they give a flattering history of the part I took in recapturing the brig. These letters may be of use to me when the time comes for me to ship on a blockader."

"I don't see how you got out of Boston with your contraband cargo," said Marcy. "How did you clear at the custom house?"

"Why, bless you, our cargo was all right," replied Jack, "and so were our papers. The cargo was brought aboard in broad daylight, and consigned to a well-known American firm in Havana; but the little articles that were brought aboard after dark and scattered around among the barrels and boxes in the hold, would have sent the last one of us to jail if they had been discovered."

"Oh, Jack!" exclaimed Mrs. Gray, "how could you do it? I can't see how you could bring yourself to take so much risk."

"I did it to keep up appearances; and hasn't Marcy done the same thing and with your consent? Didn't he join that privateer and run the risk of being captured or killed by the Yankees because you and he thought it policy for him to do so? I am not a policy man, but in times like these one can't always do as he wants to."

There were so many things to talk about, and such a multitude of questions to be asked and answered on both sides, that the little clock on the mantel struck four different hours before any one thought of going to bed; and then Jack did not go to his own room, but passed the rest of the night with Marcy, for the latter hinted very strongly that he had some things to say to him that he did not care to mention in his mother's presence.

"She has enough to bother her already," said he, as he closed and locked the door of his room ; "and although I have no secrets from her, I don't like to speak to her on disagreeable subjects. I wish she could forget that money in the cellar wall and the hints Wat Gifford gave her about 'longshoremen coming up here from Plymouth some dark night to steal it."

Sailor Jack, who was standing in front of the bureau putting away his letters of recommendation and the canvas bag that contained his money, turned quickly about and looked at his brother without speaking.

"Of course I don't know that such a thing will ever happen," continued Marcy, "but I do know for a fact that Beardsley and a few others are very anxious to find out whether or

not there are any funds in the house. Beardsley tried his level best to pump me, and Colonel
Shelby sent that trifling Kelsey up here for the
same purpose. Now what difference does it
make to them whether mother has money or not,
unless they mean to try to take it from her?"

"Marcy," said Jack, who had backed into
the nearest chair, "I wish that money was a
thousand miles from here. You haven't anything to fear from those wharf-rats at Plymouth; but if the Confederate authorities find
out about it, and can scrape together evidence
enough to satisfy them that mother is Union,
they'll come down on this house like a night-
hawk on a June bug. And, worse than that,
Beardsley may contrive to have mother put
under arrest."

"No!" gasped Marcy. "What for?"

"Don't you know that the Richmond Government has instructed its loyal subjects to
repudiate the debts they owe to Northern men
and to turn the amount of those debts into the
Confederate treasury?"

"Well, what of it? We don't owe anybody
a red cent."

"No odds. If Beardsley wants evidence to prove that we *do* owe some Northern house for the supplies we have been receiving, and that we are holding back the money instead of giving it to the Confederacy—if Beardsley needs evidence to prove all that he can easily find it."

"Why, the—the villain!" exclaimed Marcy, who had never been more astounded.

"He's worse than that, and he'll do worse than that if he sees half a chance," said Jack, with a sigh. "I wish the Yankees might get hold of him, and that some one would tell them who and what he is, for I judge from what you have told me that he is at the bottom of all mother's troubles. Now, let me tell you: you must stay at home and take care of mother, and I will ship on a war vessel and do my share toward putting down this rebellion."

"But how can I stay at home?" interrupted Marcy. "My leave is for only ninety days, and Beardsley looks for me to join the schooner as soon as my arm gets well."

"All right. No doubt you will have to do it; but you'll not make many more trips on that blockade-runner. It'll not be long before all our ports will be sealed up tight as a brick by swift steamers, and sailing vessels will stand no show of getting out or in. I know Lon Beardsley, and he will quit blockade running when he thinks it's time, the same as he quit privateering. Why, Marcy, you can't imagine what an uproar there is all over the North. They're getting ready to give the South particular fits."

"Then the result of the fight at Bull Run didn't frighten or discourage them ?"

"Man alive, if you had had as much to do with Northern people as I have, you would know that they don't understand the words. They've got their blood up at last, and now they mean business. Recruits are coming in faster than they can equip and send them off. And I can't stay behind. Mother must let me go."

"Do you think of enlisting on one of the blockading fleet ?"

"I do."

"But how are you going to get to it ? It's off Hatteras."

"So I supposed. Where's the *Fairy Belle?*"

"Great Scott!" ejaculated Marcy. "Do you expect me to take you out on her?"

"Well, yes; I had rather calculated on it."

Marcy was profoundly astonished. He threw himself upon the bed, propped his head up with his uninjured hand, and looked at his brother without saying a word.

CHAPTER XI.

"YOU seem to be very much surprised at a very simple proposition," said Jack, at length.

"And you seem to have a deal more cheek than you did the first time I made your acquaintance," replied Marcy.

Jack laughed heartily.

"Why, what is there to hinder you from taking me down to the fleet?" he demanded. "Haven't I often heard you boast of the *Fairy Belle's* sea-going qualities? If she can cross the Atlantic, as you have more than once declared, she can surely ride out any blow we are likely to meet off the Cape."

"Oh, she can get there easy enough," answered Marcy. "I was not thinking about that. But suppose I take you down to the fleet and the Yankees won't let me come back? Then what?"

16   241

"Nonsense!" exclaimed Jack. "They'll let you come back. They are not obliged to force men into the service against their will. They've got more than they want."

"But there's another thing," continued Marcy. "There are two forts at the Inlet; and suppose some of the rebels in those forts should see a little schooner communicating with one of the blockading fleet. Wouldn't they take pains to find out where the schooner belonged, and who her owner was? And then what would they do to me?"

"They would put you in jail, of course," replied Jack, with refreshing candor. "But I take it for granted that you are sharp enough to go and come without being seen by anybody. If you magnify the dangers of the undertaking by holding back or raising objections to the programme I have laid out, I am afraid you will frighten mother into saying that I can't go."

"I'll neither hold back nor object," said Marcy resolutely. "When you are ready to go say the word, and I will do the best I can for you."

"I knew you would. Now let's lie down for a while. I have tramped it all the way from Boydtown since daylight, and am pretty well tuckered out."

"If you had telegraphed to Nashville, I would have met you with a carriage," said Marcy.

"Of course. But I thought I would rather have a talk with you and mother before I let any one know I was in the country. And now that I have got here and had the talk— what would you do if you were in my place? Keep out of sight?"

"No, I wouldn't. What good would it do as long as the servants know you are here? Make it a point to say ' hallo ' to all the neighbors, talk politics with them, and tell them how you ran that schooner into Newbern through Oregon Inlet. By the way, what was done with the cargo that was intended for that house in Havana?"

" It wasn't intended for Havana. It was sold in Newbern, as the owners meant it should be, and when I left, the *West Wind* was loading up with cotton for Nassau. Well, suppose I play that I am as good a Confederate as any of the people hereabouts ; what then ? When I leave for the blockading fleet they will want to know where I have gone, won't they ? And what will you say to them ? We must think about that and cook up some sort of a story on purpose for them.''

The boys tumbled into bed while they were talking, but it was a long time before Marcy could go to sleep. He shuddered every time he thought of what the consequences would be if by any misfortune it became known in the settlement, that Jack Gray, whom everybody took to be a good Confederate, and who had been permitted, while at home, to go and come as he pleased, had seized the first opportunity to go down to Hatteras and ship on board a Union gunboat.

''This house would be in ashes in less than twenty-four hours after the news got noised about in the neighborhood,'' said Marcy, to himself, wishing that the sound sleep that so promptly came to his weary brother might come to him, also ! ''Then I should learn by experience how it seems to live in a negro cabin. But there's one consolation. They couldn't burn the cellar walls, so mother's money would be safe."

The clock struck nine before the boys got up that morning, but there was a hot breakfast waiting for them. A family council was held while they were seated at the table, during which it was decided that the only course for Jack to pursue while at home was to do as he always had done—go about the settlement as though he had a perfect right to be there (as indeed he had), and act and talk as though such a thing as war had never been heard of. If political questions were forced upon him, he could tell of his voyage on the *West Wind*, and show Captain Frazier's letter ; but he must be careful not to say anything about his short captivity in the hands of the *Sumter's* men. Accordingly, when Marcy's filly was brought to the door after breakfast, there was another horse brought with her for Jack's use. The coachman, who had been so soundly rated the day before, came also, for the two-fold purpose of making his peace with Marcy and welcoming the returned sailor.

"Sarvent, Marse Marcy. Sarvent, Marse Jack," said he, dropping his hat upon the ground and extending a hand to each of the boys. "So glad to have you back, Marse Jack, and so proud to know that you wasn't took prisoner by that pirate Semmes. We saw by the papers that he run out on the high seas las' month, and I was mighty jubus that you might run onto him. Glad to see you among us again, safe and sound, sar."

"And Morris, I am very glad to see myself here," replied Jack, giving the black man's hand a hearty shake. "So you take the papers, do you?"

"Well, no sar; I don't take 'em, but the Missus does, and she tells me what's into 'em, sar."

"I don't know that it makes any difference how you get the news so long as you get it. But I am rather surprised to see you on the plantation. I thought that of course you had run away and joined the Yankees before this time. You had better dig out, for you are an Abolitionist, and they hang Abolitionists in this country."

"Now, Marse Jack, I don't like for to have you talk to me that a way," said the coachman in a tone of reproach. "All the other niggers may go if they want to, but Morris stays right here on the place. He does for a fac'. Who going to drive the carriage if Morris runs away."

"Well, that's so," replied Jack, gathering up the reins and placing his foot in the stirrup. "I didn't think of that. Help Marcy into his saddle and then tell me what I shall bring you when I come from town—a plug of store tobacco for yourself, and a big red handkerchief for Aunt Mandy?"

"Thank you kindly, Marse Jack," said the coachman, with a pleased laugh. "You always thinking of we black ones."

"Yes; I have thought of them a good many times during the two years and better that I have been knocking around the world," said Jack, as he and his brother rode out of the yard. "Especially did I think of home when the brig was dismasted by a tornado in the South Atlantic. We came as near going to the bottom that time as we could without going, and I promised myself that if I ever again got a foothold on solid ground, I would keep it; but here I am thinking of going to sea once more, as soon as I have had a visit with you and mother."

"I can't bear to think of it," said Marcy.

"I'd like to stay at home, but these fanatics who are trying to break up the government won't let me," answered the sailor. "Now that you have had a chance to sleep on it, what do you think of the proposition I made you last night?"

"About taking you down to the blockading fleet at the Cape?" inquired Marcy. "Well, if you are bound to go, I don't see that there is anything else you can do. Of course I shall do all I can to help you, and if there was some trustworthy person to look out for mother, I would go too; but I should go into the army."

"Of course. Your training at Barrington has fitted you for that, and you would be out of place on board ship. What color is the hull of the *Fairy Belle?*"

"It's black," replied Marcy, catching at the idea. "But it wouldn't take you and me long to make it some other color. That is what Beardsley did when he turned his privateer into a blockade-runner."

"And that is what we will do with your little schooner—we will disguise her," said Jack, "and by the time we get through with her, her best friends won't recognize her. More than that, if we have to run within spyglass reach of the forts at the Inlet, we'll hoist the rebel flag with the Stars and Stripes above it, to make the Confederates think that she has been captured by the Yankees."

"But we haven't any rebel flag," said Marcy.

"What's the reason we haven't? When the *Sumter's* boarding officer told our captain that we were a prize to the Confederate steamer, he hauled our colors down, and ran his own up in their place; and they were there when we took the vessel out of the hands of the prize-crew. I jerked it down myself, said nothing to nobody, and brought it home as a trophy. It's in my valise now. When we return from town I intend to stick it up in the sitting-room where every one can see it."

"You do?" exclaimed Marcy. "Mother won't let you."

"Oh, I think she will," said Jack, with a laugh. "She will know why it is put on the wall, and so will you. Every time you two look at it, you will think of the part I played in turning the tables on Semmes and his prize-crew; but the visitors who come to the house on purpose to wheedle mother into saying something for the Union and against the Confederacy, will think they are barking up the wrong tree, and that the Gray family are secesh sure enough."

"I hope they will, but I don't believe it," answered Marcy. "When you join the blockading fleet and the neighbors ask me where you are, what shall I tell them?"

"That's a question I will answer after I have been here long enough to get my bearings," said Jack. "Did you remark that you would have to stop at Beardsley's? Well, here we are."

The rapidity with which news of all sorts traveled from one plantation to another, before and during the war, was surprising. Among the letters that Marcy Gray had been commissioned to deliver was one addressed to Captain Beardsley's grown-up daughter, and the girl was waiting for them when they rode into the yard and drew rein at the foot of the steps.

"Morning, gentlemen," was the way in which she greeted the two boys. "I was dreadful frightened when I heard that the Yankees had run onto you, and that you had got your arm broke, Mister Marcy. But it seems paw was into the same boat. Was he much hurted? Hope your venture in quinine paid you well, Mister Jack. You done yourself proud by running that schooner into Newbern with all them supplies aboard, but you oughter stayed with her and helped her through the blockade."

"Oh, the skipper will find plenty of pilots in Newbern," replied Jack, who was not a little astonished to learn that the news of his return had already got abroad in the settlement. "If I can't ship on something better than a blockade-runner, I will stay ashore."

"But they do say there's a power of money in it," said the girl. "Is that a fact, Marcy?

Paw must have got safe out and back from Nassau, or else you wouldn't be here now. Did he make much, do you reckon?"

"I believe he calculated on clearing about twenty-five thousand dollars," answered Marcy, who was looking over the package of letters he had taken from his pocket.

"I say!" exclaimed the girl, fairly dancing with delight. "If paw made that much he must get me the new dress I want, and that's a word with a bark onto it. That letter for me? Sarvent, sar. Good-bye."

"I don't see why Beardsley went to the trouble of writing to her," said Jack, as the two turned about and rode away. "She can't read a word of it."

"And I am very glad she can't," answered Marcy. "She will take it to old Mrs. Brown, most likely, and if she does, she might as well stick it up in the post-office. Mrs. Brown is a regular built gossip, and if there is anything in the letter about me, as I think there is, I shall be sure to hear of it. But don't it beat you how things get around? Just see how much that girl knows; and I haven't been out of the house since I came home yesterday afternoon. I tell you there are spies all about us. Don't trust any one you may meet in town. Tell just the story you want published, and nothing else. And don't forget that before you sleep to-night I want you to bury seventeen hundred dollars for me. You've got two good hands."

"Marcy, I am almost afraid to do it," replied Jack. "Suppose some one should watch us and dig it up as soon as we went away?"

"We'll take Bose with us for a sentry, and slip out of the house after everybody else has gone to bed. We'll take all the precautions we can think of and trust to luck. There's Nashville; now be as big a rebel as you please. I know they'll not believe a word of it, but that won't be your fault."

As Marcy expected, the first one to rush out of the post-office and greet them, as they were hitching their horses, was young Allison. He gave the sailor's hand a hearty shake, and then he turned to Marcy.

"Really, I am surprised to see you here,

and in citizen's clothes, too," said the latter. "I should have thought that your zeal for the Confederacy would have taken you into the army long ago. Man alive, you're missing heaps of fun. Look at my arm. I've suffered for the cause and you haven't." ["And, what's more to the point, you don't mean to," added Marcy to himself.]

"It's fun to have a broken arm, is it?" exclaimed Allison. "I can't see it in that light. The reason I haven't enlisted is because I thought that perhaps you would bring me a favorable word from Captain Beardsley. Did you speak to him about taking me as one of his crew?"

"I did, before I had been aboard the schooner half an hour."

"And what did he say?"

"His reply was that he couldn't accept you. The crew is full; you know nothing about a vessel; he wants nothing but sailor-men aboard of him, and if you want to do something for the South, the best thing you can do is to go into the army."

"Well, I'd thank him to hold fast to his

advice until he is asked to give it," said Allison spitefully. "I'll not carry a musket; I can tell him that much. I have seen some fellows who were in the fight at Bull Run, and they say that the privates in our army are treated worse than dogs. If I could get a commission the case would be different."

"That's the idea," said Jack. "Why don't you pitch in and get one? Begin at the top of the ladder and not at the foot. Crawl in at the cabin windows and don't bother about the hawsehole. I mean—you see," added the sailor, seeing by the blank look on his face that Allison did not understand his nautical language, "aboard ship we take rank in this way: First the captain, then the mates, then the captain's dog, and lastly the foremast-hands. And I suppose it must be the same in the army."

"You don't mean it!" exclaimed Allison, opening his eyes.

"I do mean every word of it. Ask any seafaring man and he will tell you the same. Whatever you do, don't go before the mast—I mean don't go into the ranks. Get a commission and be a man among men." ["You'd look pretty with straps on your sholders, *you* would," said Jack mentally. "I'd like to gaze upon the man who would be foolish enough to put himself under your orders."]

"Don't go into the office yet," said Allison, when the boys turned about as if to move away. "There's a crowd in there, and I want you to stay and talk to me. Tell me how you got wounded, Marcy."

"Let Jack tell you how he piloted that Yankee schooner into the port of Newbern with a cargo of supplies for the Confederacy," replied Marcy. He said this with an object in view; and that object was to find out how much Allison knew about Jack's movements and his own. Consequently, after his interview with Captain Beardsley's daughter, he was not greatly surprised to hear Allison say :

"Jack hasn't much to tell, has he? As I heard the story he had no trouble at all in bringing the schooner through—he didn't even see the smoke of a blockader. But there's one thing about it," he added, in a lower tone, "you boys have shut up the mouths of some talkative people around here who have been trying hard to injure you, especially Marcy."

"Why should anybody want to injure me?" exclaimed Marcy, looking astonished. "I don't remember that I ever misused any one in the settlement."

"I never heard of it," continued Allison. "But they say that you are for the Union, and that the only reason you shipped on Beardsley's schooner was because you had to."

"Some people around here say that I am for the Union?" repeated Marcy, as though he had never heard of such a thing before. "And that I shipped because I had to?"

"That's what they say, sure's you're born; but your broken arm gives the lie to all such tales as that. And as for Jack—did he know that the *West Wind* was a smuggler when he joined her in Boston?"

"Of course he knew it," answered Marcy. "He brought out a venture and cleared twelve hundred dollars by it."

"Whew!" whistled Allison. "I wish I could make as much money as that; but

17

somehow such chances never come my way. But what is a venture, anyway?"

"It is a speculation that sailors sometimes go into on their own hook," replied Marcy. "For example, Captain Beardsley wanted me to invest my wages and prize-money in cotton, sell it in Nassau for more than double what I gave for it, put the proceeds into medicine and gun-caps, and so double my money again when we returned to Newbern. If I had taken his advice, I might have been four or five thousand dollars ahead of the hounds at this minute."

"You don't mean to say that you *didn't* act upon his advice?" exclaimed Allison.

"Yes; that's just what I mean to say. You see, we stood a fine chance of being captured by the Yankees, and Beardsley was so very much afraid of it that he wouldn't load his vessel himself, but took out a cargo he obtained through a commission merchant. —I see Jack is going into the post-office, and we might as well go, too. If you hear anybody saying things behind my back that they don't want to say to my face, tell them to ride up to our house and look at the Confederate flag in our sitting-room, and then go somewhere and get shot before they take it upon themselves to talk about one who has risked his life while they were stopping safe at home.''

"I'll do it," said Allison, and Marcy was almost ready to believe that he meant what he said. "But are you really flying the Confederate colors? Every one says that your mother——"

"Yes, I know they do," said Marcy, when Allison paused and looked frightened. "They think she is for the Union, and have set some mean sneaks at work to get evidence against her; but you ride out to-morrow or the next day and take a look at that flag. How do you do?" he added, turning about to shake hands with Colonel Shelby and Mr. Dillon, who came up at that moment and greeted him with the greatest cordiality.

"We were very sorry to hear of your misfortune," said the latter, "but you have the satisfaction of knowing that you have suffered in a righteous cause. Did Captain Beardsley send any word to either of us?"

"No, sir; but he sent a letter to each of

you," answered the boy, thrusting his hand into his pocket. " And there they are. This other one is for the postmaster, and perhaps I had better go in and give it to him."

The Colonel and his friend were so very anxious to learn what Captain Beardsley had to say to them that they did not ask the wounded blockade-runner any questions, but drew off on one side to read their letters ; and this action on their part went far toward confirming Marcy's suspicions that these two men were the ones Beardsley had left ashore "to do his dirty work" while he was at sea. He was as certain as he could be, without positive proof, that those letters told of the unsuccessful attempts the captain had made at different times to find out whether or not there was any money hidden in Mrs. Gray's house. That money had been a constant source of trouble to the boy, but now he felt like yelling every time he thought of it. If their "secret enemies" took the course that sailor Jack was afraid they might take—if they told the Confederate authorities that Mrs. Gray, after repudiating her debts to Northern merchants (debts that she never owed), had concealed the money instead of turning it into the Confederate treasury as the law provided, then there would be trouble indeed.

When Marcy and Allison went into the post-office they found Jack surrounded by an interested group of old-time friends, to whom he was giving a humorous account of Captain Beardsley's unsuccessful effort to capture the vessel to which he belonged.

"It happened right here on our own coast," said Jack. "She first tried to fool us by showing the figures that were painted on her sails ; but that wouldn't go down with our old man. Then she hoisted the English colors, but that made us sheer still farther away from her ; for what would a pilot-boat be doing in these waters with a foreign flag at her peak? Then she cut loose on us with her bow gun, and we yelled and shot back with sporting rifles. What do you think of a fellow who will try his best to bring trouble to his only brother by showing a friendly flag, and then shoot cannons at him when he finds he can't do it? That's the way Marcy served me, and more than that, he had the face to tell me of it when I came home last night."

Of course this raised a laugh at Marcy's expense, but he didn't seem to mind it. He gave the postmaster Captain Beardsley's letter and asked for the mail in his mother's box.

"And of course when the brig escaped you yelled as loudly as any Yankee in the crew," observed one of his auditors. "I suppose you had to in order to keep out of trouble."

"But I don't reckon he'll do it again in a hurry," said another. "When he brought that Yankee schooner into Newbern he proved to my satisfaction that he is as good a Confederate as any man in the State. Why didn't you stay with her, Jack, and make yourself rich by running the blockade?"

"I had two reasons," answered the sailor. "In the first place I wanted to come home for awhile ; and in the next, there is too much danger these times in cruising about on an unarmed vessel. The next time I ship it will be aboard of something that can fight."

"Did you hear any talk of an ironclad that is

being built in the river a few miles above Newbern?" asked a third.

Jack winked first one eye and then the
other, looked sharply into the face of each
member of the group around him, and then
turned about and softly rapped the counter
with his riding-whip.

"You needn't be afraid to speak freely,"
said the postmaster, who knew what the sailor
meant by this pantomime. "There isn't a
traitor within the hearing of your voice. We
are all true blue."

"One can't be too careful in times like
these," replied Jack, turning around again and
facing the crowd. "After I have been among
you awhile, I shall know who my friends are.
I did hear some talk of a heavy vessel that is
to be added to the defensive force of the city,
and which might some time go outside and
scatter the blockading fleet, but I didn't go up
to take a look at her. I couldn't spare the
time. She'll need a crew when she is com-
pleted, and if I leave the settlement between two
days—if I am here to-night and gone to-morrow
morning—my friends needn't worry over me."

"We understand. You'll be on board an armed vessel fighting for your principles."

"You're right I will. Now, George," he added, turning to the clerk and slamming his saddle-bags upon the counter, "I want one of those pockets filled with plug tobacco, and the other stuffed with the gaudiest bandanas you've got in the store."

The clerk took the saddle-bags, and when they were passed back to their owner a few minutes later, they were so full that it was a matter of some difficulty to buckle the flaps. Then the boys said good-bye and left the store. They started off in a lope, but when they were a mile or so from the town and alone on the road, they drew their horses down to a walk, and Jack said:

"Do they take me for one of them or not?"

"They pretend to, but everybody is so sly and treacherous that you can't place reliance upon anything," answered his brother. "What you said about leaving home between two days was good. It will help me, for I can refer to it when you are gone. Now, Jack, you must put up that rebel flag the minute you get home. I told Allison about it, and if he should ride out some day and find the flag wasn't there, he would suspect that we are not just the sort of folks he has been led to believe."

"All right! And our next hard work must be to hide your money and paint that schooner of yours. We'll go about it openly and above board. We'll say she is scaling,—if she isn't she ought to be, for it is a long time since she saw a brush,—and that she needs another coat of paint to protect her from the weather."

This programme was duly carried out. Of course Mrs. Gray protested, mildly, when Jack brought down his rebel flag, and, after spreading it upon the floor so that his mother could have a good view of it, proceeded to hang it upon the sitting-room wall; but when the boys told her why they thought it best to place it there, she became silent and permitted them to do as they pleased. While they were putting the trophy in position, Jack found opportunity to whisper to his brother:

"Now, if any of our officious neighbors give the Confederate officers a hint that mother is

keeping back money that she ought to turn
into the treasury, and they come here to
search the house, they'll take a look at this
flag and go away without touching a thing.
Mark what I tell you."

"But suppose the Yankees come here and
take a look at it; then what?" whispered
Marcy, in reply.

"Well, that will be a black horse of another
color," said Jack. "They'll come here—
don't you lose any sleep worrying about that;
but when they come, you must see to it that
this flag is out of sight. I'll say one thing for
the rebels," he said aloud, turning his head
on one side and gazing critically at his prize,
"they've got good taste. I've seen the colors
of all civilized nations, and that flag right
there on the wall is the handsomest in the
world, save one."

"But think of the principles it represents,"
exclaimed Mrs. Gray. "Disunion and slavery."

"Of course," replied Jack. "But when
these fanatics have been soundly thrashed,
there will be no such things as disunion and

slavery. They will be buried out of sight. I was speaking of the rebel flag, which, next to our own, is the prettiest I ever saw. Their naval uniforms are handsome, too."

Of course it soon became known among the servants that there was a Confederate banner displayed upon the walls of the "great house," and those who came into the room turned the whites of their eyes at it and then looked at Marcy and Jack in utter astonishment. But the boys did not appear to notice them nor did they volunteer any explanation—not even when old Morris came in to satisfy himself that the astounding news he had heard was really true. The sight of the emblem, which he knew was upheld by men who were fighting for the sole purpose of keeping him and his race in bondage, struck him dumb, and he left the room as silently as he had entered it. In less than half an hour the news reached Hanson's ears, and that worthy, astonished and perplexed, waited impatiently for night to come so that he could ride into town and tell Colonel Shelby about it.

CHAPTER XII.

DURING the next three weeks Marcy Gray would have lived in a fever of suspense had it not been for the presence of courageous, happy-go-lucky sailor Jack. He could not for a moment forget the letters which, at Captain Beardsley's request, he had delivered to Colonel Shelby and the rest. Did they convey to those who received them the information that Beardsley no longer believed that there was money concealed in Mrs. Gray's house, or did they contain instructions concerning a new plot that was to be worked up against Marcy and his mother? The boys did not know, and never found out for certain what it was that the captain wrote in those letters. That night, after placing the captured Confederate flag upon the wall of the sitting-room, Jack turned the proceeds of the sale of his "venture" over to his mother, buried Marcy's prize money in one of the flower beds, and bright and early the next morning went to work to disguise the *Fairy Belle* so that "her own brother wouldn't know her." If the neighboring planters who visited them, and whom they visited in return, had any suspicion that the captured flag in the sitting-room did not express the political sentiments of the family, they said nothing to indicate it. Their life apparently was as quiet and peaceful as though such a thing as a slaveholders' rebellion had never been heard of; but one day it was broken up most unexpectedly, and young Allison was the first to tell them of it.

"Glorious victory of the Confederate arms," he shouted, jumping off the steps of the store in which the post-office was located, and running full tilt toward the place where Jack and Marcy were hitching their horses. "Didn't we always say the Northern people had no business alongside of us? The crowd in the post-office have cheered themselves hoarse, and you fellows ought to have been here to join in."

"Has there been another fight?" asked Jack. "Where did it take place and how much of a fight was it?"

"Well, you see," said Allison, "there hasn't exactly been any fight yet, but there's going to be if the cowardly Yankees will only give us a chance to get at them."

"Oh," said Jack, while an expression of disgust settled on his face. "Where is it going to come off and how do you happen to know so much about it?"

"Why, the authorities know all about it, and I suppose the papers got the information from them," replied Allison. "At any rate, there's a strong land and naval expedition being fitted out at Fortress Monroe, and it is coming down here to destroy forts Hatteras and Clark and block up Hatteras Inlet."

"And that expedition hasn't got here yet?"

"No. It's going to sail on Monday. We know all about it in spite of the efforts the Yankees have made to keep it secret."

"If the ships haven't even sailed yet, why do you raise such a row over a Confederate victory that is not won?" asked Jack.

"Oh, it's going to be won," said Allison confidently. "Everybody says so, and we thought we would begin to holler in time. What we are afraid of is, that old Hatteras will turn in and fight the battle for us by kicking up such a sea that the Yankee ships won't dare come near the Inlet. That would be bad for us, for of course if they keep beyond the range of our guns we can't sink them. Oh, they're bound to get a whipping if we can only get a chance to give it to them."

Although the Confederates boasted loudly of the strong fortifications which (so they said) had been thrown up everywhere along their coast, and even went so far as to warn the Federal government that the most powerful expedition that could be fitted out against these fortifications would be sure to meet with disaster, Marcy Gray was well aware that the coast was almost defenseless, because one of his papers, the Augusta *Chronicle and Sentinel*, was brave enough to tell the truth now and then. Only a few days before, this paper had called upon the government to provide for coast defense by "organizing and drilling infantry and guerrillas at home," so that there would be no need to call upon the Confederate President for troops. The same paper also stated that the Union naval officers knew the bays and inlets along the coast like a book from surveys in their possession, and if so disposed, there were many places where they might raid and do damage before they could be driven off. But events proved that the Union forces did not go down to the coast of the Carolinas just to give the Confederates the fun of driving them off. When once they got a foothold there they kept it, in spite of all the efforts that were made to dislodge them.

Having secured their horses and listened to all that young Allison had to tell them concerning the glorious victory that had not yet been won, the brothers bent their steps toward the post-office, where they found a crowd of men and boys who seemed to be trying to make themselves ridiculous. They acted in the same senseless way that those travelling companions did whom Marcy Gray found on the train when he left Barrington, and could not have been more excited and jubilant if the five war ships and two transport steamers, that were to operate against the forts at Hatteras Inlet, had already been wrecked on the bar or sent to the bottom by Confederate shells. One of these two things was sure to happen to that expedition ; they had not the slightest doubt on that point.

Marcy and his brother did not linger long at the post-office after they received their mail, for the boyish antics and confident boastings of the crowd that filled every foot of space between the two counters, were more than they could stand. Pleading business as an excuse, they got away as soon as they could, and unfolded their papers when they were in their saddles, only to find that Allison had told them about all there was to be learned regarding the Hatteras expedition. There were the editorials, of course, and when the boys glanced over them they knew where that crowd in the post-office got its inspiration.

"These editors remind me of Allison," said Marcy. "Seated in their comfortable rooms, hundreds of miles away from the threatened point, they speak of *our* coming victory and the pounding *we* are going to give the Yankee ships

18

the minute they come within range. But I'll tell you one thing, Jack—that expedition isn't strong enough."

"Don't worry about that," replied Jack. "Uncle Sam won't send a boy to mill as long as he's got a man handy. If they sail from Fortress Monroe on Monday, they ought to get here on Tuesday afternoon at the latest. Probably the fight will begin on Wednesday. Now let's watch the weather, and see whether or not Allison's amiable wish is likely to be gratified. Now Marcy, I will tell *you* something.   If the Federals win a victory they will garrison those forts to break up blockade running, and carry on operations farther down the coast.   As soon as we hear they are doing that, you must stand by with the *Fairy Belle.*"

" She'll be ready when you want her, but it is the hardest task one brother ever put upon another," answered Marcy.

"I am sorry to ask you to do it," said Jack, "but it is my only chance ; and you can see for yourself that I can't live at home.   Our whole family is under suspicion ; and if I don't get away while I can, there will be such a pressure brought to bear upon me by and by, that I shall be forced to enter the rebel service or take to the swamps."

"Why Jack, you know you wouldn't do such a thing as that," exclaimed Marcy.

"Hide in the swamps? I'd do it in a minute sooner than lift a hand against the flag that your grandfather and mine died under, and under which I have sailed the world over. Why Marcy, you claim to love the old flag, but I tell you that you don't know any more about it than the man in the moon. Now don't get huffy, but wait until you have laid for long weeks in a foreign port, thousands of miles from home and friends, looking for a cargo which takes its own time in coming, and surrounded by people whose hostility to all white men is such that they would cut your throat in a second if they were not afraid of the consequences, and let some one on deck report a stranger inside. You look over the side and see a handsome ship standing in with the Stars and Stripes waving in the air. When you have felt every nerve in you thrill with excitement and pride, as I have on such occasions, then you can talk of your love for the old flag. I'll fight for it as long as I can stand; but I'll starve and die in the swamp before I will fight against it."

Sailor Jack spoke with unusual warmth, and if Marcy's patriotism had been on the wane, his brother's earnest words would have infused new life and strength into it. If the Northern people, with their immense resources, were animated by the same spirit, it would not be long, he told himself, before the old flag would crowd its secession rival to the wall.

Of course Mrs. Gray was very much alarmed by the startling news the boys brought from Nashville, and she straightway began talking of hiding the money Jack had given her, and of stowing the family silver in some safe place; but Jack laughed at the idea.

"Why, mother, the Northern soldiers are not coming down here to steal our valuables," said he. "They are not robbers."

"But have you never read how lawless all soldiers are?" inquired Mrs. Gray. "They take delight in despoiling an enemy. It seems to be part of their creed. And then—look a' that," she added, pointing toward the rebel flag.

"That will not be in sight when the Federals come around here," replied Marcy. "I'll make it my business to get it out of the way, and then I'll rip up one of my bed quilts and show them my Union colors."

The fear that had taken possession of Marcy's mother—that possibly the Union forces might ascend the Roanoke River, capture Plymouth, and devastate the surrounding country—now took possession of Marcy also. Northern soldiers had not yet been given an opportunity to show the merciful way in which the inhabitants of captured cities were to be treated during the war, and Marcy may be pardoned for looking into the future with fear and trembling. The neighboring planters and their families did much to add to Mrs. Gray's fears and Marcy's, as well as to increase the general feeling of uneasiness which began spreading through the settlement as soon as the newspapers arrived. If they believed, as the Charleston and Newbern editors seemed to

believe,—that the attack on Hatteras Inlet was
sure to end in failure,—they nevertheless
thought it the part of wisdom to prepare for
the worst ; and they at once began the work of
concealing everything that was likely to excite
the cupidity of the lawless Union soldiers. Re-
membering what their Mobile papers had said
about the ragged, half-starved appearance of
the Massachusetts troops who marched through
the streets of Baltimore, they even hid their
clothing and carted the contents of their
smoke-houses and corn-cribs into the woods.
But busy as they were, some of the women
found time to run over and compare notes with
Mrs. Gray, and see what she thought about it ;
and because she tried to accept Jack's view of
the situation, and believed that there would be
no invasion of the Union forces, the visitors
went away to spread the report elsewhere that
Mrs. Gray wasn't afraid of the Yankees because she sympathized with them.

"Would you believe it, she isn't hiding a
thing," said one of these gossips. "She looks
white, but she can't make me think that she's
frightened as long as she sits there in her

rocking-chair as cool as a cucumber. I know that Jack belongs to a blockade-runner, that Jack piloted a Yankee smuggler into one of our ports, and that Mrs. Gray has a Confederate flag hung up in her sitting-room ; but I don't care for that. She's Union, the whole family is Union, and I know it."

Mrs. Gray and the boys always looked troubled after an interview with one of these busybodies, who did not scruple to magnify every rumor that came to their ears, and wished from the bottom of their hearts that they would stay at home and attend to the business of hiding their valuables ; but when the day drew to a close the gossips ceased to trouble them, for they were afraid to go out of doors after dark.

"And between you and me I don't blame them for being afraid," said Jack, when he and Marcy went up to bed. "It is in times like these that the turbulent and vicious members of the community show their hands. The rebels have been maltreating Union people all over the South, and I don't know why we should expect to escape. Well," he added, shoving a brace of revolvers under his pillow, while Marcy provided for his own defence in the same way, "if anybody comes we'll give him as good as he sends, provided he gives us half a chance."

The moment Jack Gray opened his eyes the next morning he jumped out of bed and drew the curtain. "All right so far," said he, in a satisfied tone ; "and that rebel Allison is in a fair way to be disappointed."

"But you must remember that the fleet hasn't arrived off the cape yet," Marcy reminded him. "With the best of luck it cannot get there until late this afternoon. I wish we could go down and watch the fight."

"I wish we could be in it," replied Jack, "for I just know it will end in a Union victory."

But as they could do neither one thing nor the other, they were obliged to possess their souls in patience. Of course they went to Nashville after breakfast, and of course, too, they found in the post-office the same excited and confident crowd they had met the day before, who had all sorts of stories to tell them.

"Report says that the most of the Union ships foundered before they were fairly out of sight of Fortress Monroe," shouted Allison, in great glee. "I am sorry for that, for I wanted our boys to have the honor of sending them to the bottom."

"Another report says that one of the old tubs that the Yankees were using for a transport ship sprung a leak and went down with every soul on board," said a second speaker.

"Why didn't the other vessels save them?" asked Marcy.

"They couldn't. There was a heavy gale on."

"Who brought these reports?" inquired Jack.

"The papers, of course."

"How did the papers get them, seeing that all telegraphic communication with the North is cut off?" continued Jack.

"It makes no difference how they got the news so long as they got it," exclaimed Allison. "You talk and act as though you don't want to believe it."

"It is no concern of yours how I talk and

act, you stay-at-home blow-hard. My common sense will not let me believe any such reports, which are not reports at all, but something those newspaper men made up all out of their own heads, on purpose to give such fellows as you a subject to talk about. Some of the fleet may have sprung a leak—probably they did if they were not seaworthy; but it wasn't in a gale. I watched the weather closely last night, and if there had been a blow outside we should have felt some of the force of it," said Jack. He spoke calmly enough, but he gave Allison such a look that the latter did not think it safe to say another word until the brothers were well on their way toward home.

During the rest of the day Jack and Marcy did little else but stroll about the grounds and talk—they had no heart for work of any sort. Every time Jack took out his watch he would offer some such remark as this: "If the expedition has had no bad luck, it ought to be off such and such a place by this time;" and at three in the afternoon he electrified his brother by declaring confidently: "Now the

ships are off Hatteras, and are probably looking about for a good place to put the troops
ashore." And subsequent events proved that
he guessed pretty close to the mark, for history says, "By two o'clock on Tuesday the
fleet arrived off Hatteras, and the *Monticello*
was despatched to reconnoiter the position, and
to look out a suitable landing-place."

Thus far everything had gone well. The
weather was all that could be desired, and the
hearts of the loyal people along that coast beat
high with hope ; but when Jack Gray drew the
window curtain on Wednesday morning, he
turned to his brother with a look of disappointment on his face.

"They will probably try to land some of the
troops to-day to cut off the retreat of the Fort
Hatteras garrison after the war ships have
whipped them," said he. "But if they don't
get about it pretty soon, I am afraid they'll
not make it. It's going to blow by-and-by,
and if the wind comes from the southeast, as
it generally does, the ships will have to make
an offing to secure their own safety."

And that was just the way things turned out.

That morning some of General Butler's troops were landed a few miles from the forts under cover of some of the gunboats, while the others opened a hot fire upon the fortifications. The battle thus commenced lasted from nine o'clock until almost night, and then Fort Clark was abandoned, while the flag was hauled down on Fort Hatteras in token of surrender, whereupon the *Monticello* steamed into the inlet; but when she came within a few hundred yards of the fort, the heavy guns of the Confederates opened upon her with such terrible effect that she was badly cut up, and in danger of sinking. The man in command of the fort who was guilty of this act of treachery was Commodore Barron, formerly of the United States Navy. He would have scorned to do such a thing while the old flag waved above him, but when he threw off his allegiance to the government he had sworn to defend, he threw off his manhood with it. But he gained nothing by it. The battle was fiercely renewed by the Union forces, and the next day Commodore Barron hoisted the white flag and surrendered himself and his garrison uncondition-

ally.   In going off to the fleet he was obliged
to pass close under the guns of the *Wabash*, a
a fine vessel which, six months before, he had
himself commanded with honor.

While these events were taking place at
Hatteras Inlet, Marcy and his brother remained at home, waiting with as much
patience as they could to see how the battle
was going to end.   They knew there was a
battle going on, for they heard about it when
they went to the post-office on Thursday morning ; and if they had believed all that was told
them, they would have gone home very much
disheartened.   One man assured them (and he
got his information from his papers) that the
remnant of the fleet, that is to say all the
vessels that had not been wrecked when the
expedition left Fortress Monroe, had made its
appearance in due time, begun the assault in
the most gallant manner, and the few that had
not been sunk or disabled by the seventeen
heavy guns of the forts, had been scattered by
the gale.   The flag of the Confederacy waved
triumphant, and Hatteras Inlet was yet open
to blockade-runners.

When the two were on their way home, and each had read all he cared to read in papers that did not give any reliable information, Marcy inquired :

"How much of those stories do you believe ? "

"Not quite half," replied Jack. "Perhaps some of the attacking fleet were sunk ; they are liable to be when they go into action. But I believe that if our fellows were whipped, they were whipped by the gale and not by the forts. We ought to hear something definite in the course of a few days."

And they heard something the very next morning ; but even then, to quote from Jack, who was very much disgusted when he said it, they "didn't get the straight of the story." Young Allison did not come out to greet them when they drew up their horses at the hitching-rack (he objected to being called a stay-at-home blow-hard), but Colonel Shelby and his intimate friend, Dillon, were standing close by, and the boys noticed that they looked very solemn.

"Well, the agony is over," said the colonel.

"Have you received some reliable news at last?" exclaimed Jack. "How did it come out? Which whipped?"

"Oh, the Federals overcame us with the force of numbers aided by their long-range guns," answered the colonel. "My paper acknowledges a defeat, but says it doesn't amount to anything, for it will not help the enemy in any way."

"It will close Hatteras against blockade-runners, will it not?" said Marcy.

"Oh, that doesn't amount to a row of pins," said the colonel. "We have Wilmington, Charleston, and a dozen other ports that the Yankees can't shut up for want of a suitable fleet. They haven't stationed a ship off Crooked Inlet yet, and you and Captain Beardsley——"

"I know they haven't put a ship there," Marcy interposed. "But if they didn't have the wickedest kind of a steam launch at that very place the last time I came through, I don't want to lay up anything for old age. That night's work put the blockaders on their guard, and we can't use that Inlet any more.

Beyond a doubt they pulled up our buoys, and more than that, they'll watch it as a terrier watches a rathole. Beardsley will have to lay his schooner up or go somewhere else."

"You will go with him, I suppose?" said Dillon carelessly.

"I am ordered to report at the end of ninety days," replied Marcy, who knew that the question was meant for a "feeler." "If I live I shall do so; and I expect to stay with the schooner as long as she is in the business."

"As for me, I shall report in less than ninety days," said Jack. "I've a notion to start for Newbern to-morrow; and if I find that things are working as I should like to have them, I will return and say good-bye to mother, and some fine morning you'll see Marcy ride down to the post-office alone."

"Good for you, Jack!" exclaimed the colonel, thrusting out his hand. "I looked for something like this when I heard that you had purchased a Confederate flag and brought it home with you. Where did you get the flag, if it is a fair question?"

"Of a good Confederate," replied Jack

readily. "He left it in a certain place, and when I saw my chance I took it."

"Had to take it on the sly, did you ? Then there must have been some Union men hanging around."

"There were, several of them ; and they were fighting mad, too. But I got away with the flag."

"I hope it will not be the means of bringing mischief to you and your mother," said the colonel; "but if I were in your place, I wouldn't make it so conspicuous. Now, when you go to Newbern to enlist in the army——"

"But if I go there, it will not be for any such purpose," interrupted Jack. "On land I am as awkward as a mud-turtle ; but when I am at sea, I can get about with the best of them. I shall go into the navy if I can get the chance."

"Never fear. You'll get the chance easy enough. When you return I should like to have you tell me how things look on our side, and what the Yankees are doing at the Inlet."

"You mustn't be surprised if I don't," answered Jack, " for I may slip back and slip

19

out again without taking time to say good-bye to anybody. When I fail to come to town with Marcy, you may know that I am in the navy."

When the boys went in after their mail, they found a silent and sulky-looking company leaning against the counters. They said not a word to the new-comers or to one another, but simply stared at the floor, apparently absorbed with gloomy reflections. Jack and his brother were glad to find them so, for it gave them an opportunity to secure their mail without delay and get away by themselves, where they could exult to their hearts' content over the victory at Hatteras.

"What is this new notion you have taken into your head all of a sudden?" was the first question Marcy propounded. "You haven't any idea of going to Newbern."

"Yes, I think it would be a good plan," said Jack. "I want to know just where the Union fleet is, and what it is doing, and I can't depend upon these lying rebel papers to tell me. So the only thing I can do is to find out for myself; for of course I don't want to run outside in the *Fairy Belle* unless I know of a certainty that there is a gunboat there to receive me. If Beardsley's schooner is in port I'll take a look at her, and then I can tell whether or not she is the one that chased the *Sabine*."

"She's the one," replied Marcy. "But you'll not know her. She is disguised."

Jack said he didn't care if she had been painted a dozen different colors since he saw her, she couldn't fool him. He would look at her "general make-up;" and while he was describing some peculiarities in the *Hattie's* rigging that Marcy had not noticed himself, they rode through the gate into the yard.

CHAPTER XIII.

UNION OR CONFEDERATE—WHICH ?

FOR the first time since sailor Jack came home he was the bearer of good news, and you may be sure that his mother was glad to listen to it. He declared that he took no stock whatever in the thousand and one conflicting reports that had come to him through the papers, and so suspicious had he become that the only thing that led him to believe the rebels had been worsted in the fight at Hatteras, was because they were willing to confess it themselves. Of course it would not be safe for him to try to carry out his resolve to enlist in the Union navy until he knew just how the land lay ; and the only way in which he could find out would be to go to Newbern and make personal observations. If his mother did not object he would start the very next morning and take Marcy with him. This

292

proposition startled Mrs. Gray, for she had looked upon another separation from Jack as something that was far in the future; and would not allow herself to think about it if she could help it. She said nothing discouraging, however, and Jack's programme was duly carried out.

The trip to Newbern was the most exciting and altogether disagreeable one that Marcy had ever taken on the cars. The train was crowded with soldiers, and among them were some boisterous and inquisitive ones who seemed to think it their duty to question every civilian who came on board. And they did not do it in the most gentlemanly manner, either. Before the train had left Boydtown a mile behind, a young man, dressed in a neat, clean uniform that had never seen a minute's service at the front, stopped in the aisle and laid his hand heavily on Jack's shoulder.

"Look here, my lad," said he, in a tone that was as offensive as his manner, "you are strong and able-bodied, are you not?"

"You'll think so if you don't take your

hand off my collar mighty sudden," replied Jack, jumping from his seat.

"Hallo!" exclaimed the young man, starting back in some alarm when he saw the sailor's broad shoulders rising to a level with his own. "I wouldn't throw on any airs," he added, glancing around at his uniformed companions, who straightway became interested in the proceedings.

"I won't, and I don't mean to let you do so, either—not with me," replied Jack. "You seem to feel very important because you happen to have some good clothes on, but you haven't been under fire yet."

"Neither have you," answered the Confederate.

"That's all you know about it. Now go off and let me alone, or I'll pitch you through the window."

The young man fell back to call up re-enforcements, and Jack took his seat again.

"It's all right," said he, when he noticed the troubled expression on his brother's face. "Because he wears a uniform himself, he thinks he had a right to know why I haven't one also;

but it is none of his business. Besides, it is
nothing more than you did to Allison in the
post-office at Nashville.''

''But I was among friends when I backed
Allison down, and these men are all strangers
to us,'' replied Marcy.

''No matter for that. I judge by their looks
that they are mostly Americans, and if they
are they will see fair play. There will be a
white man along to question us presently.''

And sure enough there was. The defeated
rebel drew back a little way to hold a council
of war with some of his friends, and in a few
minutes one of these friends, whose uniform
was by no means as clean and neat as the
others', arose from his seat and came down the
aisle.

''Beg pardon, sir,'' said he respectfully.
''I wish to offer a word of excuse for my im-
pulsive young companion's conduct. He is a
warm patriot——''

''So I see,'' said Jack, with a smile. ''A
good many get that way the minute they put
on a gray suit; but my brother and I, who
have already risked our lives and liberty, do

not feel called upon to give an account of our-selves to every raw recruit who may demand it. If he had asked me a civil question I would have given him a civil answer."

"Of course; certainly. But I know you will overlook it this time. But are you two really in the service?"

"My brother has been on a privateer and now he belongs to a blockade-runner," answered Jack. "You see he's got a bad arm, don't you? The Yankees gave him that."

"Well, well!" exclaimed the man, who did not know what else to say. "He ought to have a uniform on."

"His crew don't have any," replied Jack. "And if you want to know what I have done —by the way, are you going to Newbern?"

The soldier said he was.

"Well, when you get there go to Parker & Wall's and ask them whether or not the sup-plies the *West Wind* brought down from Boston are going to be of any use to the Con-federacy. I was second mate and pilot of that craft, and might have been on board of her yet if I had been inclined to stay; but if there is going to be a war I want a hand in it. I am going to Newbern to see if there is any chance for me to get into the navy."

Of course, after such a talk as this it was impossible for the brothers to keep to themselves as they would like to have done. The inquisitive rebel apologized to Jack and introduced his friends; and from that time forward there was a crowd of soldiers hanging about his seat all the while. Some of them had seen service and some hadn't; and the latter were particularly anxious to know how Marcy felt when that shrapnel came over the *Hattie's* bow and knocked him and Captain Beardsley down, and whether or not he was frightened and afraid he was going to be killed.

"The whole thing was done so quickly, and I was so excited, that I didn't have time to ask myself whether I was frightened or not," was Marcy's invariable reply; and it seemed to satisfy his questioners.

To Jack Gray's disappointment there was not a soldier in the car who could tell him anything definite regarding the situation at Hatteras Inlet; but some of them interested them-

selves in the matter, and finally discovered a
citizen who knew all about it, but who, upon
being questioned, proved to be almost as ignorant as the rest. The few things he *did* know,
however, were very encouraging to Jack. The
captured forts had not been destroyed, he said,
and that seemed to indicate that the Yankees
intended to place garrisons there. The vessels
of the attacking fleet had not been sunk or
scattered, and neither was there a sailor killed
during the whole of the fight. The war vessels
were still hanging around the Inlet, ready to
go up or down the Sound, according to the
orders they might receive from Washington,
and the rebel garrison at Fort Ocracoke, which
was located on the seaward face of Beacon Island a few miles below, as well as the troops
who occupied the camp on the opposite side of
the island, were trembling in their boots, and
holding themselves ready to run at a moment's
notice. He didn't know the first thing about
naval matters, he said in conclusion. There
might be a gunboat or two building in the
river above Newbern, but he didn't think there
was, and the only thing left for Jack was to

ship on some blockade-runner. They still had the free use of Ocracoke and Oregon Inlets.

"I thank you for the information you have given me," said Jack. "I declare it is refreshing to find a man who can tell the truth. The falsehoods I have read and listened to during the last few days are enough to disgust anybody. The possession of Hatteras Inlet is important to the Federal government, and you'll find it out."

"We have found it out already," answered the citizen. "The Yankee ships are hauling in the prizes as fishermen haul in their catch with a drag net. You see, the blockade-runners that are bound in don't know that the Inlet has been captured, and neither do they find it out until they run slap into the arms of the cruisers, who are always on the watch for them. They had hardly ceased firing. upon the forts before they captured five schooners."

"All in one day?" exclaimed Marcy.

"All in one day," repeated the citizen.

"Good enough," said Marcy, to himself. "I hope the *Hattie* was one of them." Then aloud he said: "Do you know the names of those schooners? The reason I ask is because my captain has had plenty of time to load up, run down to Nassau, and get back again. His name is Beardsley, and he commands the *Hattie*."

"Oh, yes. I heard about him, and when he gets back you will see an account of his daring exploit in the papers. That man has pluck, I tell you."

"What did he do, and why will the papers wait until he returns before saying anything about it?" inquired Marcy.

"He had taken his cargo of cotton on board, and was all ready to sail when word was received that the Yankee ships had appeared off Hatteras," answered the citizen. "No one supposed that he would think of going out, but he did; and the first thing we heard of him was that he had got safely off."

"He didn't run out of Hatteras, of course?"

"Certainly not. He stole a march on the Yankees and went down to Ocracoke."

"Then I can't see what he did that was so daring," said Marcy, to himself. "The greatest coward in the world, if he can handle a vessel at all, ought to be able to run her out of a wide inlet when there is nothing to oppose him."

"And the reason our papers didn't speak of it is because we don't want the Yankees to be on the watch for him when he comes back," continued the citizen. "We can tell by the way they have acted since they captured the forts, that they know what is going on in the city as well as we do. They must get the papers regularly; and if we ever find out who is to blame for it, I wouldn't give much for his neck."

"Now that's what *I* call pluck," thought Marcy. "Captain Beardsley didn't show a particle when he ran out to sea under the guns of Fort Ocracoke, for there was nothing for him to be afraid of, all the blockaders, if there were any, having gone to Hatteras to help the fleet. But when a Union man, in such a nest of rebels as Newbern is, risks his life by sending information to the defenders of the old flag, he's got nerve. But I am sorry to hear that about Beardsley. He'll keep on running the blockade until he is captured, and what if

I should chance to be aboard the schooner when that happens ?"

Having given them all the information he could, the citizen went back to his own seat, and the boys were at last left to themselves. They hadn't learned much, and they did not learn any more when they reached Newbern. The fortifications below the city were being rapidly pushed to completion (negroes and poor whites did the work, the officers finding life in town much more to their liking than digging in the trenches), and there had been some talk of building gunboats to assist in the defence of the place ; but so far nothing had been done about it. But, after all, there was no need of gunboats, for the thirty-one pieces of heavy artillery that had been planted on the works below, would send the Yankee fleet to the bottom in short order, should its commanding officer be so foolhardy as to bring it into the Neuse River. There was nothing to keep the boys in the city, for the *West Wind*, which Marcy wanted much to see, had already sailed for Nassau with a cargo of cotton ; and after spending two days in making inquiries that did not bring them the information they desired, they took the cars for home. Old Morris, whom they found waiting for them at Boydtown depot, was both surprised and disappointed because they did not ride on the box with him, as they usually did ; but as the boys wanted to be alone, they went inside.

"You haven't done much talking since we started," said Marcy, when Morris cracked his whip and drove away from the depot. "What's the matter ?"

"I have been laying my plans," replied Jack. "But with all my thinking I haven't been able to decide upon anything further than this : As soon as it comes dark, we'll begin and load the *Fairy Belle* with provisions and such other things as we may be likely to stand in need of, and to-morrow morning we'll slip down and out."

"To-morrow night, you mean," suggested Marcy.

"No, to-morrow morning; just as soon as we have had breakfast. I am impatient to be off; and besides I really cannot afford to waste any more time. We must go at once or run the risk of missing the Federal fleet. It may be ordered somewhere else."

"But every one along the river will see us," protested Marcy.

"Who cares if they do? In fact I should care if they did not see us. We'll hoist my Confederate flag at the peak as——"

"Why, Jack. And sail under a lie?"

"Now just listen at *you*," exclaimed Jack, shaking his finger at his brother. "Captain Semmes didn't sail under a lie, I suppose, when he ran up the English colors to quiet the fears of the *Herndon's* commander, and neither did you when you hoisted the same flag to coax my vessel within reach of your guns."

"Do you imagine that I would have done such a thing if I had been in a position to refuse?" retorted Marcy, with some spirit. "I couldn't help myself."

"I know it; and can't you see that hoisting the rebel rag will help both of us? I can, and I only wish Nashville was situated on the river so that Allison and Shelby and the rest of those blatant traitors could see us as we go by. It will save you from a heap of questioning, and may be the means of keeping a roof over mother's head."

"But what will the Union men in the settlement think and do about it ?"

"Not the first thing. There are but few of them, and they dare not say their souls are their own. They know they are watched as well as mother knows that she is watched, and there isn't one among them who dares lift his hand or say a word. For their own sakes, I hope they will not do anything to you and mother because they think we are rebels, for if they do, their houses will go up in smoke."

"But, Jack," persisted Marcy, "I wouldn't dare go alongside a Union gunboat with that flag on board my schooner."

"When the time comes, we will pull it down and hoist one of your Union flags in its place," was the answer.

"But suppose we should be seen by some one on shore who happened to have a strong spy-glass in his hand ? Wouldn't I find myself in a fix when I got back ?"

"It is no part of my programme to hug the shores so closely that our flag can be seen

20

and recognized," replied Jack. "You are not going to get yourself into trouble by taking me down to the fleet. If I thought you were, I would not ask you to go ; but that money in the cellar may be the means of turning you out of doors."

When the boys reached home, their mother saw at a glance that something had been decided upon, but she asked no questions until they were all seated at the supper table, and then they told her as much of their plans as they were willing Hanson should know, and no more.

"There isn't the sign of a navy in or about Newbern," said Jack, talking for the benefit of the girl who waited at table as well as for the information of any other eavesdropper who might chance to be hanging around. "But there must be some vessels fitting out at Edenton or somewhere else in these waters, and we intend to find out before we come back. We shall set out to-morrow as soon as we have had breakfast, and in order to do that we must provision the *Fairy Belle* before we go to bed."

Of course the news of their intended movements got noised among the servants, as the boys were sure it would, and when they were ready to set to work, there were any number of volunteers at hand to assist them, the boy Julius, who took it for granted that he was to be one of the crew, being particularly active and " bossy." He and another small darkey were sent off in a skiff to cast the schooner loose from her moorings and tow her to the shore, and the minute that duty had been performed he jumped out, seized a bundle which he had left on the bank, and was climbing back over the side with the agility of a monkey when Jack called to him :

"Avast, there. What are you about?" cried the sailor.

"Going to stow dis yere dunnage of mine in de fo'castle," replied Julius, without stopping.

"Well, come back. You can't go this trip."

"Ain't I going to sea with Marse Marcy ?" said Julius, who was almost ready to cry.

"Not this trip, I tell you. You are an Abolitionist, and we can't trust you. If I should get a chance to go into the navy I shall not want you around, for you would come back and blab it all over the neighborhood. Somebody must stay home and take care of mother. Come ashore and lend a hand with this grub."

"I jes' ain't going to do no such nigger's work as dat," replied Julius spitefully. "If I can't run on de schooner, I shan't help load her. I tell you dat for a fac'. I jes' hope she'll go to de bottom 'fore she sees Seven Mile creek agin."

The darkey emphasized his words by throwing his bundle as far as he could send it, and by flinging himself over the side as if he had been a bag of cotton. The moment his feet touched the ground he snatched up his property again and disappeared in the darkness.

" Sorry he went off mad," said Jack, " but it can't be helped. In times like these the only persons we can trust are those who can keep still tongues in their heads, and that is something Julius was never known to do. Now," he added, turning to the half a dozen blacks who remained, "if there are any among you who don't want to aid in loading a vessel that is going to hoist the Confederate colors to-morrow, you can go also."

"But, Marse Jack," exclaimed Morris, who had been waiting for an opportunity like this, "you ain't no rebel."

"Of course I am not. Who said I was ?"

"But I mean, you don't go in for the 'Federacy; kase if you did go in for the 'Federacy, the Missus wouldn't luff you in the house. I don't see what you want with that rebel flag in the sitting-room, nohow. I just believe—"

"I don't care what you believe," interrupted Jack, who was afraid that the coachman was about to give utterance to some suspicions that would come too near the truth. "Are you for the Union ?"

"Course I is, Marse Jack. And so be you."

"Are all the rest of you black ones for the Union, too ?"

"Yes, sar, we is," was the unanimous response.

"Very well. I don't try to control your opinions ; but if you are going to take sides with those who are coming down here to rob us of our property, you may trot right back to the quarter and leave us to do our own work. Off you go, now."

The astonished negroes urged and pleaded to no purpose. Jack, who thought he knew just what he was doing, would not listen to them, and finally they turned slowly and sorrowfully away, leaving Bose to act as sentry and body-guard.

"If everybody on the place doesn't hear of this in less than half an hour and set you down for a rebel, it will not be your fault," said Marcy, when the negroes were out of ear-shot.

"I don't care what they set me down for, so long as they let you and mother alone while I am gone," replied Jack. "I have been here long enough to find out what is the matter with our neighbors. They are mad because we will not declare ourselves."

"And you think the safest plan is to make them believe, if you can, that we are Confederates," added Marcy. But don't you know that this game of deception can't last forever? Now that the Yankees have got a foothold on the coast, what is there to hinder them from spreading all over the country? Suppose they should come here, and some Union man should tell them that we hoisted the first rebel flag that was seen in the settlement—then what?"

"Then will be the time for you to show how smart you are, for I shall not be here to help you. Now, Bose," he added, speaking as though the animal could understand every word he said, "you stay here and keep watch; and if you hear anybody sneaking up on us, take after him and hold him at bay till we come."

So saying he picked up the nearest basket and hoisted it over the schooner's side.

The *Fairy Belle*, having been built under sailor Jack's personal supervision, was especially adapted for the service for which she was intended, that of single-handed cruiser. Although she was provided with top-masts, she had no sails for them, and all the sheets and halliards were made to lead aft, so that they were under complete control of the boy at the helm, who could put his hand upon any of them without moving from the cock-pit. Beginning forward, there was the chain locker, which contained all the extra cordage the schooner was likely to need during a cruise, and also served as a place of storage for the ground tackle when not in use. Abaft of that was a forecastle, with bunks for two hands, and then came a small but convenient galley, with cupboards and dishes in plenty, from which a door gave entrance into a neatly furnished cabin. It was all there, too, no space being taken up with state-rooms. An upholstered locker, running the full length of each side of the cabin, not only served as receptacles for hunting and fishing outfits, canned provisions, flags, and clothing, but could easily be made into beds that would accommodate four boys. Nothing had been omitted that could in any way add to the comfort of her master and crew, and her speed, under the four sails she usually carried, was all that could be desired. She had sailed over nearly every mile of Albemarle and Pamlico Sounds, and been fifty miles outside the sand dunes; but that was before Yankee gunboats with their sharp-eyed lookouts were known upon the coast. When Marcy made those trips he had but one flag—one that was known and respected the world over ; but when he went outside this time he would have two, either of which might be the means of sending him and his brother to prison.

It did not take the boys more than ten minutes to put their supplies aboard the schooner, and while they were about it they talked in their ordinary tones, so that their words could have been heard and understood by any one who thought it worth while to come to the top of the bank and listen to them ; but they were careful to weigh the words before they uttered them, and the sequel proved that the precaution was not a needless one. After everything had been stowed in its proper place and the hatches were fastened down, Jack said :

" Of course we can't leave her alone ; we must have some one to watch her. So if you will keep an eye on her, I'll go to the house and send Morris and Julius down." At the same time he pointed to Bose ; and Marcy, comprehending his meaning, seized the dog by the neck to keep him from following Jack, who lumbered up the bank, making any amount of noise, and singing a sailor ditty as he went.

Scarcely had the words of the song died away in the distance, when something that sounded suspiciously like the breaking of twigs came to Marcy's ears, and at the same instant the faithful watch-dog tore himself loose from his master's detaining grasp and bounded up the bank, barking fierce and loud at every jump. This must have been what Jack was thinking of when he left Bose behind. As quickly as he could Marcy got upon his feet and shouted words of encouragement to his four-footed friend.

"Pull him down," he yelled. "Pull the spy down and let me see who he is."

The dog heard the command and probably tried to obey it, for his bark changed to an angry snarl, and a second later a familiar but frightened voice cried out:

"Call him off, Mister Marcy! Call him off! He'll eat me up if you don't."

"It's nothing more than I expected," thought the boy, who was in no particular hurry to give ear to the entreaty. "Now who is it that carries news to him from the house? That's the next thing to be found out."

"Is that you, Hanson?" he exclaimed, as if he were much surprised. "Come away, Bose. What brought you down here, and why did you come in that sneaking way? Jack will be mad enough to knock you down," he added, when he stood face to face with the overseer.

"Why Mr. Marcy, I had no thought of playing the part of a sneak," protested the man. "I couldn't make head or tail of what the darkey tried to tell me, but I knew there was something going on in the creek, and thought it my duty to come down and take a look at things. I didn't know you was here."

"You are Union, are you not?" said Marcy, who knew there wasn't a word of truth in the overseer's story.

"Of course I am, and so are you. So is Mr. Jack."

"Well, if he is, what is that Confederate flag doing in the house?"

"It's put there a purpose to fool folks. The

niggers don't know what to think about it, but I do ; and I think it was a good idee on your part. There's plenty of folks about here who would be glad to see harm come to you, but I'm watching 'em."

"So am I; and some day, when they least expect it, I will bring some of them up with a round turn. I hear Jack coming, and you had better get out of his way. He'd just as soon pick a quarrel with you as not."

But the overseer did not want Jack to pick a quarrel with him, so he took Marcy at his word. He went away more mystified than ever. Were the Grays Union or Confederate ? He would have given almost anything he possessed to have his doubts on this point cleared up, and the men for whom he was working in secret would have done the same thing.

CHAPTER XIV.

JULIUS IN TROUBLE.

BY the time the overseer was out of hearing sailor Jack came up, followed by two negroes, who carried blankets on their arms. They were the ones who had been selected to watch the schooner during the night, and the first words they uttered in Marcy's hearing seemed to indicate that they were not very well pleased with the duty that had been imposed upon them. Having learned from their companions that the Stars and Bars were to be hoisted at her peak on the following morning, they did not want to have anything to do with her.

"I couldn't find Julius, but I heard of him," said Jack. "He is mad clear through, and hopes some Union man will walk off with the *Fairy Belle* as soon as we rebels turn our backs upon her. I never knew him to talk as spitefully as I heard he did when he took his bundle back to the quarter. Now, boys, tow her out to her moorings and look out for her till we come again. Good-night."

"But, Marse Jack, Ise mighty jubus about dis business ; I is for a fac'. Sposen some of de Union men in de settlement——"

"Well, if any Union folks come here before morning, it will be because some of you black ones have posted them," interrupted Jack. "The people in this settlement know our business as well as we know it ourselves, or think they do, and some of you boys are to blame for it."

"Now, Marse Jack——" began the negroes, with one voice.

"I am not accusing either one of you," exclaimed the sailor. "But if the shoe fits you, you can wear it. There's one among you who runs to a certain person with everything that is done in and about the house that he can get hold of. I know who he is," Jack added, to Marcy's great amazement, "and can put my hand on him in less than ten minutes. But I'm not going to do it. I shall let somebody else punish him ; and some dark night, when the ghosts come out of the church-yard and walk around the quarter——"

"Oh, Marse Jack," cried the frightened blacks throwing down their blankets and moving closer to the boys for protection. "Don't say dem unrespec'ful words. If you do, yo' boat sink wid you to-morrer, suah."

"Well, you know it to be a fact, don't you? At any rate I have often heard some of you say that white things do walk around of nights. I know it, whether you do or not; and some night, when you are all asleep in the quarter, and I am away on the water fighting for the flag I believe in, something, I don't know just how it will look, will walk into a certain cabin down there and take a man out : and it will be a long time before you will hear of him again. You'll be astonished when you wake up the next morning. But you two will be all right if you keep still tongues in your head. If you don't, I'll not answer for the consequences."

"But, Marse Jack——" began one of the negroes.

"I can't waste any more time with you,"

said the sailor impatiently. "Haven't I told you that I don't know how the thing will look when it gets ready to go to work? I don't even know when it is coming; *but it is coming.* You may depend upon that. Now take the schooner out to her moorings and keep an eye on her till morning."

The astonished Marcy, who did not understand the situation any better than the frightened blacks did, fully expected to hear them refuse duty; but Jack had so worked upon their feelings that they were afraid to do it. Out of pure mischief he had often done the same thing before, by telling them of the wonderful adventures he had met at sea. He had seen lots of mermaids riding on the waves and dressing their hair with the combs they had taken from the pockets of drowned sailors; had often listened to the entrancing music of sirens, who, seated on submerged rocks in mid-ocean, had played their harps for all they were worth in the hope of drawing his ship to destruction; and once the vessel on which he was sailing had a two weeks' race before it could get away from the whale that swallowed Jonah. This whale got hungry once every hundred thousand years ; and whenever that happened he sunk the first ship he came to and made a meal off the crew. But Jack himself always came off safe by reason of the powers of a charm which he carried in his ditty-bag. This wonderful charm not only brought him good luck in everything he undertook, but enabled him to give a wide berth to those who sought to do him harm, and to turn the tables upon them whenever he saw fit to do so. Without saying another word in protest, the two negroes stepped into the skiff and made ready to tow the schooner to her moorings, while the boys faced about and started for the house.

"Jack, what in the name of sense are you up to now ?" demanded Marcy, when he could speak without fear of being overheard.

By way of reply the sailor laughed heartily but silently, and poked his brother in the ribs with his finger.

"I know you have made the darkeys afraid of you by telling them your ridiculous stories, and I am ashamed to say that I have backed

21

up all you have said to them," continued Marcy. "But I don't see why you stuffed them up that way to-night. It wasn't true, of course."

"All sailors are strictly truthful," replied Jack. "But seriously, Marcy, I never told a straighter story than I told those blacks a while ago, when I warned them that some morning they would find a man missing.

"Jack," said Marcy, suddenly, "what is it that has been taking you out of the house so much of nights during the last two weeks? Mother and I have often thought we would ask you, but have as often come to the conclusion that when you were ready to let us know, you would tell us."

"And a very wise conclusion it was," answered Jack. "By leaving me entirely alone, you have thrown no obstacles in my way."

"But if you were working up anything, why didn't you take me into your confidence?" said Marcy reproachfully.

"Because one can hide his movements better than two. Besides, I did not see my way clearly, and I didn't want to raise any false hopes. But I think the thing is cut and dried now, and as sure as you live," here he sunk his voice to a whisper, "there'll be the biggest kind of a rumpus in the quarter some morning; and if mother happens to be awake, she will wonder why she doesn't hear the horn."

"Why won't she hear it?"

"For the very good reason that there will be no one there who has a right to blow it."

"*Jack!*" Marcy almost gasped.

"Well, you wait and see if I don't know what I am talking about," replied the sailor.

"Where will Hanson be on that particular morning?"

"I can't tell. I only know that he will be gone, that he will not be likely to trouble you and mother any more, for a while at least, and that the whole thing will be so very mysterious that such fellows as Shelby and Allison will be frightened out of their boots; and, Marcy," added Jack, speaking in a still lower whisper, "you needn't go back to the *Hattie* if you don't want to."

"Jack, I wish you would tell me just what you mean," said Marcy impatiently.

"All right. Give me a chance and I will. But, in the first place, what was Bose barking at while I was gone? He acted as though he was getting ready to bite something or somebody. Was it Hanson?"

"That's just who it was," replied Marcy.

"And did Bose hold him until you had' opportunity to speak to him!" continued Jack. "All right. That was what I left him for. I don't care now what Hanson told you, for I don't suppose there was a word of truth in it; but what did you think when you spoke to him?"

"I said to myself that one eavesdropper had been brought to light, and that the next thing would be to find out who it is that carries news to him from the house," replied Marcy.

"Exactly. Well, there's no one that carries news, but there is a little nig who used to take him a pack of lies every day," replied Jack, "and I know who it is. That was what I meant when I told those two darkeys awhile ago that I could put my hand on the tale-bearer in less than ten minutes. It's Julius."

"Jack, you are certainly dreaming," exclaimed Marcy, growing more and more amazed.

"If you should try to take my measure on the ground right here, you might find that I am tolerably wide awake," replied the sailor, with a laugh. "I have had several talks with the overseer, all unbeknown to you and mother, and by taking it for granted that he was a good rebel, I caught him off his guard a time or two (but that wasn't a hard thing to do), and learned, to my surprise, that somebody was keeping him very well *mis*informed regarding the doings in the house. Of course that excited my curiosity, and after thinking the matter over I took Julius by the neck one day when I happened to catch him alone, and frightened the secret out of him."

And this was the secret, which Jack told in as few words as possible, for he knew that his mother was anxiously awaiting his return. Julius was one of the few servants who were allowed the freedom of the house; but, like many others of his race, he was somewhat given to laying violent hands upon things that did not belong to him. He was rarely detected, and when he was he generally succeeded in lying out of it, and of course this made him bolder; so when he saw Mrs. Gray's valuable breastpin lying exposed on her dressing-table, he slipped it into his pocket, made his way from the house without being seen, and went behind one of the cabins to admire it. But, as bad luck would have it, the overseer, who never did things openly and above board as other folks do them, came "snooping" along the lane and caught him in the act.

"What's that you've got there?" he demanded.

"Wha—what thing, Marse Hanson?" stammered Julius.

"That thing you're putting in your pocket," replied the overseer. "Hand it out, or I'll wear this rawhide into slivers on your black hide."

"Look a yer, Marse Hanson," exclaimed Julius. "My missus don't 'low no white trash of a oberseer to whop de house servants. I tell you dat." And before the words were fairly out of his mouth the little darkey took to his heels and ran like a deer.

"All right," shouted Hanson. "Run away if you want to, and I will go to the missus and tell her that you've got something of hers— some of her gold things. You won't lie me down, either, like you done the last time, for I seen you have 'em."

This dreadful threat reached the ears of the thief and stopped his flight. He turned about and faced the overseer.

"And then do you know what the Missus will say to me?" the latter went on. "She'll say, 'Mister Hanson, take this boy to the field and put him to work. He ain't fitten to stay about the house.' And when I get you into the field," he added, shaking his riding-whip at the culprit, "won't I see that you handle them hoes lively? I reckon not. Come here and give me that, I tell you."

"You'll lick me if I come back," said Julius.

"No, I won't tech hide nor hair of ye. Honor bright."

"And won't ye tell de Missus, nuther?"

"Well, that depends on whether I do or not," replied Hanson evasively. "If you'll mind every word I say to you and jump the minute you hear the word, I won't tell her. Come here, now."

Not being able just then to discover any other way out of the scrape, Julius tremblingly obeyed. When the overseer took the stolen pin in his hands his eyes seemed ready to start from their sockets.

"Do you know what you've went and done, you thieving nigger?" he said, in a mysterious whisper. "What do you reckon these yer things is scattered round 'mongst this gold?"

"Glass, ain't they?" faltered Julius.

"Glass, you fule! They're diamonds. They cost more'n a hundred thousand dollars, and that's more'n a dozen such niggers as you is worth," said Hanson, who was not very well versed in figures.

This incident happened at the beginning of the troubles between the North and South, and about the time that everybody was supposed to be "taking sides." All the people in that part of the country, with but a single exception, had declared for secession (whether they were sincere or not remains to be seen), and that single exception was Mrs. Gray, who could not be coaxed, cajoled, or surprised into saying a word in favor of one side or the other. Of course this did not suit the red-hot rebels in the vicinity, and as they could not find out anything themselves, they bribed Hanson to try his luck; but he was at fault, too. The trouble with him was, he did not live in the great house, but close to the quarter, which was nearly half a mile away; he had nothing whatever to do with the house servants; and he was pretty certain that those he found opportunity to question, did not always take the trouble to tell him the truth. He must have a reliable ally *in* the house—some one who was in a position to hear and see everything that was said and done by the inmates, who must not, of course, be given reason for believing that they were watched. Until this episode of the breastpin occurred, Hanson did not know how he was going to get such an ally; but he thought he had found him now.

"I'll keep these yer diamonds till I find out whether or not you are going to do jest like I tell you," said the overseer, putting the jewelry into his pocket.

"But, Marse Hanson," protested the darkey, "it ain't right for you to keep dat thing."

"Now listen at you," said the overseer angrily. "Wasn't you going to steal it? I ain't. I'm only going to hold fast to it a little while to see if you are going to do like I tell you. If you do, the Missus will get her pin back, and she won't never know who took it; but if you don't, I'll have you in the field where I can find you every time I retch for you. Now listen. I reckon you know that Mister Marcy is coming home from school one of those days, don't you? Well, when he comes, I want you to find out if he's Union or secesh. What's the Missus anyway?"

"She's jes' the same that you be," replied Julius.

"Look here, nigger," said the overseer, in savage tones, "that won't go down. You're Union, ain't you?"

"Oh, yes sar. Ise Union if you is."

Hanson raised his whip and Julius dodged like a flash.

"'Tain't what I want, and you know it well enough," the man shouted. "I want to know for a fact—for a fact, mind you—what them folks up to the great house is ; which side they leans to, Union or Confederate. And if you don't come down to my house this very night after dark with some news of some kind, I'll take these yer diamonds straight to the Missus and tell her where I got 'em. You know what I mean, so cl'ar yourself."

Glad to escape the whip with which the overseer constantly threatened him while he was talking, Julius lost no time in making his way to the great house ; but he did not go near Mrs. Gray till she summoned him into her presence to ask him if he had been in her room that day. Of course he hadn't been upstairs at all, not even to "tote up de wash-watah, kase dat was de gals' work and not his'n."

" I never heard that mother lost a breastpin," said Marcy, when Jack had got this far with his narrative. " Did she find it again ? Did Hanson give it up ? "

Instead of replying in words, Jack took hold of a small cord that encircled his neck, and pulled his ditty-bag from beneath the bosom of his flannel shirt. This he opened with great deliberation, taking from it a small vial and a package wrapped in a piece of newspaper.

" What have those things to do with mother's breastpin ?" demanded Marcy. " What's in that bottle ?"

"That vial contains my charm ; and a most potent one it is," said the sailor gravely.

" If you don't quit your nonsense and come to the point, I will leave you and go into the house," said Marcy angrily.

"I'll bet you won't. This thing is getting interesting now, and it will not be long before it will be more so," answered Jack. "Look at that!"

He had been unwrapping the newspaper while he was talking, and Marcy was struck dumb with astonishment when he saw him bring the lost breastpin to light.

" Jack," he faltered, "where did you get it?"

" The charm brought it. Hold on, now,"

exclaimed Jack, when his brother turned away with an ejaculation indicative of the greatest annoyance and vexation. "It helped bring it, and a little common sense, backed by an insight into darkey nature, did the rest. Now, don't break in on me any more. Mother will begin to wonder what's keeping us."

When Julius came to ponder the matter, he found that he was in the worst scrape of his life. A house servant considered it an everlasting disgrace to be sent to the field, and Julius thought he would about as soon die or take to the swamps, one being as bad as the other in his estimation. But there was one thing that could be said in his favor: He was loyal to every member of the family in whose service his father and mother had grown gray. Although he could not possibly tell the truth, and found it hard to keep his nimble fingers off other people's property, the tortures of the whipping post, if there had been such a thing on the plantation, could not have wrung from Julius a word or a hint that could be used to their injury. He didn't like to work, but he knew he would have to if he was not ready with "some news of some kind" that very night. But what could he do when there wasn't any news? In his extremity he bent his steps toward the barn where old Morris was busy washing the carriage.

"Say," he began.

"Look here, nigger," replied Morris, straightening up as quickly as a jack in the box, "who you calling 'Say'? If you can't put a Mister to my name, cl'ar yourself and don't bother me no more."

"Say, Mistah Morris," repeated Julius, taking another start.

"That's better," said the coachman approvingly. "What was you going to deserve?"

"Say, Mistah Morris, we uns is all Union, ain't we?"

"Jest listen at the chile. G' long, honey. What you know 'bout politicians? Course we is all Union; all except the overseer, and he ain't fitten to live. Run along, now."

Julius was quite willing to obey, for he had learned all he wanted to know. If Hanson was a rebel, it followed, as a matter of course, that it would afford him satisfaction to learn that the inmates of the great house were rebels also ; accordingly when the time came for him to make his report, he was on hand and eager to unburden himself. The overseer, who was waiting for him, took him into a room and carefully locked the door behind him. This not only made the darkey feel a little uneasy, but it stimulated his inventive faculties as well.

"What do you know?" Hanson inquired, taking his pipe from the mantel over the fireplace. "Have you heard anything?"

"Well—I—yes, sar," stammered Julius, as if he did not know how to begin. "I—oh, yes, sar. Is you Union?"

"Of course I am," replied Hanson. "Every white man is."

"Den you ain't got no call to have truck wid de Missus. If she find out dat you is Union, she chuck you off'n de place quick's a cat kin bat her eye. She don't like Linkum. I hearn her say so dis bery day."

"Are you telling me the truth?" asked Hanson, looking sharply at the darkey, who met his gaze without flinching.

"If I ain't telling you de fac's ob de case, you kin w'ar dat rawhide o' your'n out on me quick's you please," said the boy, earnestly. "If you's Union you best dig out, kase de Missus put de secesh on you suah," added Julius, hoping that the man would act upon the suggestion and leave before morning.

"But I don't want to give the Missus warning till I know that she's got money enough to pay me."

"Oh, yes, sar; she got plenty ob money," declared Julius, whereupon Hanson began pricking up his ears. "I seen her have as much as a dollah dis bery day. I seen it wid my own two eyes."

"A dollar," sneered the overseer. "She owes me more'n that, and she's got more'n that. She's got a bushel basketful hid away somewhere; and Julius, if you will find out where it is, and tell me and nobody else, I will give you a piece of money just like that."

As he said this he put his hand into his pocket and brought out a twenty-dollar gold piece—a portion of the liberal sum Colonel Shelby had given him for spying upon the family whose bread he ate. Julius declared, with much earnestness, that he didn't believe Mrs. Gray had concealed any money, but if she had he could find it out if anybody could, and he would bring the news straight to the overseer.

When his supposed ally took his departure Hanson was obliged to confess to himself that he did not know any more about Mrs. Gray and the money she was thought to have in the house than he did before. And we may add that he never did learn anything through the boy Julius. That astute darkey was altogether too smart for the overseer, and brought him only such news as he thought the man wanted to hear; and more than half of that had not a word of truth in it. In the first place his only thought and desire was to keep the overseer from telling his mistress that he stole the breast-pin; but as Hanson became more communicative and stood less on his guard, and the boy's eyes were opened to the startling fact that Mrs. Gray had an enemy in the overseer, he threw the fear of punishment to the winds, and set himself at work to defeat all the man's plans.

22

How he managed to keep his secret was a
mystery, for never before had the negro been
known to hold his tongue.   But he kept it,
and kept it well until sailor Jack frightened
it out of him.

CHAPTER XV.

THE ENCHANTED LOOKING-GLASS.

THINGS went on in this unsatisfactory way for a long time—so long, in fact, that Hanson began to grow discouraged. And well he might, for with all his scheming he had not been able to add a single scrap of information to the first report he made to Colonel Shelby. The boy Julius held manfully to his story—that Mrs. Gray was the best kind of a Confederate, that she had no money except the dollar she carried in her pocket-book—and the most cunningly worded cross-questioning could not draw anything else from him. In process of time Fort Sumter was fired upon, Marcy Gray came home from school, and then the overseer rubbed his hands joyously and told himself that he would soon know all about it. Well, he didn't, but Julius did; and this was the way it came about.

In the ceiling of the dining-room, to which apartment the family usually betook themselves when they had anything private to talk about, was a stovepipe hole, communicating with a store-room on the floor above. It happened that Julius was roaming about the house one day when Mrs. Gray had company at dinner, and the sound of voices coming up through this opening attracted his attention. He listened a moment, and found that he could plainly hear every word that was uttered in the room below; but he never would have thought of playing the part of eavesdropper if Hanson had not told him that he was expected to do it. Believing that he could add to his usefulness and better guard the interests of the family if he knew more about its private affairs, Julius hastened to the store-room the minute he saw Marcy and his mother going in to breakfast, and put his ear directly over the open stovepipe hole, and heard some things that made him tremble all over. There was money in the house after all—thirty thousand dollars all in gold; it was hidden in the cellar wall, and he could earn a

nice little sum by carrying the news straight
to the overseer, as he had solemnly promised
to do ; but he never thought of it.   On the
contrary he strove harder than ever to make
Hanson believe that there was not a dollar in
the house beyond the one Mrs. Gray kept in
her pocket; because why, hadn't he heard her
tell Marse Marcy so with his own two ears?
If the overseer did not say "money" during
their interviews, Julius did ; but he did not
dwell long enough on the subject to arouse the
man's suspicions.   More than that, Julius was
brave enough to "take the bull by the horns,"
and one day he disheartened the overseer by
declaring :

"I seen something dis day, Marse Hanson,
dat done took my breff all plum away; I did
so.   Marse Marcy he come home a puppose to
go into our army ; and his mother she cried
and cried, and pooty quick she say : 'My
deah boy, dat man Linkum mus' be whopped ;
dat am de facs in de case'; and den she slap
him on de back and sick him on.   Yes, sar.
I done see dat wid my own two eyes dis bery
day."

The reason Hanson was disheartened was because he had been promised a liberal reward if he could bring evidence to prove that Mrs. Gray was opposed to secession, and that her journeys to Richmond and other cities had been made for the purpose of drawing funds from the banks; and when Marcy backed up the young negro's bold statement by shipping on board Captain Beardsley's privateer, Hanson came to the sorrowful conclusion that it was not in his power to earn that reward. He was none too good to bear false witness against Mrs. Gray, but he was afraid to do it. Sailor Jack might come home some day, and—well, Hanson had never seen sailor Jack but he had been told that he was a good one to let alone.

The long-expected wanderer returned in due time, and the wide-awake little negro was the second on the plantation to find it out, Bose being the first. Julius slept in the back part of the house, so close to Marcy's room that if the latter wanted anything during the night, all he had to do was to open his window and call out, and consequently it was no trouble at all for him to catch every word that passed between Jack and his brother. He was not far off when the sailor was admitted at the front door, and when he saw the reunited family go into the dining-room, he bounded up the back stairs into the store-room and placed his ear at the stovepipe hole—not because he wanted to repeat anything he heard, you will understand, but because he wanted to know what subjects to steer clear of in his interviews with the overseer. When he heard that Jack had passed himself off for a rebel, that he had brought a smuggler into a Southern port, and that he had made considerable money out of the sale of his venture, Julius thought it would help matters if the news were spread broadcast; and he lost no time in spreading it among the negroes, and by their aid it reached Nashville before the boys went there for their mail the next morning. He told about the *Hattie's* adventure with the steam launch, also (of course he made it more thrilling than it really was), and that was the way Captain Beardsley's daughter came to know so much about it; but he never said a word concerning

Jack's short captivity in the hands of the *Sumter's* men.

After Jack had been at home long enough to find out how things stood, he set himself at work to learn who it was that kept certain people in the neighborhood so well posted in regard to his mother's private affairs. He said not a word to anybody, but worked in secret, for he believed that his efforts would result in the unearthing of a spy who lived in the house. It would add to his mother's troubles if she knew that Jack believed, as she did, that there was some trusted servant who kept an eye on her movements and went to the overseer with a report of them—so he kept his own counsel, and laid siege to Hanson the very first thing. The latter wasn't sharp enough to hold his own with any such fellow as Jack Gray, and Jack learned all he cared to know about Hanson in less than two days. The next step was to find the servant on whom the overseer depended for his information. This looked like a hopeless task, but fortune favored him. One morning he stood in front of the mirror in Marcy's room performing his toilet. The door, which was behind and a little to one side of him, was open, and the lower end of the long hall was plainly reflected upon the polished surface of the looking-glass. So was the slim, agile figure of the small darkey who slipped out of one of the rooms, ran along the hall with the speed of the wind, and disappeared down the back stairs.

"That's Julius," said Jack, whose first thought was to call the boy back and make him give an account of himself. "He has been up to some mischief, I'll warrant; but I will see if I can find out what it is before hauling him over the coals."

So saying Jack stepped into the hall, and the first door he opened was the one leading into the store-room. There was the open stove-pipe hole, and through it voices came up from the room below. He bent a little closer to it, and distinctly heard his mother tell one of the girls to put breakfast on the table and ring the bell for the boys. In an instant the whole secret flashed upon him. He said not a word, but as soon as he returned from the post-office, and Marcy had ridden to the field to carry some instructions to the overseer, Jack went up to his room, leaving orders with one of the girls to send Julius there at once. When he came, the first thing Jack did was to lock the door and put the key in his pocket.

"Now, Julius," said he, in his most solemn tones, his face at the same time taking on a fierce frown, "if you are an innocent boy, if you have been strictly honest and truthful ever since I have been at sea, if you have obeyed your mistress and kept your hands off things that do not belong to you——"

"Oh, Marse Jack," exclaimed the frightened boy. "Suah hope to die I nevah——"

"Don't interrupt me," commanded Jack, with a still more savage frown. "I'll show you in a minute that I have it in my power to find out just what you have done while I have been gone, from the time you stole——"

"Marse Jack, I nevah took dat breastpin; suah hope to die if I did," began Julius.

"Hal-lo!" thought Jack. "I've got on to something when I least expected it. That's what comes of knowing how to handle a darkey. I didn't even know that mother had lost a breastpin."

"I haven't asked you whether you stole it or not," he said, aloud. "There is no need that I should ask you any questions, for I have a way of finding out everything I want to know. If you have been an honest, truthful boy during the last two years, sit down in that chair ; but I warn you that if you are deceiving me, it will drop to pieces with you and let you down on the floor. Sit down !"

"Oh, Marse Jack," cried the darkey, backing away from the chair. "Don't I done tol' you dat I didn't took it ?"

"Do you stick to that story ?" demanded Jack.

"Yes, sar. I stick to it till I plum dead."

"All right. I hope you are telling me the truth, and I'll very soon find out whether you are or not. The Yankees are coming right through this country some day, and I don't want to give you up to them, as I am afraid I shall have to do. You have heard Aunt Mandy tell her pickaninnies what awful fellows the Yankees are, have you not ? Why, Julius, it scares me to think of them. If a live Yankee was in this room this minute,—don't get behind me, for I wouldn't try to help you if one should walk in and carry you off,—if one came in and sat down in that chair that will fall to pieces if you touch it, and you should take off his hat and his right boot, you would find that he had horns and a cloven hoof—a hoof like an ox instead of a foot like yours."

"Look a hyar, Marse Jack," exclaimed Julius, clinging to the sailor with one trembling hand while he pointed toward the wash-stand with the other. "Wha—wha' you doing da'? Wha' dat white stuff for?"

While Jack was telling the boy what terrible fellows the Yankees were supposed to be, he had slowly and solemnly filled a goblet with water from the pitcher, and then in the same solemn and deliberate way drew forth his ditty-bag and took from it a small bottle containing a harmless-looking white powder known to the druggists as citrate of magnesia. He held it at arm's length as if he were afraid of it, and that made Julius so weak with terror that he could scarcely keep his feet.

"Do you want to know what—look out for yourself, now! If it explodes when I remove the cork, look out! Do you want to know what this is?" said Jack. "Then I must whisper the words to you, for it would never do to say them out loud. It is my enchanted looking-glass—my fetich—my voodoo charm."

That was too much for Julius. With a wild scream he jumped for the door; but it was locked, and he could not get out.

"Now watch," continued Jack, who knew that he would get at the truth of the whole matter in a minute more. "To begin with, I shall command my enchanted looking-glass to show me the likeness of the villain who stole that breastpin; and in the next, I shall tell it to show me the place where it is now. Now, stand by to look in and tell me who you see there."

He poured a small portion of the white powder into the goblet, whose contents at once began to bubble and boil in the most unaccountable manner. When the water boiled up to the top and ran over on the wash-stand, Jack commanded Julius to look in and tell

him what he saw there; but the boy sprang
away and curled himself up on the floor in the
farthest corner of the room.

"Come here!" said Jack sternly. "You
won't? Then I'll look myself. Ah! What is
this I see? Julius, come here this instant and
tell me who this is."

Jack emphasized the order by taking the
negro by the back of the neck and lifting him
to his feet; but he soon found that he could
not hold him there without the use of more
strength than he cared to put forth. Julius
was like an eel in his grasp. As fast as he
raised him from the floor he would somehow
manage to slip back again; and all the while
he begged and pleaded so loudly that Jack
was forced to desist for fear that his mother
would hear the uproar, and come to the door
to ask what was the matter.

"You are afraid to look in that goblet and
you dare not sit in the chair," said Jack at
length. "That proves that you did take the
pin. Now where is it? If I have to fill my
enchanted glass again, I'll make you look in it
whether you want to or not. Where is it?"

THE ENCHANTED LOOKING-GLASS.

"De oberseer got it," was the reply that made the sailor wonder whether he was awake or dreaming. "Suah's you born, de oberseer done made me gib it to him."

Jack had not the least doubt of it, but in order to test the boy's sincerity, he told him to sit down in the chair, assuring him, at the same time, that he had nothing to fear. As he had atoned for his guilt by making a confession, the chair would hold him up as it would anybody else. Julius tremblingly obeyed, and when he found that the chair really did support him, he gained courage, and with a little questioning told the whole story pretty nearly as we have told it, with this difference: He omitted some important items which we have been obliged to explain in order to make the narrative clear to the reader. It was a very nice scheme, Jack told himself, but he had not yet got the game as completely in his own hands as he determined to have it.

"Julius," said he impressively, "do you know what will happen to you if you fail to prove the truth of this most remarkable tale? You'll be sold down South before the week is over. A darkey who has been as carefully brought up as you have wouldn't last long in the cotton fields.''

''But, Marse Jack,'' said Julius earnestly, ''I kin prove dat I ain't tole you nuffin but the gospel truth. I kin fotch you de pin; but you musn't luff de oberseer whop me.''

''He shall not put a hand on you,'' Jack assured him. ''Keep away from the quarter, take no more reports to him, and I will stand between you and all harm.''

As he said this he unlocked the door, and the darkey disappeared like a flash. He was gone about half an hour, and when he returned he handed Jack the breastpin, which was wrapped in a piece of newspaper. The overseer being away in the field and his cabin unlocked, it was a matter of no difficulty for the darkey to rummage his bureau drawers until he found the object of which he was in search. Whether or not Hanson ever discovered that he had been robbed of the '' charm'' that gave him such power over Julius, Jack never knew. If he did, he never said a word about it while he remained on that plantation.

But this was not the only good work Jack Gray did during the first two weeks he passed at home.   When the *West Wind* was a day out from Boston, he accidentally learned that one of his best foremast hands was a resident of his own State, and that his father, who was a strong Union man, lived but an hour's ride from Nashville.   Of course the two became friends at once.   All the lightest and easiest jobs about deck seemed to fall into Aleck Webster's hands, and Jack won the good will of his mess by taking it upon himself to see that their food was not only abundant, but that it was well-cooked and properly served. They talked over the situation as often as they could get together, and not knowing just how matters stood at home they concluded that they had better not recognize each other after they reached Newbern.   If, after they had passed a few days at their respective homes, they thought it safe to do so, they could very easily bring about a meeting, and who could tell but that they might find opportunity to work together for the good of the old flag, or for the relief of some persecuted Unionist ?   Jack

23

knew of one Unionist who was persecuted by being watched by rebel neighbors, and that one was his mother. He and Webster met at the post-office one morning, but they met as strangers. In fact his shipmate was a stranger to all present, for his father, who was a small farmer, had moved into that section from Georgia while Aleck was at sea. Having the misfortune to be a "cracker," or a poor white, Mr. Webster was rather looked down on by such men as Colonel Shelby and Major Dillon, but Jack Gray was not that sort. Aleck was a good sailor, and such a man was worth more in a gale at sea than a landsman who could call upon his bank account for a hundred thousand dollars.

During his first interview with his old shipmate Jack Gray heard some things that made him open his eyes. It was true, as he afterward told Marcy, that the Union men in the neighborhood were few in number, and that they dared not say out loud that their souls were their own; but they were well organized, and by no means afraid to follow the example set them by the rebels, and act in secret.

Aleck said that there were about twenty of them all told, and no one could join their company unless he was vouched for by every man in it. They calculated to defend themselves and one another. They would not go into the Confederate service, and if they were crowded upon too closely they would take to the swamps and fight it out with any force that might be sent against them. They were well armed and resolute, and Aleck said they would be in just the right humor to deal with Hanson's case when it was brought to their notice at their next meeting.

"My mother rather took me to task because I helped that smuggler into port, but if you can give me the assurance that these Union men will stand between her and that cowardly overseer she's got on the place, I shall be glad I became a smuggler for the time being," said Jack.

"I can give you that assurance, Mr. Gray," said Aleck positively. "That's just what the company, or society, or whatever you have a mind to call it, was got together for. I know, because I was present at their last meeting, and the whole thing was explained to me before I took the oath to stand by it. Why can't you come down and join us?"

"We're not on board ship now, and my name is Jack. There's no Mister about it," was the reply. "I am in full sympathy with you and with the object for which you have been brought together, and if I was going to stay at home I should surely ask you to hand in my name. But my mother will be defenseless when I go into the navy and Marcy leaves to join that blockade-runner, and if Shelby and Beardsley and Hanson should find out that I knew there was an organization like yours in existence, they would burn up everything we've got. We can't discharge Hanson without bringing ourselves into serious trouble; and if you fellows could think up some way to drive him off the place, and bring old Beardsley home so that my brother wouldn't have to go blockade running any more, you would make us all your everlasting debtors."

"If you wanted to write to this Captain Beardsley you would address him at Newbern, wouldn't you? All_right. We meet somewhere in the woods next Wednesday night, and then we will talk it over and see what can be done for you."

Jack Gray always was light-hearted and jolly, no matter whether things worked to suit him or not; but Marcy and his mother thought they had never seen him quite so much at peace with himself and all the world as he appeared to be after this interview with Aleck Webster. If those Union men were in earnest and did what his shipmate thought they certainly would do, there might be a fight right there on the plantation; and that was the reason Jack did not take his mother into his confidence. To quote from Marcy, she had enough to trouble her already. If the attempt to drive the overseer from the place was made and resulted in failure, it would probably lead to some vigorous action on the part of Colonel Shelby and his friends; and that was the reason Jack did not tell Marcy of it. If a difficulty arose, he wanted Marcy to be able to say that he did not know a thing about it. But this particular night might be the last one he would ever spend with his brother, and he thought it prudent to make a clean breast of the matter.

"That is my story," said Jack, in conclusion. "What do you think of it?"

"I think you have worked to some purpose," replied Marcy, who could not yet understand how Jack had done all this without his knowledge. "But there is one thing you have yet to explain. You told me that I need not go back to the *Hattie* if I don't want to. I certainly do not want to, but how shall I get out of it?"

This was the way Jack explained that. On the Thursday morning following the day on which he held his first interview with Aleck Webster, he met him again, and the young fellow had startling news for him. After the two had seated themselves on a low fence a little way from the store, Aleck fastened his gaze upon a paper he held in his hand and said:

"It is just as I told you it would be. Our men were all mad when I told them that Unionists, and women at that, were being mistreated right here under their very noses, and them setting around like bumps on a log and doing nothing to stop it, and it's my private opinion that if that overseer of your'n had been handy last night, they would have used him rough. He'll get out; I can promise you that."

"Well, look here, Aleck. My brother is going to take me down to the blockading fleet in a few days, and I wish you wouldn't make a move until we are gone. Then folks can't say we had a hand in it or knew anything about it."

"Very good, sir. We'll look out for that. And perhaps you and your brother will be glad to learn that Captain Beardsley will be warned to-day that if he don't quit blockade running and bringing in supplies for the Confederacy, he will miss some of his buildings when he gets back."

"That will bring him sure," said Jack gleefully. "You can't touch him in a worse place than his pocket. But you didn't say anything about his forcing Marcy into the rebel service, did you? For if you did, he'll bounce my folks the minute he gets home."

"If he tries it, may be he'll miss some more buildings when he gets up in the morning," said Aleck.

"But he'll not let you or anybody know that he is working against them," said Jack. "He's too sharp for that."

"If anything happens to your folks we will lay it to him and act accordingly," said Aleck, with a laugh. "But the man who was told to write that letter to Beardsley will take care to word it so that he can't lay the blame on any one person's shoulders. You tell your brother that if he doesn't want to go blockade running again, he needn't go; for his schooner is about to quit the business."

"Do I know any of those Union men?" inquired Marcy.

"Probably you are acquainted with all of them, but they will make no sign," replied Jack. "The only one I know is Aleck Webster. I tell you it was a lucky thing for all of us when Captain Frazier took me aboard the *West Wind*. Now you take charge of this pin, and when the agony is all over, when Beardsley has been brought home and Hanson has been taken care of, give it to mother and tell her how you came by it. Perhaps the story will prove as interesting to her as I hope it has been to you. Now, let's go into the house. She will wonder what is keeping us out so long."

CHAPTER XVI.

OFF FOR THE FLEET.

MRS. GRAY was always uneasy when the boys were out of her sight, and that was not to be wondered at, for they so often brought her bad news when they came back. But on this particular evening they had no news of any sort, except that which shone from their radiant faces. Marcy thought he had good reason to feel light-hearted, for was he not getting the better of the secret enemies of whom he and his mother had stood so much in fear? Julius would carry no more reports to Hanson ; Hanson himself would soon disappear from their sight; Captain Beardsley would be compelled to stop blockade running ; and Colonel Shelby and his friends would have to act with the greatest caution in order to escape the vengeance of the Union men who held secret meetings somewhere in the woods. That was good news enough for one night, and

302

Marcy was sorry that he was obliged to keep it from his mother. It was long after midnight when the boys went upstairs, and there they passed another half hour in ripping up one of Marcy's bed quilts to get at the flags that had been stitched into it.

"I hope there are no more privateers on the coast," said Marcy, as he drew one of the flags from its hiding place.

"So do I," replied Jack, "for if we should happen to run foul of one of them, my Confederate colors would be no protection whatever. The boarding officer would very naturally inquire: 'What are you doing out here so near the blockading fleet?' and no answer that we could give would satisfy him. Why don't you take the old one? It would be a pity to have that nice piece of silk whipped to tatters by a Cape Hatteras gale."

"My friend Dick Graham gave me that old flag," answered Marcy; "and I told him that the next time it was hoisted it would be in a breeze that was not tainted by any secession rag. I want to keep my promise if I can. Now, I will put what is left of the quilt in my trunk where mother can find it in the morning."

After that the boys went to bed, but not to sleep. Marcy was too nervous. Thinking over the details of the remarkable story his brother had told him during the evening, and speculating upon the possible results of his trip to the blockading fleet, effectually banished slumber; and seeing how restless he was, Jack was considerate enough to stay awake to keep him company. The time passed more rapidly than it generally does under such circumstances, and it did not seem to them that they had been in bed an hour before they heard their mother's gentle tap at the door, and her voice telling them that the day was breaking.

"I told her we shouldn't need a warm breakfast," said Marcy. "But this looks as though she had stayed up all night on purpose to have one ready for us."

The only thing the boys had to do before they left the room was to hide some papers which they did not want anybody to see while they were gone—to wit, Marcy's leaves of absence, signed by Captain Beardsley, and the letter of recommendation that the master of the smuggling vessel had given Jack. These they slipped under the edge of the carpet, where the boys thought they would be safe (they little dreamed that the time would come when that same carpet would be torn up and cut into blankets for the use of Confederate soldiers); but the papers which related to the part he had taken in rescuing the brig *Sabine* from the hands of the *Sumter's* men, Jack put carefully into his pocket. They were documents that he would not be afraid or ashamed to show to the officers of the blockading fleet.

That was the last breakfast that Jack Gray ate under his mother's roof for long months to come. Realizing that it might be so, it required the exercise of all the will power he was master of to keep him from showing how very gloomy he felt over the coming separation. He was glad when the ordeal was over, when the last kiss and the last encouraging words had been given, and he and Marcy, with the two rival flags stowed away in a valise, were on their way to the creek. Greatly to Marcy's surprise, though not much to Jack's, they found the little skiff which did duty as the *Fairy Belle's* tender drawn out upon the bank, and Marcy was almost certain that he saw the woolly head of the boy Julius drawn out of sight behind the schooner's rail.

"What's the meaning of this?" he demanded. "Where are the ship-keepers?"

"Let's go aboard and find out," replied Jack, with a twinkle in his eye which said that he could tell all about it if he were so inclined. "I was afraid we would have to tow out to the river; but this is a topsail breeze that will take us down there without any trouble at all. Take the valise and get in and I will shove off."

Marcy had plenty of questions to ask, but knowing that his brother would not take the least notice of them unless he felt like it, he stepped into the tender and picked up one of the oars. A few sturdy strokes sufficed to lay the skiff alongside the schooner, and the first thing Marcy did when he jumped aboard, leaving Jack to drop the small boat astern, was to look down the hatchway that led into the forecastle. There stood Julius, as big as life, with his feet spread out, his hands resting on his hips, and a broad grin on his face.

"What are you doing there, you imp of darkness?" exclaimed Marcy. "Didn't you understand that we don't want any Abolitionists aboard of us this trip?"

"G'long now, honey," replied the boy, turning his head on one side and waving Marcy away with his hand. "Ise heah 'cording to Marse Jack's orders."

"That's all right," said Jack, who had come aboard by this time and was making the skiff fast to the stern. "You see," he added, coming forward, "I wanted to make all the darkeys on the place think that I am going down to Newbern to join the rebel gunboat that so many people seem to think is being built there."

"Aw, g' long now, Marse Jack," said Julius. "Mebbe de niggahs all fools, but dey ain't none of dem b'lieves dat."

"You hold your tongue," said Jack good-naturedly. "Perhaps our darkeys are all right, and perhaps they are not. It won't do in times like these to trust too many with things that you don't want to have scattered broadcast over the neighborhood. Our nigs all know, Marcy, that you have been in the

habit of taking Julius with you on all your
trips about the coast, and when I told him to
stay behind I did it with an object. I meant
to take him and he knew it. You will need
his help coming back, and his presence will
give weight to the story we are going to tell
the blockaders."

"But what will the hands say when they
miss him?" inquired Marcy. "What will
mother think?"

"Dey'll all think I done took to de swamp,"
declared Julius, with such a hearty guffaw
that it made the boys laugh to hear it. "Dat's
what I tole 'em all I going to do, and I ain't
nevah coming back no mo' till Marse Marcy
come too."

"You see he played his part well. There's
the chink I promised you," said Jack, tossing
a gold coin down to the boy, who scrambled
for it as though some one was trying to get it
away from him.

"But what has become of the two ship-keepers?" said Marcy. "They were told to remain on board till we came."

"Law-zee, Marse Marcy," exclaimed Julius,

with another laugh, "you jes' oughter see dem niggahs hump demselves when I swum off to de schooner and cotch de bob-stay. 'Oh, dere's one of dem white things,' dey holler ; but I ain't white and I knows it, and den dey run for de skiff and jump in and go off to de sho' so quick you can't see 'em for de foam dey riz in de watah.''

"Did you scare them away ?" exclaimed Marcy.

"I reckon so, sar; kase dere ain't nobody but Julius been on de schooner or 'bout it sence dat time."

"Well, let's get to work," said Jack. "Julius, you stay below till I tell you to come up, do you hear? If I see so much as a lock of your wool above the combings of the hatch, I'll chuck you over for the catfish."

A laughing response from the black boy showed just how much he feared that the sailor would carry this threat into execution ; but it kept him below, and that was what Jack wanted. As matters stood now, Julius could account for his absence from the plantation by saying that he had got angry and run away be-

24

cause Jack ordered him to stay ashore ; but he couldn't say that with any hope of being believed if any of the settlers along the coast saw him on board the schooner.

If Jack Gray had been so disposed, he could have taken the *Fairy Belle* into Pamlico Sound without showing her to the Plymouth people at all, for a small stream, called Middle River, and its tributaries, ran entirely around the city behind it, and out of sight of the fortifications that the Confederates had thrown up on the banks of the Roanoke. Starting from Pamlico River below Roanoke Island, a small boat, manned by those who were acquainted with the windings of the different channels, could come up through Middle River and Seven Mile Creek, passing within a few hundred yards of Captain Beardsley's house and Mrs. Gray's, and strike the Roanoke two miles above Plymouth. Please bear this in mind, for it is possible that we may have to speak of two expeditions that made use of these rear waterways to avoid the Confederate batteries. But there was no danger to be apprehended from the Plymouth people. The danger would come when the schooner passed outside and drew near to the blockading fleet; and that was the reason Jack had thought it best to disguise her.

The breeze being light and the channel crooked, it took the schooner an hour or more to work out of the creek under her jib, but when the rapid current of the Roanoke took her in its grasp, and the fore and main sails were run up, she sped along at a much livelier rate. As the *Fairy Belle* approached the town the roar of the morning gun reverberated along the river's wooded shores, and the Confederate colors were run up to the top of a tall flag-staff.

"Now comes something I don't at all like," said Jack. "We will run our own rebel rag up to the peak, and when we come abreast of the town we'll salute the colors on shore."

"How do you perform that ceremony anyhow?" asked Marcy.

"By lowering and hoisting the flag three times in quick succession," replied Jack. "It takes two to do it as it ought to be done, but of course you can't manage the halliards with only one hand. All I ask of you is to hold the wheel. I don't suppose those haymakers in the fort will have the sense to answer the salute, but we don't care for that. It may save us the trouble of going ashore to listen to questions that we can't answer with anything but lies."

The first gray-coated sentry they passed looked at them doubtfully, as though he did not know whether it was best to halt them or not, but probably the sight of the flag they carried settled the matter for him. At any rate he did not challenge them, and neither did any of the other sentinels they saw along the bank; but one of the numerous little groups which had assembled, as if by magic, to see them go by, hailed them with the inquiry:

"Where do you uns think you are going?"

"We hope to see Newbern some day or other," was Jack's reply. "Now stand by the wheel, Marcy, and I will see what I can do with the halliards."

The ceremony of saluting the Confederate flag was duly performed, but, as Jack had predicted, no notice was taken of the courtesy.

The soldiers looked on in silence, and probably there was not one among them who knew why the *Fairy Belle's* colors were hauled down and up again so many times; but when Jack made the halliards fast to the cleat and took his brother's place at the wheel, the same voice called out :

"Will you uns bring us some late papers when you come back ?"

The sailor replied that he would think about it, and then he said to Marcy :

"You want to have your wits about you when you pass this place on your way home. If they hail you and ask where your partner is, you can tell them that I am in the navy. If they inquire where Julius was that they didn't see him when we went down, he was below attending to his duties ; and if they ask about the papers, you were so busy that you couldn't get them."

The next place where Jack wanted to show his captured flag was in Croatan Sound. The Confederate force which had been mustered to defend these waters, having been compelled to abandon, one after the other, all the forts they

had erected to defend the various inlets leading to the open sea, were concentrating on
Roanoke Island, which they were preparing to
hold at all risks. They were building forts,
fitting out gunboats, and sinking obstructions
in the channels. Everything was well under
way when the boys went through, their captured banner serving as a passport here as it
had done at Plymouth. They took the deepest
interest in all they saw, little dreaming that
the day would come when the big guns, which
now offered no objection to their progress,
would pour a hot fire of shot and shell upon
both of them. Sailor Jack would have been
delighted if some one in whom he had perfect
confidence had assured him that such would
be the case, but Marcy would have been over-
whelmed with astonishment.

"This island is already historic," said Jack,
as the little schooner dashed by the unfinished
walls of Fort Bartow, and he waved his hat in
response to a similar salute from one of the
working party on shore, "and it'll not be
many weeks before it will be more so."

"What has ever happened here to give this

lonely island a place in history?" inquired
Marcy.

"I am surprised at you," answered Jack.
"Here you are, a North Carolina boy born
and bred, and you don't know the history of
your own State. Well, I didn't know it,
either, until I happened to pick up an old
magazine, thousands of miles from home, and
read something about it—not because I cared a
snap for history, which is awful dry stuff to
me, but because I had nothing else to do just
then. Of course you know that many of the
Croatan Indians, who have gray eyes and speak
the English language of three hundred years
ago, claim to be descendants of Sir Walter
Raleigh's lost colony, don't you? Well, that
colony was planted here in 1585 on the shores
of Shallow Bag Bay, which lies on the seaward
side, and a little to the northeast of the fort
we just passed. They were the forerunners of
the English-speaking millions now on this side
of the big pond. Here, on the 18th of August,
1587, Virginia Dare, the first white American,
was born. The county of which this island
forms a part was named after her family.

Now tell Julius to bring up some supper, and while we are eating it we'll take a slant over toward the main shore. There may be some sailor men among those soldiers for all we know, and, if they are watching our movements, we want to make them believe that we are holding a course for the lower end of the Sound, and that we have no intention of going near any of the inlets."

Up to this time Julius had kept below out of sight; but his forced inactivity did not wear very heavily upon him, for he had been asleep all the while. He was prompt to respond to Marcy's call, and took Jack's place at the wheel while the two boys were eating the cold supper he brought up for them. It was quite safe for him to stay on deck now, for it was almost dark, and besides it was not likely that he would be seen by any one on shore who knew him. When he had satisfied his appetite Jack hauled down the Confederate colors and asked his brother where he should hide them.

"It looks to me like a dangerous piece of business for you to hide them anywhere," replied Marcy, who had been thinking the matter over. "It looks sneaking, too. We are all right and we know it. We are never going to get through Crooked Inlet without meeting that steam launch or another one like her, and if the officer in command shouldn't be satisfied with your story or with your papers either, and should take it into his head to give the *Fairy Belle* a thorough overhauling, then what? If he found that flag stowed away in some secret place, he'd make prisoners of us, sure pop."

"If I didn't think it would be of use to you when you come back I would tie a weight to it and chuck it overboard," said Jack. "On the whole I think we'd better not try to hide it. The honest way is the best where Yankees are concerned. I'll put it in the locker alongside our own flag."

It was about twenty-five miles across the Sound to Crooked Inlet, and the schooner covered this distance in four hours. Of course Captain Beardsley's buoys had been lifted and carried away long before this time, and the only safe way to take the vessel into open water was to pull her through with the skiff which was towing astern. Although that would involve three or four hours of hard work, it was not a thing to be dreaded; but the thought of what they might meet before or after they got through, almost made Marcy's hair stand on end.

The night being clear and starlight, Marcy had no trouble in piloting the *Fairy Belle* into the mouth of the Inlet. Then the sails were hauled down, the skiff was pulled alongside, and a tow-line got out.

"Now, Julius," said Jack impressively, "stand by to turn over a new leaf. Quit lying and tell the honest truth."

"Now, Marse Jack," protested Julius.

"I know what you want to say," interrupted the sailor, "but we have no time for nonsense. I don't care what sort of lies you tell those rebels round home, but nothing but the truth will answer our purpose here. We've got to go aboard some ship—we can't get out of that; and while the captain is questioning Marcy and me, some other officer may be questioning you. If your story doesn't agree with ours in every particular, all of us will find ourselves in trouble. Tell them who we are, where we came from, why we are here, and all about it."

"But, Marse Jack," said the darkey, who seemed to have forgotten something until this moment, "I dunno if I want to go 'mong dem Yankees. I don't want to see no horns an' huffs."

"It's too late to think of that now," replied the sailor. "But I will tell you this for your encouragement: You won't see any horns and hoofs if you do just as you are told. But if you begin lying, you'll see and hear some things that will make your eyes bung out as big as my fist. Crawl over, Marcy, and I will hand you the boat-hook."

Marcy clambered into the skiff followed by Julius, Jack lingering behind long enough to lash the rudder amidships. Then he also took his place in the tender and picked up one of the oars, Julius took the other, Marcy knelt in the bow to feel for the channel with his boat-hook, and the work of towing the schooner through the Inlet was begun. There was not a buoy in sight, and when he removed them the officer whose business it was to guard that par-

ticular part of the coast must have thought he
had done his full duty, for the active little
launch that Marcy so much dreaded did not
put in her appearance. They passed through
the Inlet without running the *Fairy Belle*
aground or seeing anything alarming; and it
was not until the broad Atlantic opened before
them that the long-expected hail came.

"Not a thing in sight," said Jack, with
some disappointment in his tones. "I was in
hopes we could get through with our business
so that you could return to the Sound before
daylight, but perhaps it is just as well as it is.
You want to keep away from those soldiers
long enough to make them believe that you
have been to Newbern. Haul the skiff alongside, and we'll fill away for Hatteras."

"Jack, Jack!" exclaimed Marcy suddenly,
"there comes something."

Looking in the direction indicated by his
brother's finger, the experienced sailor distinctly made out the white canvas of a natty
little schooner that was holding in for the Inlet.
It was the most unwelcome sight he had seen
for many a day.

CHAPTER XVII.

AN UNEXPECTED MEETING.

"WHAT is she, Jack?" said Marcy, in a suppressed whisper. "Do you make her out?"

His voice was husky, and he trembled as he asked the question, for he knew by the exclamation that fell from his brother's lips that those white sails were things he did not like to see.

"I make her out easy enough, in spite of her disguise," was Sailor Jack's reply. "And I would rather meet all the gunboats in Uncle Sam's navy than her."

"Disguise!" Marcy almost gasped. "You surely don't think——"

"No, I don't think anything about it," Jack interposed. "I know that that is Captain Beardsley's schooner. I wish from the bottom of my heart that she had been sunk or captured before she ever caught us here; but it is too late to get away from her. She will go by within less than twenty yards of us."

"And do you think Beardsley will know the *Fairy Belle* in her new dress?" asked Marcy, who had never before been so badly frightened.

"Being an old sailor he can't help it."

"Of course he will mistrust what brought us out here, and spread it all through the settlement," added Marcy.

"That is just what he will do," said Jack truthfully.

"And what will Shelby and Dillon and the rest of them do to us—to mother?"

"You must make it your business to see Aleck Webster as soon as you get home," replied Jack. "Tell him that Beardsley has returned, that he caught us out here, and that the time has come for him and his friends to show their hands. I think you will have time to see Aleck before Beardsley gets home, because he's got to go to Newbern with his cargo."

All this while Captain Beardsley's blockade-runner had been swiftly drawing near to the mouth of the Inlet, where the *Fairy Belle* lay rising and falling with the waves, and now she dashed by within less than a stone's throw of them. The boys, who were standing up in their skiff holding fast to the *Fairy Belle's* rail, could not see a man on her deck except the lookout in the bow and the sailor at the wheel. The lookout was Beardsley himself; Marcy and his brother would have recognized his tall form and broad shoulders anywhere. He kept his eyes fastened upon the *Fairy Belle* as he swept by, but he did not say a word or change his course by so much as an inch. In five minutes more he was out of sight.

"Now will somebody tell me what that old villain wants of a pilot?" exclaimed sailor Jack, as he climbed over the rail and turned about to help Marcy up. "He knows more about Crooked Inlet than you do, or he couldn't run it with all his muslin spread and no buoys to mark the channel."

"I always said he didn't need a pilot," replied Marcy. "He has kept me with him on purpose to torment mother."

"He'll not do it any longer," said Jack

confidently. "You must send word to those
Union men as soon as you get home. If you
don't, Beardsley will make it so very hot for
you that by the time the fire gets through
burning mother won't have a roof to go under
when it rains. Stand by, Julius."

Jack and the darkey went forward to hoist
the headsails, and Marcy, filled with the most
gloomy forebodings, undid the fastenings of
the wheel and laid his uninjured hand upon
one of the spokes. One after the other the
sails were given to the breeze, lights were
put out to show the first cruiser they met
that they were honest folks going about
honest business, and Jack came aft to relieve
his brother.

"I have been thinking of Barrington," said
the latter, as he backed away and leaned up
against the rail. "It has somehow run in my
mind that our little settlement would escape
the horrors of war, but the events of the last
half hour have opened my eyes. We're going
to see trouble."

"I really believe you are," answered Jack.
"And when it comes, you must show what

you are made of. I have no fear but that you will stand up to the rack like a man."

"It isn't myself I care for ; it's mother."

"I know ; but when it comes to the pinch you will find that she's got more pluck than you have. That money is what scares me. If the suspicions of the authorities become aroused, look out. But don't lisp a word of that where mother can hear it."

"Oh, Marse Jack," exclaimed Julius, who just then came aft in two jumps, "de Yankees out da'."

"Out where?" inquired Jack, while Marcy's heart began beating like a trip-hammer. "Oh, yes ; I see them now. Stand by with a lantern, Julius."

The darkey hastened forward to obey the order, muttering as he went that Marse Marcy would have to take de light kase he wasn't going nigh dem Yankees till he seed 'em fust, and the schooner held on her course. What the boys saw was a bright light shining through the darkness a short distance off the starboard bow, and what they heard a moment later was the puffing of a small but exceedingly active

25

steam engine. The light presently disappeared but the puffing continued, increasing in force and frequency as the approaching launch gathered headway, and then came the hail :

"Schooner ahoy !" And almost in the same breath the same voice added : "All ready with that howitzer."

"Ay, ay, sir," answered Jack promptly ; and anticipating the next command he gave the wheel a rapid turn and spilled the sails, while Marcy took the lantern Julius gave him and held it over the side.

In five minutes more a large launch, carrying a crew of twenty men and a twelve-pound howitzer in the bow, came alongside, half a dozen pairs of brawny hands laid hold of the *Fairy Belle's* rail, and an officer, dressed in an ensign's uniform, came over the side, being immediately followed by four or five blue-jackets, armed with cutlasses. What sort of a reception they expected to meet at the hands of the *Fairy Belle's* crew it is hard to tell, but they were plainly surprised when they looked about her deck and found that there was no one there to oppose them.

" Who are you ? " demanded the officer, as Jack slipped a becket over one of the spokes in the wheel and came forward to meet him. " What schooner is this and where are you going ? "

" This schooner is the *Fairy Belle*, and she is the property of my brother," answered Jack, waving his hand in Marcy's direction. " We are going to the blockading fleet. And as to who I am—will you be kind enough to run your eye over these ? They will answer the question for you."

As Jack said this, he placed his papers in the officer's hand, while Marcy held up the lantern so that he could see to read them. He was by no means so surprised as Marcy expected him to be, and the reason was simple enough. Since the forts at Hatteras Inlet were captured, scarcely a day passed that some vessel of the blockading fleet did not hold communication with Union people on shore. There was more love for the old flag in that secession country than most of us dreamed of. If Marcy Gray had known this he would not have felt as uneasy as he did.

"I have been on the watch for an audacious little blockade-runner that slipped by one of our boats into this Inlet a few weeks ago," said the officer, as he folded the papers and handed them back to their owner. "You're quite sure you're not the fellow?"

"Do I answer his description?" asked Jack, in reply.

"Well, no; I can't say that you do. But it is very easy to disguise a vessel of this size."

"And it is just as easy for you to look around and see if I have any place to stow a cargo," said Jack. "Come below, if you please."

Taking the lantern from his brother's hand Jack led the way through the standing-room into the *Fairy Belle's* cabin, where he stopped to throw back the cushioned top of one of the lockers.

"Here's the flag I have sailed under ever since I was old enough to shin aloft," said he, taking up the carefully folded Union banner. "The other is the one Semmes's boarding officer hoisted on the *Sabine* when she was captured. When we took her out of the hands of the prize crew I hauled it down and kept it. It brought us safely by Plymouth and Roanoke Island, and I hope it will take my brother safely back.''

With this introduction Jack went on to give the officer a hasty description of the state of affairs in and around the settlement in which his mother lived, and told, what the Confederates were doing at Roanoke Island ; and all the while he was leading the officer from one room to another and showing him all there was to be seen on the *Fairy Belle*. But he did not say a word about the *Hattie*. The officer did not know that that ''audacious little blockade-runner'' had slipped through his fingers, and Jack thought it would be the part of wisdom to steer clear of the subject of blockade-runners if he could. A reference to them might lead to some questions that he would not care to answer.

''I am entirely satisfied with your story,'' said the officer, when they returned to the deck. ''But, all the same, I shall have to send you to my commander. I have no authority to act in a case like this.''

"Very good, sir," replied Jack. "We are quite willing to go. Do I understand that you take the schooner out of our hands?"

"By no means," was the prompt reply. "I will put a petty officer aboard of you to act as your pilot, and you can run the vessel down yourselves. I must stay about here till daylight and look out for that blockade-runner. Bo'son's mate!"

The petty officer stepped forward and received some brief instructions from his superior, which were given in Jack's hearing.

"These are Union boys, and one of them has come out here to ship," said the officer. "I want you to pilot him to the *Harriet Lane*. You are not to interfere with the management of the schooner in any way, for she is not a prize. She sails under our flag. Tell the captain the same story you have told me," he added, turning to Jack, "and I think it will be all right. Good-bye."

With these parting words the officer and his boarding party clambered down into the launch, which put off to resume her useless vigil at the mouth of the Inlet; the boatswain's mate, at Jack's request, took his place at the wheel, and the *Fairy Belle* filled away on her course.

"All right so far," said Marcy, who breathed a great deal easier now than he did when the launch first hove in sight. "If the captain of the *Harriet Lane* treats us as well as that ensign did, I shall be glad I came out here."

"He will, sir," said the boatswain's mate, letting go of the wheel with one hand long enough to raise his forefinger to his cap. "He always does. We have often had shore boats come off to us since we have been on the blockade."

"You have!" exclaimed Marcy, who was very much surprised. "And do you let them go ashore again when they get ready?"

"Cert'ny, sir. They come and go betwixt two days—not because they are afraid of us, but because they must look out that the rebels ashore don't hear of it. Some of the boats get news from Newbern every day or so."

"We know that," answered Jack. "And we heard a rebel say, not long ago, that if the Newbern people could find out who it is that sends off the papers so regularly they would make short work of him. How much farther have we to go?"

"Not more than ten miles, sir. We'll see our lights directly."

"Do you know anything about this little blockade-runner that your launch is watching for?" inquired Marcy. "Who is she? What's her name and where does she hail from?"

"We know all about her, sir, for we chased her once when she was the privateer *Osprey*. She belongs up Roanoke River, but she runs the blockade out of Newbern. Her captain—what's this his name is again?—Beardsley, used to be a smuggler; and if we get our hands on him we'll be likely to remember him for that. Our Uncle Sam ain't so broke up yet but what he can deal with men who have violated his laws."

"I hope to goodness you may get your hands upon him," thought Marcy, who was surprised at the extent and accuracy of the blue-jacket's information. It proved beyond a doubt that there were Union men ashore who kept the Yankee commanders posted, and Marcy wished he knew who they were. He might find it convenient to appeal to them if he and his mother got into trouble with Captain Beardsley.

The strong breeze being in her favor, the *Fairy Belle* made good speed along the coast, and in due time the warning lights of the Union war vessel showed themselves through the darkness. It was not customary for the Union cruisers to show lights and thus point out their position to vessels that might approach the coast with the intention of running the blockade, but being anchored off an inlet that was known to be in full possession of our forces, the captain of the *Harriet Lane* knew that no such vessels would come near him. While the blue-jacket was explaining this to the boys, a hoarse voice came from the gunboat's deck.

"Schooner ahoy!" it roared.

"No, no!" replied the man at the *Fairy Belle's* wheel.

"That's a little the queerest answer to a hail *I* ever heard," was Jack's comment.

"Be ready to stand by the sheets fore and

aft, for we must round to under her stern and come up on her port side," said the boatswain's mate. "The answer was all right, sir, and in strict accordance with naval rules. Had I been a captain, I should have given the name of my ship. Had I been a wardroom officer, I should have answered, 'Ay, ay!' But being neither one nor the other, I gave the same reply that the steerage officers have to give."

"And what answer would you have given if the admiral was aboard of us?" inquired Jack.

"I should have said 'Flag,' sir. You give different replies for different ranks so that the officer of the deck may know how to receive the people that are coming aboard. It would make him awful mad if you gave such an answer that he would extend wardroom honors to a steerage officer. Now, stand by to slack away and haul in."

Five minutes' skilful manœuvring sufficed to bring the schooner around the stern of the gunboat and up to an open gangway, in which stood the officer of the deck and one of the ship's boys, who held a lighted lantern in his hand. To the former the boatswain's mate reported :

"A shore boat, sir, with a couple of Union boys aboard. Mr. Colson sent me down here with her. One of 'em wants to ship, sir. He's got papers."

"Let them come aboard," said the officer.

"It was easy enough for Jack to obey the order, for the gangway was low ; but Marcy, having but one hand to work with, required a good deal of assistance. As there was considerable swell on, Julius and the boatswain's mate remained on board the schooner to fend her off with the aid of boat-hooks.

"I have come off to ship under the old flag, sir," was the way in which Jack introduced himself and his business.

"Are you an able seaman?" inquired the officer.

"I am, sir, and there is the proof."

Jack produced his papers, and the officer of the deck read them by the light of the lantern, Marcy improving the opportunity to make a hasty inspection of his surroundings. He didn't see much except the big guns which had aided in the reduction of the forts along the coast, the quartermaster on the bridge, and a few men lying on deck, apparently fast asleep, but he took note of the fact that everything was as neat as his mother's kitchen. By the time he had made these observations the officer had finished reading Jack's letters of recommendation. When he handed them back, all he had to say was:

"So you have had some experience with that pirate, Semmes, have you? I wish we had been around there about the time he captured your vessel. We will attend to your case in the morning. The doctor and paymaster are asleep, and it isn't worth while to rout them out just to ship one man."

"It will not be necessary for my brother to lie alongside all night, will it, sir?"

"Oh, no. Boatswain's mate, you go back and report to Mr. Colson."

"Very good, sir," replied the petty officer, with his finger to his cap.

"May I make bold to inquire if you have any papers aboard that you can spare?" continued Jack, who would not have thought of asking such a question if he had had a blue shirt on and been sworn into the service. "We'd like some Northern papers, if you have them, for as we are situated we get the news from only one side."

In response to this request the messenger boy was commanded to run down to the ward-room and bring up any papers he might find on the table there, and while awaiting his return Jack turned to say a parting word to his brother.

"Now Marcy," said he, "you've got to look out for yourself—and for mother. Not knowing what dangers you are likely to meet, I can't give you a word of advice; you will have to be on the alert and act according to circumstances. See Aleck Webster at the post-office, and tell him to put a stopper on those secret enemies of ours the first thing he does. You have seen me talking with him, and will know him the minute you see him. I shall trust you to communicate with me as often as you can, though I can't ask you to write to me. Tell mother you left me well and in good spirits. Good-bye."

"Why, my lad, things must be in a bad way in your part of the country," said the officer of the deck, who had heard all Jack had to say to his brother.

"They are indeed, sir," answered the sailor. "It is easy enough for you Northern folks to be loyal to the old flag, but it is as much as one's life is worth down here."

The messenger boy having returned by this time, Marcy took the papers he handed him, gave Jack's hand a parting shake, and was assisted over the side.

"Shove her bow off, Snowball," commanded the boatswain's mate, as he moved aft to take his place at the wheel, and let her drift astern. "Come back here, sir, and sit down," he added, in a vain effort to cheer Marcy up a little. "He's a fine lad, I'll warrant, that brother of yours."

"He is, indeed," replied Marcy proudly. "And a sailor man, too, I think you will find."

He had never before felt so gloomy and downhearted as he did at that moment, and he didn't care to talk. Calling Julius aft to strike a light for him, he went into the cabin and tried to read, leaving the man-of-war's man to sail the schooner, which he was able to do without help from anybody. In the bundle of papers that the messenger boy gave him, Marcy was glad to find three that were published in Newbern. These he kept out to be read at once, intending when he passed Plymouth to throw them ashore for the soldiers; but the Northern papers he stowed away in one of the lockers beside the flags. He wanted time to read them carefully, for he believed they would tell him the truth; and that was something he had not heard for many a day. It seemed to him that he had not been below more than half an hour when he heard a hail, to which the hoarse voice of the man at the wheel responded. A moment later it added:

"On deck, if you please, sir. I've got to leave you now. My launch is close aboard."

She was almost alongside by the time Marcy reached the deck, and five minutes later the officer in command of her again came over the rail; but this time he came alone. There were no blue-jackets with drawn cutlasses at his heels.

"I guess you've had luck," were the first

words he said. "I don't see the other fellow anywhere."

"No, sir. We left him aboard your vessel," replied Marcy. "He will be examined and sworn in in the morning. By the way, what did the officer of the deck mean when he said that the paymaster was asleep as well as the doctor? What has the paymaster to do with swearing him in?"

"He or his clerk has to take the descriptive lists, you know, sir," replied the sailor. "Then he gets an order from the captain to give the men their clothes and small stores—tobacco, soap, sewing silk, and the like, you know, sir. I was told to come back and report to you, Mr. Colson."

"Very good. Get aboard the launch. Can you and the moke get along by yourselves?" he continued, turning to Marcy. "I see you have but one hand."

"Oh, yes, sir; we'll get along all right," answered Marcy, who was very much afraid that the officer would ask him how he had got hurt. "Seen anything of that blockade-runner since we left?"

"I haven't seen a thing except this schooner to-night," was the reply ; and Marcy judged from the tone in which the words were uttered that the officer was much disgusted at being obliged to stay out there all night in an open boat for nothing. No doubt he would have been still more disgusted to learn that if he had been two miles farther up the coast he would have had a chance of capturing the "audacious" little vessel that he was looking for.

The officer wasted no words in leave-taking, but went at once, and Marcy Gray felt more gloomy than ever when he found himself alone on the ocean with nobody but the boy Julius for a companion. He sent the latter to the wheel and went forward to act as lookout and pilot, intending to follow Captain Beardsley's example and run through Crooked Inlet under full sail. He thought he could remember about where the buoys had been placed, and besides he had the flood tide to help him. If he succeeded, he would run across the Sound and hunt up some little bay in which he could go into hiding until such time as he thought it safe to come out and start for home.

26

This programme was duly carried out, and the good luck that had thus far attended him stayed with him to the end. He piloted the schooner through the Inlet without the least trouble, ran across the Sound without being seen by anybody, and put into the mouth of a little bayou, where he tied up and turned in for a much needed rest. He remained there all that day and the ensuing night, and at sunrise on the following morning ran Sailor Jack's Confederate flag up to the *Fairy Belle's* peak, and stood boldly out for Roanoke Island.

CHAPTER XVIII.

CONCLUSION.

AS soon as the schooner was straightened on her course so that Marcy could manage her with one hand, he came aft' and took the wheel.

"Go below and hide that Union flag," said he. "These rebels may not be as easily satisfied this time as they were when we went down, and if they send a boat aboard of us I don't want them to find anything. I don't care to know where you put the flag. All you have to do is to hide it where we can find it again when we want it."

Julius was gone not more than five minutes, and when he returned to take the wheel Marcy walked forward, carrying in his hand one of the Newbern papers which he had folded and twisted, newsboy fashion, so that it could be thrown a considerable distance.

403

The first thing that attracted his attention, after the *Fairy Belle* passed the foot of the island, was a steamer, whose crew were busy adding to the obstructions that had already been placed in Croatan Sound. But there was a wide clear space close under the guns of Fort Bartow, and into this Julius held his way, passing so near the steamer that Marcy was able to throw his paper among the crew.

"Newbern," he shouted to the Confederate officer, who picked up the paper and waved his thanks. "It isn't a very late one, but it was the best I could do."

That blockade had been run in safety, but when they reached the head of the island Marcy found himself menaced by another danger which he was afraid could not be so easily passed. One of Commodore Lynch's gunboats was lying there, and when she saw the schooner approaching, she sent one of her boats off to intercept her. Marcy's hair began to stand on end.

"What have you done with that Union flag, Julius?" he asked.

"Now, jes' listen at you," replied the boy.

"What for you want dat flag now? It hang you, suah."

"I only wished to be assured that you had it safe," said Marcy, as he ran into the cabin to bring up another paper; and when he returned with it, he shook it at the men in the boat and beckoned them to come alongside, just as if he didn't know that that was what they intended to do. As the small boat came nearer and began to swing broadside to the schooner, Marcy raised his hand and Julius spilled the sails.

"You needn't stop," said the young master's mate, who sat in the stern-sheets. "Throw us a line and we'll tow alongside. Our old man had a little curiosity to know who you are, where you have been, and where you belong. Thanks for the paper. What's the news?"

"I didn't get any," replied Marcy. "I saw one Yankee cruiser riding at anchor off the coast, and also saw one blockade-runner come in. What sort of a cargo she brought I don't know, for I didn't exchange a word with any of her crew."

"What's the matter with your hand?" inquired the master's mate.

"De Yankees done guv him dat hand, sar," said Julius promptly. "Dey done knock him 'mos dead wid a shell."

"The Yankees!" exclaimed the young rebel. "Are you in the service?"

"I was running the blockade when I was hurt," answered Marcy. "But I wasn't hit by a shell. I was knocked down by a heavy splinter."

"Pass us down your other flipper," said the officer, standing up in his boat and extending his hand. "I am glad to meet you. When you get the use of your arm again come aboard of us. We need men, and I know the captain will be glad to take you."

"He got one brother in de navy now," added Julius, who thought that Marcy wasn't trying half hard enough to make the boat's crew believe that he was loyal to the flag that waved above him.

"Is that so? Then if he comes in himself that will make two, won't it? Well, I will detain you no longer. Come aboard of us if you can, for we think we are going to see fun here in the course of a few weeks. Good-by till I see you again. Shove off, for'ard."

"Julius, I am afraid you talk too much," said Marcy, when the boat was left out of hearing. "If you don't keep still you may get me into trouble."

"Look a yere, Marse Marcy," said Julius, "Marse Jack done tol' me it plum time for me to stan' by to tell what's de troof, an' I ain't done nuffin else sence he tol' me dat. De Yankees did guv you dat hand, you done got one brother in de navy, an' dat's all I tol' dat rebel. I didn't say you a rebel you'self, kase dat would be a plum lie; an' all de black ones knows it."

At the end of two hours a bend in the shore hid the island and Commodore Lynch's gun-boat from view, and as night was drawing on apace, Marcy began looking around for a suitable spot in which to tie up for the night. He knew better than to try to pass Plymouth after dark. The countersign would be out, and not only would he be obliged to go ashore to *get* it, but he would also be compelled to land to *give* it to every sentry on the bank. That would be a good deal of trouble and might prove to be dangerous as well. It would give the soldiers off duty a chance to board the schooner, and that was something Marcy did not want them to do. They would go all over her, peeping into every locker and corner, steal everything they could get into their pockets or put under their coats, and one of them might accidentally find that Union flag. For these reasons Marcy thought it best to lie by for the night.

" It will bring us home in broad daylight, Julius, and some of the servants will be sure to see you when you leave the schooner to take me ashore," said he. " So the story you made up to tell them about running away to the swamp, will have to be changed to something else. It would have to be changed any way, for of course Captain Beardsley saw you when he ran by us at the mouth of the inlet."

"I been thinkin' 'bout dat," answered Julius, " an' I going to tell nuffin but de troof. Dat's de bes'. I was stowed away on de schooner, an' you nevah knowed it till you come off in de mawnin' an' cotch me.''

Marcy said nothing more, for he did not believe that either of them could tell a story that would save them from the trouble that Captain Beardsley would surely try to bring upon himself and his mother. He would take Jack's advice and lose no time in seeking an interview with Aleck Webster.

Marcy easily found a hiding-place for the night, and bright and early the next morning set out to run the last of the blockade—the garrison at Plymouth. This was accomplished without any trouble at all, the depth of the water permitting Julius to hold so close in that Marcy could throw his last Newbern paper ashore. The soldiers scrambled for it as if it had been a piece of gold, and shouted for him to send off some more ; but Marcy could truthfully say that he had no more, the garrison at Roanoke Island having got the others. The Northern papers were too precious to be given to rebels. Those were to be saved for his mother.

In due time the *Fairy Belle* reached the mouth of Seven Mile Creek, the sails were hauled down, and Julius, with such slim aid as Marcy could give him with one hand, began the work of towing her to her moorings. It took them two hours to do this. When Marcy had seen her made fast to her buoy he did not get out of the skiff, but sent Julius aboard the schooner with instructions to put both the flags and the Northern papers into his valise and hand it over the side. To his great surprise there was not even a pickaninny on the bank to say, "How dy, Marse Marcy?" and he usually found them out in full force whenever he returned from his sailing trips. Presently Julius got into the skiff to row him ashore, and followed him to the house, carrying the valise in his hand ; but even when they passed through the gate they did not see a person about the premises, nor a dog, neither. Bose seemed to have "holed up" the same as the rest. The doors and windows were wide open, but where were the house servants that they were not singing at their work? Marcy did not know what to make of it, and Julius gave it as his opinion that something done been going wrong on the plantation.

"I believe you and Jack, between you, have frightened everybody off the place," declared Marcy, little dreaming how near he came to the truth when he said it. "But we'll soon know all about it, for here's mother."

He ran lightly up the steps to greet her as she appeared at the door, but stopped short when he reached the gallery, for he saw that his mother was as solemn as her surroundings. She tried to call a cheerful smile to her face, but the effort was a sad failure.

"What in the world is the matter here?" demanded Marcy, as soon as he could speak. "Have the hands all run away? Where is everybody? Why is the place so quiet?"

"Oh, Marcy!" exclaimed Mrs. Gray, motioning to Julius to take the valise into the house, "such a strange thing has happened since you went away. Hanson has disappeared as completely as though he had never been on the place at all."

"Good enough," cried Marcy, giving his mother a bear-like hug with his one strong arm. "Now we shall be free from his—eh? You don't mean to say you are sorry he has gone, do you?"

"I don't know whether I am or not," was the astounding reply. "If he had left of his own free will I should be glad, I assure you; but the manner of his going frightens me."

"The manner?" repeated Marcy, who was all in the dark.

"Yes. The night after you went away, some of the field hands were awakened by an unusual noise and went to the door of their cabins to see a party of fifteen or twenty masked men making off, with Hanson bound and gagged in the midst of them. They were so badly frightened that—Marcy," exclaimed Mrs. Gray, holding the boy off at arm's length and looking searchingly into his face, "do you know anything about it? Is Jack at the bottom of this strange affair?"

These last words were called forth by the exclamation of surprise and delight that Marcy uttered when the truth of the whole matter flashed suddenly upon him. The absent Jack had told him that the morning was coming when his mother would not hear the field hands called to work because there would be no one to call them, and his prediction had been verified. Aleck Webster was true blue, the Union men who held secret meetings in the swamp could be depended on to hold their rebel neighbors in check, and Marcy Gray could hardly refrain from dancing with delight at the thought of it.

"Come in and I will tell you all I know about it," said he, throwing his arm about his mother's waist and leading her into the hall. "You needn't worry. Every one of the men who came here that night were your friends and mine, and they——"

"But who were they?" asked Mrs. Gray.

"It is probable that one of them sailed with Jack when he was on the *West Wind;* but who the others were I don't know, and it isn't at all likely that I shall ever find out," replied Marcy. "Not in the dining-room, please, because there's a stove-pipe hole in the ceiling that leads into a room upstairs. Oh, it's a fact," he added with a laugh, when his mother stopped and looked at him. "A certain person, whose name I shall presently give you, listened at that pipe-hole time and again, and took messages straight to Hanson. But you'll not blame him when you hear my story. Let's go into the back parlor. By the way, did you find your breastpin ? "

His mother said in reply, that she had neither seen nor heard of it since the day it was stolen.

" Well I've got it safe and sound," continued Marcy ; and then he settled back in his chair and repeated, almost word for word, the story sailor Jack had told him the night before he left for the blockading fleet. He told how Julius had taken the pin in the first place, how the overseer had worked upon his fears to compel him to give it up, and how he had used the power which the possession of the stolen pin enabled him to exercise over the timid black boy. Then he described how sailor Jack and his " Enchanted Goblet " appeared upon the scene ; and from that he glided into the history of Jack's acquaintance with Aleck Webster, and the interviews he had held with him at the post-office. But there were two things he did not touch upon—the meeting with Captain

Beardsley at Crooked Inlet, and sailor Jack's fears that the Confederate authorities might interest themselves in the matter if they learned, through any of her "secret enemies," that Mrs. Gray kept money concealed in the house. His mother was profoundly astonished, and when Marcy finished his story she did not know whether to be glad or frightened. The boy thought, from the expression of her countenance, that he had added to her fears.

"You don't act as if you were pleased a bit," said he dolefully. "Are you not glad to know that I can stay at home now? Beardsley has got to quit business, and of course he can't make any more excuses to take me away from you. He never did need a pilot, the old rascal. When he reads the warning letter that is waiting for him in Newbern, he'll fill away for home without the loss of a moment."

"Of course I am glad that you will not be obliged to go to sea any more," said Mrs. Gray. "But I don't want those Union men to destroy Captain Beardsley's property. When you see this man Webster I hope you will say as much to him."

"If it's all the same to you, mother, I'll wait and see how Beardsley conducts himself," answered Marcy, who did not like the idea of trying to protect a man who had done all he could to annoy his mother. "If he lets us alone, we'll let him alone; but if he bothers us, he had better look out. When he finds out what those Union men did to Hanson, I think he will haul in his horns. I wonder if Shelby and Dillon know it?"

"That's another strange thing that happened while you were absent, and I did not know what to make of it," replied Mrs. Gray. "Of course the story of the overseer's abduction spread like wild-fire, and I know it must have reached the village, for the very next afternoon Mr. and Mrs. Shelby rode out to visit me; and that is something they have not done before since these troubles began."

"Aha!" said Marcy, in a significant tone. "They began to see that you were not so help-less as they thought you were, and that it might be to their interest to make friends with you."

"That is what I think now that I have

heard your story," replied his mother, "but I did not know what to think at the time they made their visit. I am sorry that I was not more courteous to them, but they were so *very* cordial and friendly themselves that it made me suspicious of them."

"That was perfectly right," said Marcy approvingly. "You did well to stand on the defensive. Don't let them fool you with any of their specious talk. They're treacherous as Indians, and would burn your house over your head to-morrow, if they were not afraid."

"Oh, I hope they are not as bad as that. What do you think these Union men did with the overseer? They didn't—didn't——"

"Kill him as they ought to have done?" exclaimed Marcy, when his mother hesitated. "No, I don't think they did ; and neither can I guess what they did with him. But Jack said, in effect, that after he was taken away he would not bother us again for a long while. Did Shelby ask after Jack and me?"

"He did ; and I told him that you had gone off in the *Fairy Belle*. Mrs. Shelby hinted that Jack might be on his way to New-

27

bern to join the navy, and I did not think it worth while to deny it. It seems Jack told young Allison that if you rode into Nashville alone some fine morning, Allison might know that Jack was aboard a gunboat. Of course Mrs. Shelby thought he meant a rebel gunboat."

"Don't you believe it," said Marcy earnestly. "She knew better than that and so did Allison. Did the hands seem to be very badly frightened over Hanson's disappearance?"

"There never was such a commotion on this plantation before," answered Mrs. Gray. "According to the coachman's story, Jack predicted that 'white things' would some night appear in the quarter and carry Hanson away with them; and although the abductors were not dressed in white, the fact that they came and did just what Jack said they would do was terrifying to the minds of the superstitious blacks. I wish Jack would not tell them such ridiculous tales."

"He'll not be likely to tell them any more for some days to come," replied Marcy. "But there was nothing ridiculous about his last story. It was business, and I think that villain Hanson found it so. Now, if you will come up to my room and stitch my Union flag into the quilt where it belongs, I will hand over your breastpin."

When this had been done, Marcy strolled out to the barn to tell Morris to saddle his horse, and to see what the old fellow thought of the situation. Just as he stepped off the gallery he heard a piercing shriek, and hastened around the corner of the house to find the boy Julius struggling in the grasp of the coachman, who flourished the carriage whip over his head.

"What are you about, there?" demanded Marcy.

"He going whop me kase I say Marse Jack in de navy," yelled Julius. "Turn me loose, you fool niggah."

"No, I ain't going whop him for dat, but for lying," said Morris, releasing his captive with the greatest reluctance, and with difficulty restraining his desire to give him a cut around the legs as he ran away. "He say Marse Jack gone on a *rebel* boat, an' I know in reason dat ain't so."

"You won't get nuffin mo' outen Julius if you whop him till he plum dead," shouted the black boy, who had taken refuge behind Marcy and was holding fast to him with both hands. "I reckon I know whar Marse Jack gone, kase I was dar."

"Go into the house, Julius. You will be safe there ; and, besides, your mistress wants to see you. Put the saddle on Fanny, Morris, and I will ride to Nashville. Where's the overseer ?"

"Oh, Marse Marcy, we black ones so glad you done come back," exclaimed the coachman, throwing his whip and hat on the ground, and shaking the boy's hand with both his own. "We safe now. Nobody won't come to de quarter and tote folks away to de swamp when you around."

"Who did it ?" asked Marcy.

Morris laughed as he had not laughed before since Marcy went away. "Now listen at you," said he. "How you reckon a pore niggah know who done it ? Everybody afraid of de niggahs now-days; everybody 'cepting de Union folks. Going get 'nother oberseer, Marse Marcy?"

"Yes. I think I shall take the place my-self."

"Dar now," said Morris, with a delighted grin. "Dem niggahs wuk demselves to death for you. Now you go in de house an' tell your maw whar you going, an' I bring de hoss an' holp you in de saddle."

Marcy good-naturedly complied, and hearing voices coming from the dining-room he went in there, and found Julius listening to a lecture from Mrs. Gray on the sinfulness of stealing. But Julius defended himself with spirit, and declared that for once his habit of picking up any little articles he found lying around loose had been productive of good to every member of the family.

"When I put dat pin in my pocket, missus, I know I ain't goin' to steal it," he protested, with so much earnestness and with such an appearance of sincerity that almost anybody except Mrs. Gray would have believed him. "I don't do no stealin'. I jes' want to look

at de pin, an' I goin' put it back when I get
done lookin' at it. But de oberseer he done
took it away from me, an' dat's de way you
find out what sort of a man he is. No, missus;
I don't steal. I always tell de troof."

Marcy Gray did not ride to Nashville with
any hope of meeting Aleck Webster that day,
and consequently he was most agreeably surprised when he saw him standing on the steps
of the post-office. He did not look or act like
a man who had been engaged in any under-
hand business, and neither did Colonel Shelby,
who hastened down the steps and came across
the road to the hitching-rack to help Marcy off
his horse.

"So glad to see you safe back," was the way
in which he greeted the boy. "Your brother
said that if you came down here without him
some day we might know he was in the navy;
so I suppose that is where he is. He didn't
waste much time in going, did he? What's
the news from Newbern?"

Marcy cut his replies as short as he could
without being rude, and went into the office to
look at his mother's box, which had been emp-

tied by the coachman half a dozen hours before. He exchanged a very slight nod and a wink with Aleck Webster as he passed him, and the latter, who seemed to know just what he meant by the pantomime, mounted his horse when no one but Marcy was watching him and went down the road toward Mrs. Gray's plantation. There were plenty of loungers in the office, young Allison, of course, being one of the most talkative ones among them, and although they seemed to know where Jack was, they could not imagine what had become of Hanson.

"I tell you honestly, Marcy, that if it hadn't been for that Confederate flag in your mother's dining-room, we should have laid his abduction at your door," said Allison. "But the flag proves that you are all right; and, besides, you couldn't have had a hand in it, for you were on your way to Newbern when it happened. It opened our eyes to the fact that there are traitors among us, and that we must be careful who we talk to."

"Traitors," repeated Marcy. "I don't know what you are trying to get at. Hanson told me with his own lips that he was a Union man. Kelsey told me the same, and brought word to the house that Colonel Shelby and Mr. Dillon wanted Hanson discharged ; but I sent back word that if they wanted the overseer run off the place they could come up and do the work themselves, for I would have no hand in it. I don't want to get my neighbors down on me if I can help it. If Hanson was a Union man, as he professed to be (and I don't know whether he was or not, for I would not talk politics with him), it was Confederates living right around here who came to the quarter and took him away."

Marcy saw by the astonished look that came to Allison's face that all this was news to him, and this made it plain that he was not in Colonel Shelby's "ring." He backed up against one of the counters and glanced around at his companions, but had not another word to say. The time came when he was admitted into the "ring," and showed himself to be one of the most active and aggressive ones in it. To keep up appearances Marcy bought a paper, took another look at his mother's box and left the office; and as no one went with him to help him on his horse, he led her alongside the fence and mounted without assistance. A mile and a half from Nashville the road followed the windings of a little creek whose banks were thickly wooded. As he drew near this point he dropped the reins upon his horse's neck and pulled his paper from his pocket—not with any intention of reading it, but to be in readiness to answer Aleck Webster's hail when he heard it. It came before he had ridden twenty yards farther. The man had hidden his horse in the bushes, and now stood in the edge of them within easy speaking distance, but out of sight of any one who might be watching Marcy Gray.

"You are Mr. Jack's brother, ain't you?" said he, as Marcy stopped his horse and fastened his eyes upon the paper he held in his hand. "I thought so; and I want to know if you are satisfied, by what we did while you were gone, that we will do to trust."

"We are more than satisfied," replied Marcy. "We'll never forget you for it. What did you do with him?"

"Turned him loose with orders never to show his face in the settlement again. We wanted to take him off to the fleet; but of course we couldn't, for he wasn't in the rebel service. Shelby was sort of civil to you, wasn't he? Well, he got a letter, same as Beardsley did, or will when he gets to Newbern——"

"He's in Newbern now," interrupted Marcy, still keeping his gaze fastened upon the paper. "We passed him at Crooked Inlet just as we were going out. That frightened Jack, and he told me to lose no time in telling you of it."

"That's all right; but Beardsley will not trouble you. We've written letters to him and Shelby and all the rest telling them that if they don't stop persecuting Union folks we'll burn everything they've got; and if that don't quieten them, we'll hang the last one of them to the plates of their own galleries. Go home and sleep soundly. We'll take care of you. Where did you leave Mr. Jack?"

Marcy gave a brief history of his run to the blockading fleet and back, told how very badly frightened his mother's servants were when they saw the overseer carried away by armed men, and how the circumstance had affected some of the "secret enemies" of whom they stood so much in fear; hinted very plainly that if at any time Aleck or any of his .friends found themselves in need of bacon, meal, or money, they could have their wants supplied at his mother's house, and wound up by urging him to keep a sharp eye on Captain Beardsley.

"I don't think he will ever trouble you," was Aleck's reply. "At any rate, he will never make you go to sea again against your will. But if anything does happen to you after the warning we have given him, we'll blame him for it, whether he is guilty or not, and some night you will see his buildings going up in smoke. Is there any one on the road who will be likely to see me if I come out? Well, then, good-bye."

Marcy put his paper into his pocket and rode away with a light heart, little dreaming how soon the time would come when another of sailor Jack's predictions would be partly fulfilled, and he, the well-fed Marcy Gray, standing sorely in need of some of the bacon and meal he had promised Aleck and his friends, would steal up to his mother's house like a thief in the night to get them, starting at every sound, and keeping clear of every shadow he saw in his path for fear that it might be an armed man lying in wait to capture him. But that time came. It is true that Captain Beardsley and his friends did not do anything against him openly (they were afraid to do that), but they worked against him in secret and to such purpose that Marcy Gray, forced to become a fugitive from his home, was glad to take up his abode for a while with the Union men who lived in the swamp. How this unfortunate state of affairs was brought about, what young Allison did after he became a member of the "ring," and how Captain Beardsley, Colonel Shelby, and the rest paid the penalty of their double dealing, shall be told in the next volume of this series of books, which will be entitled, "MARCY, THE REFUGEE."

THE END.

www.ingramcontent.com/pod-product-compliance
Lightning Source LLC
Chambersburg PA
CBHW030947110726
47900CB00004B/1161